THE OCEAN GIRL

The Sylvania Series

The Forest Bride
The Village Maid
The Ocean Girl
The Woodland Stranger (coming in 2024)
The Fire Apprentice (coming in 2025)

A FAIRY TALE WITH BENEFITS

The Ocean Girl

JANE BUEHLER

All rights reserved. No part of this book may be reproduced or transmitted in any form or by any means, electronic or mechanical, including photocopying, recording, or by any information storage and retrieval system, without written permission from the author, except for the inclusion of brief quotations in a review.

Published by Emily Jane Buehler
PO Box 1285, Hillsborough, NC 27278 USA
https://janebuehler.com

Publisher's Note: This is a work of fiction. Names, characters, businesses, places, events, locales, and incidents are either the products of the author's imagination or used in a fictitious manner. Any resemblance to actual persons, living or dead, or actual events is purely coincidental.

Copyright © 2023 Emily Jane Buehler
Cover illustration © 2023 by Cory Podielski
Cover design by Cory Podielski
Book design by Emily Jane Buehler
Author photograph © 2018 by Cory Podielski

The Ocean Girl (Sylvania Book 3) / Emily Jane Buehler
ISBN (print): 978-1-957350-02-8
ISBN (ebook): 978-1-957350-03-5

Library of Congress Control Number: 2022919741

To all the mermaids in Niantic Bay

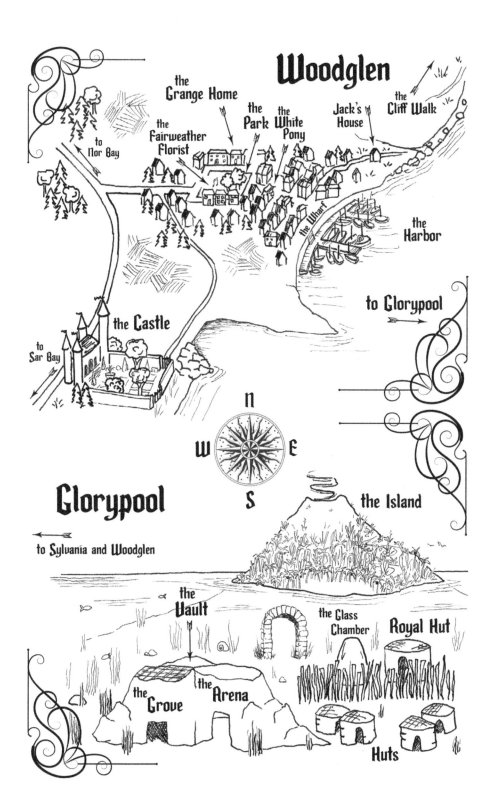

Chapter 1

Muri's tail churned below her in the water, holding her body vertical as she stared up at the surface. The dark shadow of the boat blocked the sunlight that sparkled through the shifting sea. She secured the strap of her satchel over her shoulder and swam a little closer. Overhead, someone moved on the boat, flickering in and out of sight. The underside tipped back and forth, sending out a ring of waves.

The fleet of boats had appeared overhead when she'd entered the bay. Her relief at arriving in the bay, safe from the creatures of the deep, had battled her new fear of interacting with the land dwellers.

Muri mulled over everything she knew about land dwellers. The humans were the ones who went out in boats to gather food—not the fairies. The fairies didn't like being out on the ocean because they couldn't swim. Which was lucky, because the fairies were the ones she had to watch out for. They were treacherous, with their magic spells and illusions, and they were selfish as well. The humans were more like animals, slow-witted and easy to stay clear of. But they could still be dangerous, especially when they became angry.

Muri had never seen either a fairy or a human. The merpeople had stopped visiting the land villages when she was a merchild. But she had learned about them from the other merpeople. How was she ever going to survive among them long enough to complete her mission—to find the missing merking?

And what if King Strombidae had encountered a fairy on land? What if he'd had one of their spells cast on him? Was that why he'd never come home?

Muri pushed the thoughts aside. She had a quarter-moon to find him before he forfeited his standing in Glorypool—before he lost the throne and the other mermen fought over who would be the next merking. Probably, King Strombidae had simply lost track of the time he'd been away—almost a full season. He was probably enjoying life on land with his newest wife. His human wife. Number nine.

Muri was to be number ten.

Her stomach twisted the way it always did when she thought of her impending marriage.

Maybe the merking wouldn't want to come home, though. Maybe he liked this new wife so much, he'd stay on land with her forever and Muri could avoid marrying him. Maybe she shouldn't even try to find him. She could wait here in the bay until the final day and then swim home and tell everyone he wasn't coming back.

But if he didn't come home, his merwives would lose their positions as well. She couldn't let that happen, even if it meant her own unwelcome marriage.

The boat above her rocked sharply, and the person on board appeared at the edge, leaning over the side. Muri drifted closer as the myriad fish in the water darted away. The person was large—a human man, she guessed, as she watched his shimmering form through the surface. Did the men on land help with the work? In Glorypool, the merwomen were the ones who gathered the seaweed and checked the nets for fish. The mermen protected the settlement. No one had dared to attack as long as Muri could remember—except for that one incident involving Janthinidae.

The man's arms plunged into the water and Muri flinched back. The hands closed around a rope and gripped it hard before pulling up and out of the water. Muri could see the brute force of the man, and terror swirled inside her, but so did a hint of fascination.

His arms—they weren't tinted green like hers, but bronze like the stripes on the nautilus shell. The sun made the humans that way, Lottiidae had told her, all different shades from pink to brown, while the moon-loving fairies glowed with silvery-gold skin and had eyes like sea lettuce.

All of them had sounded hideous when Lotti described them.

But the man's arms didn't look hideous. They looked warm, reminding her of the warmth when lying in the sun on the sand on the island. If only she could see his face . . . . She caught herself before drifting off into a daydream. She *should* try to see his face— one glimpse into his dim-witted eyes would quell her curiosity fast enough.

A rush of shining fish flooded past, obscuring her view with their silver bodies. Muri flicked her tail and moved up toward the boat. The shark-eye shell tied on a cord around her neck floated up and bumped her chin when she stopped. Lotti had tied it on as Muri prepared to leave Glorypool. Muri would need the shell on her mission.

Lotti would have a fit if she saw how close Muri was to the fishing boat. But if Muri had to walk on land, she needed to see what she faced. If the man spotted her, she'd be gone so fast he'd think he'd imagined her.

He appeared again over the edge of the boat, hauling on the ropes and blocking the beams of light that pierced the water. She tried to piece together his face from the broken slivers she could make out between the glints of sunlight. His nose was as coppery as his arms, and a peak of hair crowned his head, completely different from the long locks of the merpeople. The fish swam closer around her, and she flicked herself up again. Everything was blue up there—bright blue, not murky like at the bottom of the sea— not like in Glorypool. The colors were like those of the island, but it would be peaceful here, without any merpeople to contend with. She almost thought she'd—

The fish pressed in on her, writhing in panic. A net was closing around them—and around her.

Muri's heart thudded. She grabbed for the net, trying to pull herself up, but the opening at the top shrank into nothing, held tight by the grip of the man above. She dragged her body through the fish toward the edge of the trap. She tugged at the stiff ropes, trying to widen the clam-sized holes as the net pulled tighter, but the ropes were too strong. The fish-catcher had trapped her in his net and was pulling her toward the surface.

She glanced up. She had only a few moments before those hands were on her. The rough fiber of the net scraped her cheek as she twisted through the fish, positioning herself and reaching for the knife in her belt. She jerked it out and pressed it to the net. She sawed at the rope and felt a snap as the first strand of twine broke. Faster, she had to go faster. She worked the sharpened stone blade of her knife until the entire rope split, ripping open a wider hole. She sawed at a second spot and another rope popped open, and another. The hole grew, with fish bodies spilling from it to wriggle away toward the dark depths.

The whole net jerked upward, and warm water hit Muri's head. Surface water, warmed by the sun.

She snapped one last rope and ducked her head through the opening. Her hair swirled up and around the net. She pulled it down and pushed with her tail. Something else caught at her neck. She strained against it and it broke, releasing her from the trap as the man hauled the net up, with fish spilling from the hole she'd cut.

She inhaled a lungful of seawater and let it out slowly, willing herself to stay calm. That had been so close . . . and she wasn't even on land yet! Why had anyone thought *she* should be the one sent to find the merking?

She focused on the silvery fish slipping through the water around her, letting the flicker of their glimmering scales sooth her nerves. She could do this. She just had to go up on land and sneak around until she found the merking, and then she'd dive back into the sea and swim home and no land dweller would be able to stop her.

A cluster of fish tumbled past. As their chaotic motion sorted itself out, a prickle crept up Muri's spine. She ducked her head, stealing a glance over her shoulder. The fish-catcher's net still hung in the water beside her, with fish wriggling out of the hole. Muri turned and lifted her head.

The man in the boat stared down at her. Her heart thudded as she stared back. This close, she could see his wide, dark eyes and his parted lips. He clutched the ropes of the net, the motion of his muscled arms arrested. She stared back, horrified. But also . . .

A wave rocked the boat and the man stumbled forward. Muri's view wavered as the water sloshed above her. He caught himself on the edge of the boat and began to lift his head back toward her.

Muri darted down, away from the warm sun and the danger. A few moments passed and nothing came after her.

A muted shout reached her. He must've seen what she'd done to his net. She didn't need to hear the words to know the man was angry. The stories were true, then—the humans' anger came like a summer squall, the surface calm one moment and battered by rain the next. She never should have swum so close to look. What if she met the man in the village later today? What if he saw her and knew she was the one who'd cut his net?

That thought was silly. He'd never notice her once she had legs. And as fast as his anger had come, maybe it would leave just as fast—he wouldn't be angry forever. And Lotti would never know Muri had almost been caught.

When she neared the cold seafloor, she dared to look back. Far above, above the water, the muted shouting had stopped. The net was gone, pulled all the way into the boat. Only the dark hull remained on the twinkling surface.

Muri checked for her satchel as she swam along the sand, continuing on toward the village. The bag still hung around her body, and nothing had spilled out. She reached for her shell necklace. It was gone.

Chapter 2

Muri had lost Lotti's shell. Ten seas, what had she been thinking?

She knew how dangerous the humans could be. Lotti had warned her not to get too close until she was disguised. And she'd almost been caught in a fishing net! She'd been so distracted by that man, and it could have cost her everything.

What would he have done if he'd caught her? Land dwellers didn't see merpeople often, Lotti had said. They revered the merpeople as mythical beings, with superior abilities and the merking's magic. That's why it had been such an honor for the merking to choose one of the humans as his next bride. So, the fish-catcher probably would have been surprised to find her in his net. But what an introduction—she certainly wouldn't have looked like a mythical being, pressed among the fish and trapped within the ropes.

But Lotti had also said humans wanted the merpeople's power for themselves. What would the man have done? Would he have let her go? Or kept her as a hostage to barter with, with the merking? Muri was strong, but against those arms, would she have been able to escape?

Now she'd lost Lotti's shell and wouldn't be able to communicate with her sisters—to call for help or to ask for advice if she needed it. Every time she disobeyed orders, it ended in disaster.

Muri tamped down the worries. She'd simply have to find King Strombidae without help or advice. And she wouldn't get distracted again. She'd complete her mission and be safely back in Glorypool as soon as possible.

She swam up until her head poked above the ocean surface. The bare masts of the fishing boats were far out in the water. A cliff rose up from a rocky beach a few hundred tail-swishes away. Farther on along the coastline, the buildings of a village came down to the water—Woodglen, they called it.

Muri gaped in awe as a thrill shot through her. Woodglen was only a small village for the humans, but compared to Glorypool, it was sprawling. Glorypool had only a cluster of huts beneath the water, and the only building on the island was the merking's hut at the hot springs, high up in the jungle. But here in Woodglen, row upon row of rooftops climbed up the hillside over the bay. At the top, the colorful tops of unusual trees rose over the buildings. And behind that were smooth towers with pointed tops soaring up toward the clouds.

In a short while she would walk through a human village!

It was dangerous. But as she examined the village, excitement wove its way through her dread. She had never been anywhere away from Glorypool in her twenty-three seasons.

Everything she knew about the land dwellers had come from the older merpeople like Lotti. The merwomen talked to pass the time while they gathered food or wove baskets, telling the stories passed down for generations about the other creatures of the world. Many of the merwomen, even the ones just a few seasons older than Muri, had been to land villages before. Regular patrols to the nearest villages—those on the islands east of Glorypool and along the northern coast of Sylvania to the west—had been maintained for ages to ensure the land dwellers weren't plotting against the merpeople. While the mermen had patrolled, the merwomen had stolen into the villages to gather supplies. But even with their desperate need of provisions, the merking had ended the visits. It was just too dangerous to venture onto land.

But now Muri would actually see the outside world and one of the villages for herself. Those stories she'd heard would help her blend in among the humans. They might even save her life. The exhilarated tingle spread to her tail fins. She would see humans firsthand. Maybe she'd even bring home her own stories to share with the other mermaids.

The angled houses and the taller buildings in the village had unnatural corners—like gigantic crystals of rock filling the hillside. What else would she see once she walked down the lanes between them? From this distance, nothing moved.

She again gazed along the towers rising up into the clear sky. That must be the castle where the human king lived. Strombidae had intended to marry a human princess, so the castle might be a good place to start searching for him. Maybe he'd gone on living at court after the marriage. He'd intended to bring the bride back to Glorypool—he'd had an air-filled glass chamber built specially for her and placed it beside his royal hut on the seafloor—but maybe he'd been enjoying life on land and didn't want to return.

Lotti always said nothing was as nice as Glorypool, with the island right there for trysting and spawning—despite the island's monkey population—and the beach water warmed by the volcano . . . but Lotti always thought everything was better in Glorypool. And she always thought everything was better if it stayed exactly as it already was. Maybe Strombidae had found something on land that he liked better.

Muri ducked back under the water and swam for the beach. She pushed through a cloud of eelgrass and the sand bumped her tail. A moment later, she pulled herself out of the waves and onto the sand. She exhaled her last breath of seawater from her lungs as she began using them to breathe air.

It had been a while since she'd been above the surface. Ever since Strombidae had noticed her the previous spring and chosen her as a future bride, none of the other mermen had dared lie with her. Not that she'd minded losing their attentions—sometimes trysting was fun, but sometimes it was more like a chore. And the mermen never liked it if they saw her yawning in the middle of it.

But she *had* liked visiting the island—seeing the flowers and eating fruit and being in the warm sun . . . and she'd visited many times before the merking chose her. But after he chose her, no one would take her to the island and risk the displeasure of King Strombidae Murkel of Glorypool.

A gull flew over, its cry piercing. Everything sounded high-pitched in the air, fast and clear. "I am Muricidae," Muri said aloud, testing out her voice in air as she lay on the sand and waited for her tail to dry. She spread her fingers over the gritty texture beneath her, packed hard as the tide went out and left it to dry. She inhaled the cool spring air, inhaling the stink of eelgrass, baking where it had caught on the rocks. Strange scents crept in beneath it—maybe from the grasses up at the top of the cliff, covering the hillsides between her and the village. Near the island, the seasons were less obvious because of the constant heat emanating from the base of the volcano.

"I am Muri," she said again, her voice clearer. "I seek Prince Murkel of Merlandia." A prince! Ha, what a bizarre lie. And to say he was the prince of a distant coastal kingdom called Merlandia, with prosperous farms and mountains filled with gemstones. That was the story the merking had concocted to woo his human bride. Muri snorted. Lotti's explanations about humans never added up—if the merpeople were mythical beings revered by the humans, why had the merking had to tell lies to win over his human bride? The humans didn't tolerate multiple wives, Lotti had said, as if that explained it.

What was bride number nine like? How would she adjust to living in the sea? Muri had seen the air chamber that would be the new bride's home and gotten chills up her spine. She'd tried to imagine the opposite situation—herself kept in a tank of water on land. To be trapped like that would be awful. But the humans were different. They didn't think much or have many emotions.

Still, would bride nine be happy in Glorypool? How would she react when Strombidae turned away from her and moved on to a new wife?

When Strombidae moved on to Muri?

Ugh. She never liked to think about what it would be like as the merking's wife. It was a great honor, and that was what mattered, not whether she liked the look of him or took pleasure in lying with him. The other merwomen thought him handsome with his long, dark locks and regal nose. But Muri's heart had sunk the moment he'd noticed her—which had happened only because she'd spoken out of turn. She had to learn to obey, or she'd never survive as his wife.

Which she never would be, if she failed to find him.

She pulled herself up the sand until the tip of her silvery blue tail was out of the water. Already the breeze was drying her scales and her legs were forming. She pulled off her satchel and removed its contents: a human dress, a pair of foot coverings, a scallop shell filled with clay to hide the green tint of her skin, and a length of twine to tie back her shiny dark hair. Her golden eyes with their large pupils for seeing in the depths of the ocean would be impossible to hide, but Lotti said humans weren't careful enough to notice each other's eyes.

Muri gathered up her hair, remembering how it could have snagged in the fish-catcher's net. Having hair down to her waist was such a bother, especially now that she'd be out of the water for days. It would be tangling in snarls and catching on things. But merwomen never cut their hair. Once when she'd suggested it, Lotti had been horrified.

But what if Muri had gotten stuck in the net? And what if her hair drew attention—that fish-catcher's hair had been short as a monkey's. Wasn't she safer without it?

She took her knife from its sheath and held a fistful of hair out, pulling the tresses taut against the blade. No one was here to stop her.

But soon she'd be home, where the rules applied.

Down the coastline, the village beckoned, as if it were daring her to make the first cut. Muri closed her eyes. She would say . . . She would say no one else in the human village had had clothes like hers, and they'd mostly had short hair, and the humans had all been staring at her. Cutting her hair had been necessary to blend in. She sucked in a deep breath and felt a surge of joy at defying the rules of Glorypool. She sliced the knife through her hair and tossed the cuttings into the water with the swirling eelgrass.

She gathered another fistful, then another, shearing them away one after the next until her hair had all been cut. The damp ends brushed her shoulders. A shiver of unease ran through her, thinking of Lotti, but the feeling was too late to prevent what she'd done. Lotti had sent her on this dangerous mission. She was doing what she needed to do to succeed.

Out on the bay, the sails had risen on a few boats that moved toward the village. The sun was still high, but noon had passed. Maybe those fish-catchers had filled their boats and were done fishing for the day. Or maybe one had given up for the day because of the gaping hole in his net.

Muri imagined his face again, broken by the sunlight and waves, and his strong arms reaching into the water. The way he'd stared down at her. Maybe she *would* see him in the village, but he wouldn't know she'd cut his net. He wouldn't notice her once she had legs and with her now short hair, but she'd get a closer look at the man who'd almost captured her.

Or maybe he *would* notice her—maybe he'd think she was a pretty human and try to talk with her. Or maybe she'd speak to him—she could ask him which road led up the hill to the castle as an excuse to hear his voice in the clear air.

Nonsense. She couldn't let anyone notice her, and she definitely couldn't talk to any of them.

With a sound like the shushing of windblown sand, her scales disappeared and her shimmering tail faded into legs. She stretched them out and slowly pushed herself up to her knees, getting used to the feel of them after so many moons. The rock wall that towered over the narrow strip of sand blocked some of the wind, but a few gusts tossed her shortened hair. She stood, balancing in the wind until she grew steady.

She bent for the dress and wrung out the seawater. Once the dress stopped dripping, she flapped it open and hung it over a rock hot from the sun. Lotti had shown her how to put it over her head with her arms through the holes.

Clothing made sense for land dwellers in the wintertime, but now? In the hot sunshine? Muri was tempted to ignore Lotti's advice, but the older merwoman had insisted—humans did not walk about naked, and if she did, they were sure to notice her and maybe even lock her away for it. And the human men reacted strangely to nakedness, unable to control their animal-like lust at the sight of even a single bared female breast. Muri was used to the mermen pulling her up on the beach for a tryst, but the ten seas help her if she let a human touch her.

Well, she'd better enjoy the breeze on her bare skin while she could. Muri sat on a warm rock and opened the shell containing the clay. It would hide her green skin to prevent the humans from guessing she was a merperson. Supposedly it wore off in about a week, but hopefully she'd be long gone from the land village by then.

She scooped up two fingers' worth and rubbed it onto her arm, spreading it thin to cover as much skin as she could. The green disappeared where she rubbed it. The new color wasn't as tan as the fish-catcher's skin, but it was warmer than the cool green tint of merperson skin. She smeared more clay on. Strombidae must have disguised himself this way, too, since he'd had to pretend to be human while he courted his land bride. Was he still hiding his identity? They'd been married almost a full turn of the seasons—or bonded, as the humans called it. Surely bride nine knew the truth by now. And no doubt she'd been honored to learn it. So why hadn't she returned to Glorypool with him?

Muri kept working at her disguise until her entire body was covered, even the parts the clothing would hide. She scratched a fingernail across her forearm, and the tan color held. She scooped up some sand and rubbed with it, scouring her skin, and only after numerous passes did the green start to show through. Well, she didn't plan on rolling around in the sand while she was here. She pulled on the foot coverings and dress, tied what remained of her hair with the twine, and gathered up her satchel.

She started along the shore toward the village. She walked on a strip of flat sand broken by half-submerged rocks. The tide was out, but when it was high tide, the waves must crash against the base of the cliff because the sand was smooth and packed. Her steps left a row of faint prints behind her as the sun moved behind the cliff. As she drew nearer the village, she had to scramble over boulders. After a while, the way became so difficult that she climbed to the top of the cliff where the rocks met grass. The human clothing made it awkward but she managed.

If only she could dive back into the sea! She'd be at the village in a few heartbeats. Instead, she started walking along the clifftop where a path had been worn in the grass. Sunlight slanted across her, glinting on the water where it shone beyond the cliff's shadow. All the fishing boats were sailing for shore now. Figures moved in front of the buildings where the village ended with a wharf along the edge of the harbor. Wooden docks lined with boats stretched out into the water.

Ahead of her on the clifftop, a small stone cottage nestled in a dip in the land. Scraggly trees curled over it. Behind it, more cottages dotted the landscape until the taller buildings of the main village began.

Muri tugged at the neckline of the dress. It itched against her skin. The dress was loose and shapeless, hiding her form as well as the knife belted around her waist. Hopefully she wouldn't need her knife, as she'd have to reach under her skirt to get it.

The worn path widened as she approached the lone cottage. It was about the size of a hut in Glorypool but much sturdier with its solid stone walls and wooden shingles on the roof. The cottage didn't move a smidge as the wind buffeted it. She'd never seen a human cottage before—or any cottage, for that matter, although as far as she knew, only humans lived in cottages. The fairies lived in magical rooms they created inside trees in the forest.

Nothing moved as she neared the cottage. In a garden on the far side from the bay, land plants pushed above the soil. Fishing nets hung from hooks on the cottage wall, giving off a faint earthy smell in the sun. A barrel at one corner of the building connected to a channel running up to the roof.

In spite of the barren open landscape, the location was sheltered from the wind. It had been built down in the natural curve of the hillside, but also the ground rose up a bit on the ocean side, further shielding it, and the trees blocked the wind off the ocean. But the three trees were thin enough that should one fall, it didn't seem likely to damage the solid-looking stone and wood of the cottage.

Muri frowned, noticing all of this. She peeked into the barrel beside the wall. Water filled it about halfway. The channel flowed down from the cottage roof—was the barrel full of rainwater? Her frown deepened. The sheltered cottage and this strange water system seemed too intelligent to have been built by humans.

Muri stepped onto a path of flat stones set in the grass between the cottage and the trees. The cottage wall had a window covered with glass, the same material as the air chamber King Strombidae had brought to Glorypool for his human bride. So glass had other uses. Gingerly she touched it—it was cold and smooth. She tried to see inside the cottage, but the glare off the glass obscured the view. Maybe that was for the best—someone could be in there.

She turned to move on but bright colors at the base of the cottage wall caught her eye: land flowers! The flowers were in clumps, one blue, one purple, and two white, and each cluster of flowers was on a thick stalk surrounded by numerous green fronds. She knelt to examine them. Each cluster contained tiny star-shaped blossoms, and a sublime scent wafted off. She bent even closer and inhaled. The scent was like nothing she'd ever smelled in Glorypool or on the island.

Something moved to her left and Muri jumped up. An animal watched her from the end of the path, blocking her exit. It was black and covered with fur. When she met its gaze, its mouth dropped open to reveal rows of pointed teeth. Muri stepped back but it didn't follow. It leaned sideways, lifted its rear leg, and lazily scratched its ear. Its tongue rolled out and it started panting.

This was what humans called a dog. They kept them as pets, and they were usually tame and came in all shapes and sizes. Their distinguishing feature was the tongue lolling outside the mouth. Muri crept closer and held out a hand, and the dog sniffed it. She scratched behind its ear where its foot had scratched, and it leaned into her fingers. When she stopped, it padded around and hobbled back to the front of the cottage. Muri followed. The dog flopped down onto a sunny stone patio before the cottage door, yawned, and closed its eyes.

The path, now wide enough for a cart, ambled away from the cottage and past the next few homes. Muri followed it as it widened into a dirt lane and the village spread out before her. This was it, the moment she'd been anticipating since Lotti had decided to send her to land to search for the merking. Her heartbeat sped up, and she wiped her sweating palms against the dress. It was useful as a towel, at least. She checked her palms for any hint of her green-tinted skin, but the clay that hid her true color had stayed on.

Muri took a deep breath and walked in between the buildings.

The dirt lane turned to hard stones beneath her feet. It led straight to the lowest area of the village, the part by the docks. The buildings here had glass windows, too, but the glare of sunlight plus the darkness inside hid what they contained. The doors were brightly painted, with colors as vibrant as those of the land flowers she'd seen, and some buildings even had flowers growing in containers below the windows or in barrels beside the door. Were the flowers edible? Or were they merely for decoration?

Everything in Glorypool had a practical use. But the humans had a habit of amassing possessions they didn't need—they valued belongings instead of relationships. Still, as Muri passed more barrels of flowers, the flowers brought her joy. She'd like it if Glorypool had things this beautiful.

Something moved overhead. An animal perched on the roof, watching her pass, its eyes gleaming. Small, pointed ears, whiskers, twitching tail—it was a cat. They were also pets of the humans, although this one eyed her as if it wanted to eat her. She hurried past.

A short human in a dress appeared ahead, walking toward Muri with a basket over her arm. Her clothing covered her skin from her shoulders to her knees, as Lotti had said. Muri held her breath as the woman neared. The woman nodded a greeting and passed by. Muri's disguise had worked.

The lane opened onto the wharf, crowded with humans. Muri stopped in the shelter of a doorway to take it all in. The people were walking this way and that, both men and women, and all of them did, in fact, have clothing on. As she stepped out from the doorway, someone moved beside the wall and she stumbled back. But it was only two women, standing close and whispering. They didn't even glance over. Muri ducked her head as they kissed. Those two were so smitten, they'd not have noticed if she'd had three heads and a tail.

To her left, boats were arriving at the docks, their sails billowing in the breeze as the fish-catchers fastened ropes to cleats and reached to pull down the sails. Muri scanned the faces for the man she'd encountered, but none of them were familiar.

The fish-catchers were about half male and half female. Apparently human men *did* help with gathering food—no one in Glorypool had told her that. And what's more, a woman strode about on the docks, shouting at the others and writing on a ledger, and the men reacted with smiles. One of them whistled at her and she simply ignored him. He went right back to his work. What strange and fascinating behavior. Muri wanted to keep watching. But she had a mission. And the last time she'd been distracted, she'd almost ruined everything.

Ahead of her was some sort of market with bins and tables, some covered with fish. So much fish! Was this one day's catch? The fish on display would have fed everyone in Glorypool for weeks. Her stomach rumbled at the thought, but now wasn't the time for eating. She could find some seaweed later.

The land dwellers exchanged coins for packages of fish, and others stood in groups talking or laughing. Muri had expected to feel scared among the humans, but their mild behavior seemed harmless, even friendly. When a woman in a shawl looked her way and their gazes met, the woman actually smiled. Well, the humans weren't very smart, which might explain the reaction. And they were most dangerous when angry, not happy and laughing like this placid crowd.

Muri moved forward, circling around the crowd at the market. Next to the stalls was a shop with tables out front where people sat drinking from mugs. Muri wanted to sit at one of the tables and watch the people go by. What a strange feeling—the urge to sit in a human chair and watch the humans! In Glorypool, the merwomen never stopped moving—even when they were immobile, weaving a basket or sleeping, the water endlessly swayed around them. That was one thing Muri liked so much about the island: lying on the sand being perfectly still. After the trysting was done, at least, and before you were hustled back into the sea.

Several streets led away from the wharf, with the center one running steeply uphill. It would lead to the castle. Muri headed toward it. As she started up the steep lane, a word caught her attention.

"Merlandia."

Muri stopped. The word had come from a group gathered at the corner. "Says they're dangerous," the voice said.

"You really think there's more than one?"

"Seems likely."

Muri edged into the back of the group. They faced a poster tacked up on the wall. Human words filled half of it beside a picture of . . . was that a merman and a merwoman? They had ridiculously big tails and fangs in their mouths. What in the ten seas . . . ?

An older man joined the group, squinting at the poster. "Read it to me, will you?"

The first man read aloud, "Danger: Mermen on the loose." He paused to scan the crowd. Some people smirked, while others stood wide-eyed in horror. He returned to the poster. "The merfolk are real! They lurk in the depths of the sea in the land called Merlandia. Last spring, one came ashore to kidnap Princess Rose."

Muri started. Kidnap?

The reader continued. "A man twenty hands tall was spotted on the docks last quarter-moon at midnight. He dove into the water and never surfaced. Are the mermen returning, and why? Are they here to kidnap more women? Are our daughters safe?" The reader turned to the crowd. "There's a meeting at the public house tonight."

"Which pub?" someone asked.

The man gestured at the shop with the seats out front. "The Mast."

As the crowd murmured, he turned back to the wall. "There's more." He pointed at another poster, tacked up beside the first, and the crowd shifted to let him near. This poster pictured a realistic merman and merwoman, smiling. "This one says they're just like us. With war-mongering kings and oppressed peasants. That Murkel was a lousy king who oppressed the merfolk."

Murkel! The man reading the poster continued, but Muri couldn't focus on his words. Murkel was a lousy king? The man spoke as if he knew the merking. Should she ask where he was? The man didn't strike her as friendly toward Strombidae.

"That old drunk Murkel was really one of these things?"

Muri's gaze snapped to the speaker, a short woman in front.

"The princess said so—that's good enough for me."

"Has anyone asked him about this recent visitor?"

"He was up in the park earlier," someone said, waving an arm up the hill, "but I couldn't get anything useful out of him. Just kept moaning—'It's over,' and 'They're coming for me.'"

The crowd shifted, and no one spoke.

Muri didn't need to hear any more. If the merking was in the park—and moaning in distress, it sounded like—then the park was where she needed to go. She turned from the crowd.

She bumped straight into a man. He stood behind her, right behind her and too close, close enough that she could catch the stale smell of sweat on his skin. His shirt was stained, with thick ugly chest hair poking out the top. She lifted her gaze up—way up—to his leering face and tangled hair. He glared down with baleful green eyes and his skin shone. Muri gulped. He had to be a fairy.

"Excuse me, sir," Muri whispered, barely able to get the words out without shaking.

But the fairy didn't step back. If anything, he moved in closer. He leaned down and quietly snarled, "And just what are you doing here?"

Muri glanced to the side. The moment she moved, the fairy's hand was on her arm like a shut clamshell.

"Just listening to the gossip," she said, swallowing her panic. "They were reading the poster about the merman." There had to be an escape.

The fairy's grip tightened, and his breath hit her face. Muri cringed and held her own breath.

"I know what you are, ocean girl," he whispered.

Into her mind popped all the times mermen had grabbed her arm, ordering her this way or that. Each time, she'd struggled against her own will and made herself obey, knowing she had no right not to.

But she wasn't in Glorypool.

Many seasons of motion through the water had made her arms and legs strong—stronger than a land-dwelling fairy's. Muri stepped forward and shoved, and the fairy stumbled back. His grip on her arm loosened as he bumped against the person beside him, cursing. She tore her arm away and ran.

Chapter 3

ಏ ✶ ಌ

Muri fled up the hill and away from the fairy. She ducked into the first alleyway she came to and into a recessed doorway. She was pretty sure the fairy hadn't been right behind her. Maybe he'd pass by the alley if he followed her.

She waited, catching her breath and counting her heartbeats until she reached one hundred. Then two hundred, which took longer since her heart's rapid pace was slowing. When her heartbeat was back to normal, she peeked out from the doorway. The alleyway was deserted. She crept to the corner with the street leading up to the park. The steep lane was empty to her left, if you didn't count all the cats lying in the sun. Most of the villagers were still down at the market. And the horrible fairy was nowhere in sight. She'd lost him.

The humans milled about on the wharf, in the bit visible between the buildings at the bottom of the hill. After a moment, she shook her head. She was looking for the fish-catcher again. She closed her eyes and knocked her head gently on the wall. She wasn't going to see her fish-catcher. She shouldn't even want to—look how dangerous the fairy had been. The muscular fish-catcher would be worse! But his face—the fractured glimpse of it—kept appearing in her mind.

She turned away and stole up the hill past more doorsteps and shopfronts. The cats barely opened an eye as she passed where they lay. Every few buildings, another lane crossed hers, leading away on both sides. She tried to move calmly, as if she were any other villager walking along the street, but her instincts urged her to look behind and overhead, expecting an attack.

At the top of the hill, the lane flattened and had turns to the left and right. Buildings continued along the outside of the street. More people moved between the shops, but none of them glowed the way the fairy had. Straight ahead was an open, grassy area. Across the grass stood tall trees, budding into brilliant pale greens and reds. The island had palm trees, not colorful trees like this. Afternoon sun glinted on a metalwork fence surrounding the grass. This must be the park. Hopefully Strombidae was still here.

Muri stepped into the street and crossed over to the park. No one looked her way. How had the fairy recognized her? Did he have a special sight? Lotti was right—the fairies *were* tricky.

The park gate opened onto a path between flowerbeds. Farther on, the path led into the tall trees. She passed more of the wonderfully scented flowers she'd seen at the cottage and followed the path under the trees. Some branches were bare, while others were sprinkled with tiny blossoms in yellow or red or green. The stone walkway radiated a faint heat, welcome in the chill wind of early evening.

A man carrying a parcel passed her, and ahead, a man in rags lay sprawled on a bench, mumbling to himself. Muri made a wide circle as she passed the mumbler, surveying the trees for any sign of Strombidae. The path ahead was—

"Muricidae."

The voice was a hiss like steam through a fissure. Muri spun around, but no one was in sight, only the man with the parcel far down the path, and the mendicant on the bench. The mendicant was leaning up on one elbow, staring at her.

Muri gasped. "Your highness?"

King Strombidae Murkel was a wreck. His skin was sallow, his face sunken, and his once-gleaming locks of hair brittle and dull. His regal nose was the only familiar feature he had left. Even his once full lips were shrunken. A gray scruff covered his chin. His body lay across the bench as if he were dead, except for his faded golden eyes, which flicked from her short hair down to her shoes and then back up to hold her paralyzed.

"Muricidae," he rasped. "Come closer."

She didn't want to go any nearer than she already was, but the command was an order from her king. She took one step.

"Closer," he demanded, his voice louder.

Muri took another step, then another, fighting back her revulsion until she stood before him. This was her future husband. She'd never been attracted to him, but now he horrified her. The thought of marrying him made her want to dry out her tail and never go home.

He propped himself upright on the bench until he sat with his face slightly below hers. "Why have you come?" His breath was rancid.

"Your highness, we've been worried about you. And about the kingdom. If you're not back in seven days, the throne is forfeit."

"It's been a full season," he murmured. "I thought so."

But he didn't move from the bench. Why didn't he care? Didn't he understand?

His eyes narrowed. "And you're just coming to find me? Is that what I'm worth?"

"No, your highness. We thought you were spending time with your bride. And when we started to worry, it was too late. Bull stopped anyone who tried to leave."

"Bullidae," Strombidae hissed.

Bull was the most likely to replace Strombidae on the throne. He was handsome, but mean—mean enough that the mermaids avoided him if they could.

"Lotti came up with a plan for me to get out of Glorypool to come find you."

"Why did they send you?"

"Bull has guards all around the perimeter. No one's allowed to leave. But—"

"How did you escape?"

"Lotti caused a distraction." Muri wasn't about to tell him his first wife had lured the guards into the air chamber for a quick bout of trysting.

"But why you?"

"I would not be missed."

"Why not?"

Muri blushed and looked down. "You know why not, your highness."

When she looked back, a gleam had come into his eyes. "A full season has passed and you were still in isolation."

"It was your order, your highness. I stayed in the royal hut and went out to work only with your wives. No one else would notice I was gone right away."

The gleam was growing and with it, the dread that had formed in Muri's chest when she'd first recognized him.

"You follow my orders," he said, grinning, "even now?"

Muri swallowed. "Of course, your highness," she whispered. She barreled on. "But there's no time. You must come home and reclaim the throne." Maybe he'd forget whatever was on his mind.

"You said there's a quarter-moon."

"But—"

"Come here." His hand was out and on her thigh.

Muri forced herself not to flinch away from his touch. "Your highness, please."

He licked his lips and squeezed her tighter.

"Prince Murkel!"

Muri started and jumped back the moment Strombidae's hand released her. He shrank back on the bench, withering before her eyes.

A woman hurried up and stepped in front of Muri, knocking her back and blocking her from Strombidae. The woman had long, dark curls and wore a simple dress that fit against her body much closer than Muri's did.

"You leave this child alone!" the woman said to Strombidae.

"She's no child—" Strombidae replied, but the woman cut him off.

"You've behaved so well this winter. You know if you start bothering the women again, they'll move you back to the jailhouse."

Muri gawked at the woman. Who was she, who spoke like this to the merking? Like he was a misbehaving merchild. She called him "prince" as if he had never told anyone his real title. And what did she mean, "bothering the women"?

And why in all the seas was the human woman helping Muri?

Strombidae uncurled, sitting taller. "I wasn't bothering her. She came willingly. Isn't that right, Muri?"

"Sir, I—"

But the woman didn't even wait for Muri's answer. "That's enough. She's coming with me, and don't let me see you grabbing anyone again. I'll report you, I swear I will."

"You wouldn't, wou—"

"I will, Murkel. You're not in Merlandia anymore. I don't know what it was like there, but here you follow the rules. Our rules." The woman turned and took Muri by the arm. She started away, hauling Muri alongside her. Muri didn't dare try to pull away. She glanced back once at Strombidae, who watched them go in silence.

"You must be new in town," the woman said, letting go of Muri's arm once Muri was following along. Her voice remained sharp, but the anger wasn't directed at Muri.

Muri looked up into her eyes—blue, like the ocean under a winter sky. "Why did you help me?"

"I'm not going to let him paw at you. He's a lout."

Muri winced at the disrespect. What had happened to the merking in this terrible place?

The woman regarded her again. "Are you lost? I can walk you to the inn."

It seemed the quickest way to be rid of her. Muri followed the woman out from the trees. The sun rested at the tops of the buildings, and the sky had a pinkish hue.

"There you are."

Muri stiffened at the voice. The wide trunk of the nearest tree flickered, and the fairy appeared, leaning on the trunk with his arms crossed in front of his chest. As he uncrossed them, he seemed to shrink. His tangles of hair smoothed and the stains disappeared from his shirt, and his height continued to diminish until he was only a little taller than her. His skin still had a strange shine to it, as Lotti had said.

Muri's heart pounded. She'd heard of their magic and illusions, but seeing it in use was terrifying. The fairy might look scrawny now, but who knew what he was capable of.

"It's okay, Avi," he said, standing upright and coming toward them. "I lost her in the crowd earlier. I've been looking for her. I know where she's going." In a flash, he reached for Muri's hand and gripped it tightly, pulling it into the crook of his elbow as if to escort her. If she pulled away, he'd only hold tighter. And he knew the woman. She'd helped Muri get away from Strombidae, but she must be in league with the fairies or afraid of their power. She wouldn't help Muri escape this time.

"Thanks, Gray." The woman turned to Muri. "Take care of yourself, pet, and stay away from Murkel. At least keep out of arm's reach. He doesn't move very fast otherwise." And with that, she flashed a smile at the fairy and headed away.

Chapter 4

ᴥ✴ᴑ

THE FAIRY STOOD MOTIONLESS, WATCHING the woman go. He wasn't that tall, but his hand was tight on her wrist. He probably expected her to push him again and wouldn't let go this time.

Maybe Strombidae would come after her. Muri twisted to look over her shoulder, and the fairy's grip tightened. When the woman was thirty paces away, he spoke in a low voice. "Thanks for knocking me over earlier."

In spite of her fear, Muri's voice rose. "You tried to grab me, like you're doing again. You can't expect me not to fight back."

"Fair enough," he said. "But it's not like I'm going to tumble you in an alley. I just want to know what you're up to."

"It's none of your business what I'm—"

"After the trouble your rotten king caused? I think it is. The humans can't tell what you are, but I can. I've a responsibility to keep them safe."

What in the ten seas was he talking about? Why did a fairy care what happened to the humans?

He peered down at her. Other than his creepy green eyes, he resembled the humans—snub nose, thin lips, and shaggy brown hair, only his hair had weird blond streaks. "Now why are you here?" he asked.

"What do you mean, the trouble he caused?" Muri said. "King Murkel came to land to meet his bride."

"You mean he came to *kidnap* his bride."

"Kidnap?" There was the word again, the same accusation made by the poster at the wharf.

"And it's not like she was going to be his only mate, right? But he didn't share that he was already bonded. He made everyone think she'd be the only one. How many mates does he have down in Merlandia, anyway?"

Muri stared at the stone path. Why was the fairy asking her about this? Did he really mean her no harm? She scuffed her foot. "Eight."

"Are you one of them?"

"I'm to be ten," she said more quietly.

"And you want to bond with him?"

She inhaled, trying to stay calm. "It's a great honor."

"Do you want to?"

Muri didn't answer.

"Didn't think so."

"He's my king. I have to do as he says."

"I don't think he'll be your king much longer," the fairy said.

"That's why I'm here," Muri said, looking up. "He's been gone almost a full season. If he's not back in Glor— in Merlandia in a quarter-moon, the throne is forfeit."

The fairy stared intensely at Muri. "If I let go of your hand, will you run?"

"No," she mumbled. Where would she even go?

"I'm not going to hurt you, I promise. I just wanted to make sure you weren't planning to kidnap any more humans." His grip on her hand loosened, but he kept it in the crook of his elbow.

"Of course I'm not."

"Promise?"

"Yes." She pulled her fingers out of his elbow. "Did he really kidnap her? Didn't she want to marry him?"

"Would you want to be dragged onto land and forced to bond with a human and then made to live in a tank of water you could never escape from?"

His words described exactly what she had imagined. Strombidae's air chamber popped into her mind and she shivered. "But didn't he court her?"

The fairy was shaking his head. "Ocean girl, you have been deceived." She looked up into his unnerving green eyes. "Murkel paid off the human king so he could take her against her will. He ripped her dress off on the beach and dragged her into the sea. He planned to drag her all the way to Merlandia. She would have likely drowned on the way."

Muri shivered again. This was awful. Was it true? Janthinidae had said once that fairies didn't like to tell lies—they'd rather tell a twisted truth if they needed to hide something. And why would the fairy make up something like this? Was he trying to cover up whatever they had done to the merking?

"What happened?" she whispered.

"Her lover saved her."

"Her *lover*?" Strombidae's bride had a *lover*?

"The fairy prince Broadleaf."

"A *fairy*?" This story was getting less and less believable.

The fairy's face took on a dreamy expression, and his hand came to his breast. "He plucked her from the sea and hid her away in the forest, and like a stubborn fool, Murkel followed. But when Murkel's phony gold turned back to seashells, the human king went after him. He was locked in the castle dungeon for many moons."

"Moons?"

The fairy smirked at her. "I can see you're too shocked to form coherent sentences."

"But if he was in the dungeon, how did he stay hydrated?"

The fairy held her gaze and said nothing, and the truth dawned on Muri. The way Strombidae's body was all shriveled and sickly . . .

"He's dried out," she whispered.

As the truth sank in, Muri's knees wobbled. The fairy reached for her arm, and this time she didn't pull away.

Muri gasped in a shuddering breath, but it wasn't enough air. She kept at it, sucking in air until the dizziness passed. The fairy still supported her, holding her up by her elbow. She nodded as her balance steadied, and he tentatively let go.

The sun had dipped below the buildings and shadows deepened around her. The merking was no longer a merman. Her mission was over, just like that. What would she do now?

"Come with me," the fairy said, speaking more gently. "I'll get you some food, and you can . . . figure things out."

Muri hesitated.

"My sister will be there," he added. "We have a flower shop."

The word "flower" settled Muri. A whole shop of flowers? She felt disoriented over the news about the merking, but when would she ever get to see a flower shop again? And besides, anyone who ran a shop selling flowers couldn't be that bad, could they?

The fairy turned toward the edge of the park, leading her along beside him. He didn't speak at first.

Strombidae was dried out. He could never return to Glorypool. What would happen when the merpeople heard the news? Muri had to tell Lotti as quickly as possible, and without the shell necklace, she'd have to return to Glorypool to do it.

"What's your name?" the fairy asked.

"Muricidae. They call me Muri."

"I'm Gray."

Janthinidae had said that fairies named their children after trees and plants, because it gave them special magic when they used the plant they were named for. Muri wasn't sure what kind of a plant a gray was.

Gray passed through the park gate and headed across the street to the door of a shop. Land flowers filled the window as if they were growing inside the building. The colors and shapes were fantastical. A blue and white bird with a russet breast perched on the sign hanging over the door and chirped a few times as they passed underneath.

Gray pushed open the door and ushered Muri inside. The flower shop smelled wonderful, with bouquets of flowers in jars lining the wall behind a counter. Pots with leafy vines hanging down and fronds sticking up filled the space. A woman appeared in the doorway behind the counter. She resembled Gray, green eyes and all, but with longer, darker hair swept up in a knot.

The woman's eyes widened at Muri, and her lips parted.

"This is my sister, Hyacinth," Gray said. "Hy, this is Muri. We've been talking in the park."

Hyacinth turned to him, shutting her mouth and tilting her head.

"She's here to retrieve Prince Murkel. I've been filling her in on what happened last spring. She's in a bit of shock." He lowered his voice into a loud whisper. "She was the bride scheduled after Rose."

Hyacinth's face filled with pity, and she stepped out from the counter, limping on one foot. She reached for Muri. "You poor thing," she said, resting her hand on Muri's arm. Muri didn't flinch, although all this touching and squeezing was a bit unnerving. It must be a land custom.

"Do we have any biscuits? Or tea?" Gray asked. He turned to Muri. "You're probably hungry, right?"

"Do you eat biscuits?" Hyacinth asked.

"I don't know what a biscuit is," Muri said, "but I'd like to try fairy food."

"Very good." Hyacinth smiled and limped into the back room.

"Is she hurt?" Muri whispered to Gray.

"What? Oh, no, she hurt her foot when we were kids, but it doesn't cause her pain."

"But—"

Gray looked at her.

Muri's face heated. "Never mind." She'd been making assumptions about Hyacinth's abilities. She'd never known of any merpeople hurting themselves in such a way, but she wondered how an injury would be received in Glorypool if it hindered a merwoman's productivity. Janthinidae had been the only elder in Glorypool, and in her last few years, she hadn't been able to help as much with the gathering and some of the other tasks, and some of the mermen had suggested—

Muri shook her head. She didn't like to remember it. Besides, Muri had never believed that the complaints about Janthinidae were truly about her ability to work as hard as she once had. The mermen had never liked Janthinidae because she talked back to them and refused to defer to them. As soon as they had an excuse to complain about her, they did.

Hyacinth returned with a plate of round yellow blocks stacked like a pyramid. She placed it on the counter along with a clay jar. She uncovered the jar and dipped a thin metal knife in. It came out bloody. Muri recoiled. But it wasn't blood; it was lumpy and too pale. Hyacinth began smearing the spread onto the objects—the biscuits.

Gray nudged Muri up to the counter. A sweet scent wafted up from the plate.

Hyacinth watched Muri's face as she dipped her knife into the jar again. "It's strawberry jam," she said. "Do you know what a strawberry is?"

Muri exhaled in relief. "A fruit."

Gray swiped the jar out from under his sister's knife and held it out to Muri. "Try it."

She sniffed the open jar and got a heady dose of a delicious, sugary smell.

He tilted the jar toward her. "Scoop some on your finger."

Muri glanced at Hyacinth, who smiled encouragingly. Muri scraped a little of the jam from the lip of the jar and put her finger in her mouth. Ten seas, it tasted divine—like every sea grape on the island had been condensed into one swallow. Gray grinned.

Muri looked away, licking her finger clean and drying it on her dress. As Hyacinth resumed spreading the jam, Muri remembered her mission. What was she doing eating jam with fairies when the merwomen back home were waiting for her news? She fidgeted with the folds of her dress. Everything was happening too fast. She'd come to land to find Strombidae. But Strombidae was reduced to being a human, and she was eating "biscuits"! With fairies! Who were treating her kindly. The longer she was with them, the less threatening they seemed.

Was it all a trick? Lotti would think so. But why would the fairies trick her? She didn't have anything they'd want. And just look at Hyacinth—her face was kind and caring. If this was all a trick, it was a masterful one.

Did Gray and Hyacinth know the fish-catcher? Maybe they could—

Muri stopped herself. She was *not* asking the fairies if they knew any handsome fish-catchers. Gray had already questioned her motives for being on land. Asking about a human man would make her sound like a potential kidnapper for sure.

"Hyacinth," Muri said to end the silence, "is your name a plant name?"

Hyacinth nodded.

"What kind?"

"It's a flower—right now is the season for them. There's some blooming out in the park—pinks, blues, low to the ground."

"The ones with the scent like paradise?"

Hyacinth smirked, and across from her, Gray rolled his eyes. "Don't encourage her. She's the one who planted them all through the park. We'll have them sprouting between the cobblestones next."

"They're useful," his sister said.

"To you, maybe. Not to anyone else."

"What kind of plant is Gray?" Muri asked.

Gray's face fell, and Hyacinth's lips twisted in a grin. "Are you going to tell her, or should I?"

Gray sighed. "Our mother named us. She was a bit . . . eccentric?"

"I'd say 'whimsical,'" Hyacinth said.

"And she didn't know she was carrying two children."

"We're twins," Hyacinth added.

"Hyacinth came out first and got the proper name, and when I popped out, mum wasn't expecting me, so . . ." He paused and bit his lip.

"She named him Grape Hyacinth," Hyacinth rushed out, scrunching her face in delight. "It's adorable!"

"Stinkin' grape hyacinth, the most useless flower in the world."

"I love grape hyacinths!" Hyacinth said. "You could at least try to appreciate them."

"What are grape hyacinths?" Muri asked.

Hyacinth put down the knife and gestured to the biscuits. She turned and pulled a large book off the shelf behind the counter. Gray snagged a biscuit and took a bite, and Muri followed his lead. The jam was truly delicious, leagues better than sea grapes. The biscuit was a bit strange, though, like eating greasy chalk. It crumbled in her mouth and she had to catch a bit before it fell out the corner of her lips. But the jam made up for the biscuit.

Hyacinth opened the book further down on the counter, away from the sticky jam, and moved it to catch the dwindling evening light on the pages. Muri had never seen a book before. It had flat sheets of papery bark all bound together and filled with colorful sketches of flowers. Hyacinth flipped past one after another.

"Did you draw those?" Muri asked.

"Yes." Hyacinth stopped on a page. It showed a stem coming up from the earth with a cluster of purple nodules on top, just like the sea grapes. "That's a grape hyacinth. It's just that size, too. They're precious things, hiding in the grass."

"Oh, it's so cute!" Muri said. Beside her, Gray groaned.

"That's what I tell him," Hyacinth said, "but he insists on complaining about it. Ever since we first saw them last spring."

"I don't want to be 'precious' or 'cute,'" Gray muttered. "I want to be 'majestic' or 'sturdy.'"

Muri turned to him. "Why had you never seen one until last spring?"

"Until last spring, the fairies lived in underground caverns. We weren't allowed to go up in the forest."

"What happened?"

"Princess Rose came and set us free."

"Wait . . . King Murkel's bride?"

"I told you, she was never his bride."

Hyacinth flopped the book closed. "After Rose escaped Murkel, she found her way to the caverns where our people lived. She could see the entrance because it turned out she was half fairy."

"His bride was half *fairy*?"

"Would-be bride," Gray said between bites of his second biscuit.

"And then," Hyacinth continued, "she thwarted the fairy queen and rescued her slaves, and the fairies chose her to be the new queen because of her bravery and kindness, and we were freed to leave the caverns."

"His bride is the *fairy queen*? Would-be bride," she added quickly, glancing at Gray. His mouth was full of biscuit but he nodded.

Muri couldn't take it all in. The more she learned about bride number nine, the smaller she felt. This Rose was incredible. How would Muri ever live up to her?

Or did she have to?

Was she still expected to marry Strombidae if he was no longer a merman? He couldn't force her to, not if he wasn't the merking. Muri's pulse accelerated, but her smile faded into shame. How could she be so glad when the merking was suffering?

"So, ocean girl," Gray said, slapping his hands together to clear off the biscuit crumbs.

"Don't call her that," Hyacinth said. "And fetch me a lamp, would you?"

Hyacinth reached for a large jug packed with tall stems of flowers and brought it to the counter. Gray disappeared in back and returned carrying an object glowing with the light of the sun. A fire burned inside a glass enclosure. How had Gray made a fire so fast? Maybe he'd used fairy magic. Muri stepped back as he placed the lamp beside the flowers.

Gray leaned with one arm on the counter, watching Muri. "What's your plan, now that you've found your lousy king?"

"I have to tell Lotti and the other wives. When the merking doesn't return, there'll be fighting over who succeeds him and all his wives will lose their places."

"But you can't leave!" Gray said. "You only just got here. We've barely started to get to know you." He gestured at Hyacinth. "We've never met a merperson before. We could learn so much from each other."

"I would love to hear about your home," Hyacinth added. "Have you ever been on land before?"

"Only our island."

"You should definitely see the castle gardens before you go," Hyacinth said. "Gray could take you tomorrow."

"You *have to* see the gardens," Gray said. "Hy has worked so hard planting since fall and everything is starting to bloom."

Muri shouldn't stay on land any longer, but she wanted to. When the news about Strombidae reached Glorypool, things would be bad regardless. What did another day matter?

But Lotti and the others were waiting for her report, living in fear of their future. If only she hadn't lost Lotti's shell! She could have sent a message without having to go home.

"I don't have anywhere to stay," Muri said, hoping the excuse would be enough.

"You can stay here," Gray said. "Take my room and I'll sleep on the floor."

"I couldn't!"

Hyacinth peeked up from arranging her bouquet. "They'd let her have a room at the grange home. They told me I could have one any time since I send all the flowers."

Gray clapped his hands. "Perfect!"

"What's the grange home?" Muri asked.

"It's like the inn," Gray said, "but for older folks without anywhere to go. People who don't have families to help them. The village supports them."

"Older folks . . ." Muri murmured. Like Janthinidae. These older humans couldn't catch fish out on the bay or tend a garden, but the younger humans kept them around. This behavior was the opposite of how the mermen had behaved with Janthinidae.

Gray was smiling down at her. She could sleep in a human home? In one of their beds with the blankets and pillows? She should go back to Glorypool—she *knew* she should go—but making herself leave was hard with Gray insisting and with how much she didn't want to return home yet. Nothing here on land matched what she'd been told under the sea. The first two fairies she'd met were perfectly decent, and the human woman earlier had had a mind as sharp as any merperson's. Muri wanted more time to observe, to see if other humans were the same, or if they changed into monsters when they grew angry. She wanted to know the truth.

And what was another day?

"I would love to see the gardens," she said. "I love the flowers here. On the island most of the flowers are little ones up in the trees."

Hyacinth's eyes lit up. "You must have all kinds of flowers we don't have here. I wish I could visit your island."

Gray reached for another biscuit. "You mean you wish you could harvest all the island flowers and reap all their magic and use it in your devious plans."

Hyacinth lifted her chin. "There's nothing wrong with learning about new plants."

"You'd have to brave the monkeys to pick the flowers, though," Muri said. "We harvest fruit from the ground using long poles so we can get away quickly if a monkey comes."

"Monkeys," Hyacinth whispered, and her eyes were shining.

"They're terrifying," Muri continued, but Hyacinth was half smiling.

Gray rolled his eyes and spoke with his mouth full of biscuit. "Hy just sees them as new animals to dominate."

"*Befriend*," Hyacinth said, "and learn from."

"We should let Muri get to sleep," Gray said.

"The grange is across the square," Hyacinth said. "Gray can show you when he takes—"

The door opened behind Muri, letting in a burst of cool air.

Hyacinth looked up. "Oh, Jack," she said, smiling. "What brings you up here?"

Muri turned. It was the fish-catcher.

Chapter 5

The fish-catcher stood in the doorway, halfway blocking the opening with his broad frame. Muri's face heated but she couldn't look away. He faced Hyacinth, and the warm lights of the flower shop glowed off his cheeks and the curls of his hair.

It was the same man—Muri's heart thudded so hard she knew for certain. She'd thought his face would look different than what she'd glimpsed through the waves, and that she might not recognize him, but she did.

Jack.

He was so tall he had to duck a little to get in the doorway. Muri was used to being shorter than everyone, but Jack was as tall as Strombidae, or taller. She couldn't stop herself from studying the arms she'd seen from below the surface. It hadn't been a misperception caused by the water—they were every bit as muscled as they'd appeared then. The dim lamplight softened his tan, and now he wore a linen shirt. His hair was short on the sides, practically not there at all, but curled invitingly on top of his head.

His gaze flicked over to Gray and he nodded in greeting. He turned to Muri and stopped, startled, with his lips parted. Muri stared back, her heart hammering. Would he recognize her? Everything she'd learned about humans raced through the back of her mind—brainless doltish beasts, dangerous when upset—and she knew she should be scared, but all of the tales she'd heard were swept away by how much she wanted to gaze at Jack.

Gray cleared his throat loudly. Muri tore herself away. Gray was studying her with narrowed eyes, and he smothered a smile.

"I hope I'm not intruding," Jack said. His voice was deep to match his size. He was still watching Muri when she turned back, but he quickly looked away.

"Not at all, sir," Gray said, motioning Jack into the shop. "In fact, you're just in time to meet our new acquaintance. Muri has arrived in town for a few days. Muri, this is Jack. He's one of the local fish-catchers. He catches fish. In nets. Except for sometimes, when his nets rip in extra-large holes for no apparent—"

"Gray, hush," Hyacinth interrupted.

Muri's eyes had widened. Did Gray know?

But Jack only came forward and said, "He's teasing me. I pulled up my net today and half the fish had escaped. I've no idea how the net ripped." He regarded Muri again, and again her heart threw itself against her ribs. "Muri. I'm glad to meet you."

When he spoke her name, his lips moved as if he were kissing the air. She held her breath and blinked a few times, trying to clear her head. Was he truly a human? Maybe he was a fairy, too, and using one of their spells on her. He'd spoken to her. She nodded, hoping a nod was an appropriate response to whatever he'd said.

"I'm sorry to hear about the net," Hyacinth said.

"It's no matter," Jack said. "I can mend it. But that brings me to why I'm here. When I pulled up the net, I found this caught in it." He moved to the counter beside Muri. His hand came out of his trouser pocket and he lay down her shell necklace. The cord was broken.

Muri almost gasped aloud. She snapped her mouth shut and peeked at her necklace. The shell was a curled shark eye, small enough to fit in her palm. It was plain for a seashell and unremarkable if anyone happened to see it, except for the cord tied through it.

Hyacinth leaned in to study it.

"It seemed a bit . . . different," Jack said. "Aside from the cord tied through it. Like it shimmers, but then I blink and think I must've imagined it. And since I've had it, I can't stop thinking about it. It's like it's calling me."

Calling him? Muri knew the shell's power but she'd never seen it "shimmer," as Jack described it, or felt it call to her.

Hyacinth reached for the shell. As soon as she touched it, the wrinkle at her brow smoothed. "You're right. It has a spell on it."

Everyone leaned in closer. "A spell?" Jack asked.

"A fairy spell."

Muri stopped herself from blurting out her surprise. It wasn't a fairy spell—it was an ancient merspell, the power given only to the merking. Strombidae had given the necklace to Lotti when they'd married, back when she was his only bride.

"What does it do?" Jack asked.

"I can't say—I can just feel it's there. We can ask the elders, but there's no telling how long it's been floating around the ocean. Whoever created it may be gone. Keep it safe, and I'll let you know what I find out."

Jack scooped the shell back up. It disappeared into his pocket.

Muri had to get that shell.

Jack tilted his head at the gigantic bouquet Hyacinth had assembled. Muri didn't know the names of all the flowers, but she recognized some hyacinths. The others were a rainbow of pinks, purples, and yellows, some with stripes on the petals, some with frilly edges. Taken all together, the flowers were as beautiful as a coral reef.

"Is that for the grange?" Jack asked. "I've a box for them. I can take it across."

Gray had been unusually silent since Hyacinth shushed him, but now he stepped forward. "If you're going to the grange, would you show Muri the way? She'll be staying there, courtesy of the Fairweather Florist."

"Of course." Jack turned to her, and the moment she met his gaze, her heart thundered all over again. "I'd love to."

What was Gray up to? He wouldn't send her out the door with a human if the human were dangerous. And now that she'd heard Jack speak, he didn't seem dangerous. Maybe the humans varied, with some being more or less aggressive, the same as with the merpeople.

Muri remembered her wish to see the fish-catcher in the village, and that she might hear him speak. Her wish had come true, and here she was, about to walk out into the evening with him!

Gray touched her elbow. "Go get some rest. And tomorrow I can show you the castle gardens. Don't even think of leaving town before you see them."

Jack lifted the huge bouquet in its water jug off the counter and turned to go. Gray held the door open. As Jack stepped out, Gray's fingers tightened on Muri's arm. He leaned in close to her ear.

"And remember," he whispered, and Muri turned. A smile broke across Gray's face. "No kidnapping the humans. You promised." Gray nudged her out the door, still grinning, and closed it behind her.

Jack stood on the cobblestone street. He held the jug of flowers tightly in one arm, and somehow, he'd picked up a small crate that must've been out on the stoop. As Muri came out, he hefted the crate up onto his shoulder. As he did, the edge of his shirt lifted, revealing a narrow band of skin.

Muri shivered. The sun had set long ago, and with the onset of twilight, the air temperature had dropped. She was used to the cold depths of the sea, but somehow the land breeze made the chill worse. Her dress had been fine during the daytime but now felt thin. Behind Jack, fiery lamps flickered and glowed atop tall posts around the square.

Jack smiled as she came out into the street. His smile was warm and friendly. She couldn't help but contrast it with the facial expressions she commonly saw in Glorypool—mermen always looked arrogant. She found herself smiling back a little, but she had to look away for fear she'd blush all over again and he'd notice her awkwardness.

"Muri," Jack said as they started away from the flower shop, "where are you visiting from?"

Muri had planned out a story for this moment. "I'm from Nor Bay, and my cousin's in Sar Bay. We planned to meet here, but I've no idea when she'll arrive."

He took a moment. Was he trying to tell if she was lying? "What does your family do in Nor Bay?" he asked at last.

"I've no family." That statement was true enough.

Jack turned to her and she looked back, managing to meet his gaze until he looked away. Behind him, the sky had faded to a strange purple color, like the tallest flowers in the bouquet he held.

"Nor do I," Jack said, and the note of sadness surprised her. Why did he care? Humans didn't form lasting family bonds.

"What happened?" Muri asked.

"Both my parents were killed out on the bay. They used to work together on their boat and they didn't come back one day. It must have been an accident, but no one witnessed it. The whole boat disappeared."

"How old were you?"

"Fourteen winters. Old enough to start working on other boats until I saved enough for mine."

"And now you're a fish-catcher?"

"Yes."

They rounded the corner of the park. Where had Strombidae gotten to? What if he saw her walking with Jack? She had an excuse—she needed to get her necklace back. But Strombidae would be angry. That's how mermen were, always jealous and leaping to conclusions. Perhaps he had passed out on his bench.

"The grange is all the way on the far side," Jack said.

Muri spoke carefully, trying to keep her voice sounding calm. "What do you think that shell does?"

"I've no idea."

"I've never seen a fairy spell."

"I guess you wouldn't have as much chance to up in Nor Bay." He stopped to adjust his hand on the jug holding the flowers, pinning the jug against his body to avoid dropping it. It must've been heavy, but he carried it in one hand. "Until recently, most people here hadn't seen a fairy spell either, or a fairy, because the fairies were kept underground. Only the older folks believed fairies existed. But when Princess Rose freed the people from the king's tyranny, she freed the fairies as well, and things changed."

Princess Rose again! She was everywhere. And she had freed the humans, too? What couldn't this woman do?

"Some of the fairies live in Woodglen now," Jack continued, "like Gray and Hyacinth, and they've helped us. Seeing their spells work"—he smiled and shook his head—"it never loses its thrill. Has Gray shown you all his tricks?"

"His tricks?"

Jack grinned. "You'll see. Ask him to show you. He'll love it. I don't want to spoil the surprise."

"Can you use the shell?" she asked, even though she knew he couldn't. Only the merking could use a merspell.

"I don't see how."

"What will you do with it? Sell it?"

"I suppose I could, but no. It feels like a lucky charm to me."

"Even though you found it in a ripped net?"

He laughed and the sound warmed her. "I guess it doesn't make sense."

"Will you take it home?" Her questions were becoming suspicious, but she couldn't think how else to keep track of the shell.

He tilted his head and stared off at the treetops. "No, I think I'll keep it on my boat. Maybe it will protect my nets from now on."

His boat. That would be easy enough. She could go in the middle of the night and steal it.

But at least a hundred boats were docked at the wharf. How would she ever find the right one?

"Have you been to the castle gardens before?" he asked.

"No," Muri said, and genuine enthusiasm flared inside her. "I've not been much of anywhere. I hoped I might see some—" She stopped. She'd almost said some human places. "Some new places," she finished carefully.

He gestured at the windows they were passing. "Most of the shops are up here in the square, but there's more down at the wharf. If you were wanting a memento."

"I don't need that," Muri said. "I'll have the memories." Although if she'd had any human coins, she'd have loved to peruse all the items in their shops. How much fun it would be to bring a gift to Caly and the other mermaids, a bright and shiny gift from land to brighten their monotonous days of gathering seaweed and fish.

"That's how I feel about it," Jack said. "I would much rather see something new than buy a token to prove I'd been somewhere."

"Where I'm from—" Muri caught herself again. Talking to him was too easy—the truth kept trying to slip out. "The cottage I live in is sparse. We don't have a lot of trinkets like in the shops here."

"Well, I'm glad you're able to be here and visit with your cousin. What else do you want to see, aside from the gardens?"

"A public house," Muri blurted out.

"A pub? But you have those in Nor Bay."

Muri's brain scrambled for an explanation. "But none my father will let me go in."

"You have a father, then?"

Oh right. She had no family. "Not my real father. I live with a family. But it's been so long, I've been lumped together with his daughters." She smiled and hoped it would cover her patched-up story. "He won't let any of us go to pubs."

"Let me recommend The White Pony. Some of the other pubs can be a bit rowdy."

He stopped in front of a large blocky building. It was made of solid stones fit together with mortar between them and had smooth stone steps leading up to the door. All the stones in the wall were smoothed flat on the outside and colored grays and whites. The impressive building looked important, as if the land dwellers might run the village from inside it. But this was the grange home, where older humans were sent to live. And that meant Jack was about to leave her.

She had to see him again—to get the necklace, of course. But a tiny thread of something else laced the thought. She *wanted* to see him again.

"Would you go with me?" Muri said. "To the pub?"

His eyebrows moved up. Her face flushed hot. No merwoman would have made such a suggestion in Glorypool, if they'd had places like pubs, but Muri hadn't had any other idea of how to see him again.

"If my cousin's not here, I mean," she said, hoping she hadn't affronted him, "so I wouldn't have to go alone. You seem to know the way."

"Of course," he said, his face relaxing. "I— You caught me by surprise is all. I'd be glad to go."

"I told Gray I'd visit the gardens tomorrow."

"I'll be out on the water all day," he said. "I could find you when I get in?"

He stood waiting for her answer, balancing the crate with one hand, while the cluster of flowers danced beneath his face. She was going to see that face all night in her dreams. Muri couldn't help the smile that bloomed across her own.

"That would be wonderful."

He smiled back. "Would you mind getting the door?" he asked, and she blinked herself back to reality. She climbed carefully up the steps to the door. It had a handle that must open it. Her hand fitted into the handle, and thankfully, as soon as her thumb rested on the top part, it dropped down and the door clicked open. She pushed it wide and stepped away to let him enter.

As Jack went inside, Muri turned back and scanned the park.

The trees were dark in the fading twilight. She squinted. Strombidae stood in the shadows and watched her. Had he overheard what she and Jack had said? She shuddered and turned into the light of the doorway.

Chapter 6

ঔ ✹ ৎ

Inside the grange building, Jack introduced Muri to several withered-looking human women sitting in a gathering room. A bright lamp standing on a side table cast a warm glow on their faces and darkened the windows as they welcomed Muri and Jack in. Colorful blankets were draped across the furniture, and books filled a shelf.

First, the humans oohed and aahed over Hyacinth's bouquet, which Jack set on the center of a table near the door. Then they oohed and aahed over Muri when Jack introduced her as a visitor in town. And finally, after Jack delivered his crate of fish, said goodnight, and departed, they did quite a bit of oohing and aahing over Jack. Their faces lit up when Muri told them she had plans with him the next evening, which they called a "date."

Her head was fairly spinning as she took in all the furniture and the odds and ends lying around the home while the women buzzed with talk around her. The moment she yawned, one of the women offered to show her to a room. She led Muri up slippery wooden stairs, lit by one of the glowing lamps attached to the wall. Muri clung to the railing as she climbed the stairs, which were steeper than the trails she'd climbed uphill into the jungle when harvesting fruit. She followed her host to the top of the stairs and down a hallway into a room. It was smaller than the other rooms she'd seen, with a bowl and a pitcher of water on a small table and a bed. A window looked over the village. The woman apologized for not having a lamp to give her and left, shutting the door behind her.

Standing in the dark, quiet room, Muri took a moment to savor being alone. Of course it happened sometimes at home that she'd find herself with no one else around, but without solid walls, you never knew who might come swimming up. Here, safely enclosed inside the building with only the muffled voices of the women below and the occasional noise from the village square outside, she was truly alone.

She crept to the window first. Through the glass, the streetlamps glowed in the dark below her, but she couldn't see much else. She stepped over to the bed. In Glorypool, they rested under weighted mats on the seafloor, with several merpeople inside each small hut. The bed here was beyond anything she'd imagined. As she crawled onto it, her knees sank in like it was mud. She gave up trying to cross it and simply flopped down. She rolled onto her back in the softness and stared vacantly at the ceiling. When the merpeople talked about land dwellers, everyone focused on their behaviors. But, she realized, the descriptions of their habitat had been sparse. She knew what a bed was, but no one had ever said it would be like lying on a cloud. Or that it would be held up high on wooden legs, or have gigantic pillows she could move around and lie on top of.

Lotti would have a fit if she knew Muri was at the grange home, rolling about in a human bed. She'd say Muri should be sleeping hidden on a beach for safety. Or that she should be out in the park, tending to Strombidae. Ugh, Muri didn't want to think about him. The women in the grange home seemed perfectly safe, even friendly.

Eventually Muri wiggled her way to the top of the bed and squeezed herself under the blankets. In spite of the soft comfort, she lay awake for hours with thoughts of her day replaying on a loop in her mind. The village outside gradually went silent, and the women's voices from downstairs quieted.

The palest pink-tinted light woke her. She watched the small patch of sky visible through the room's window until the color compelled her out of the warm bed and over to look out. She worked on the window latches until they opened and she could push up the sash and inhale the clear smell of morning. Birds sang from the tree branches. Over the tops of the buildings and trees, a glorious pink and gold sunrise filled the cloud-strewn sky.

She rested there and watched the sunrise. She hadn't been to the island in a full season, so she was used to the endless darkness of Glorypool. From her high window, she could see into the treetops in the park and could just make out the sign hanging over the flower shop beyond.

Muri sighed and left the window. She had to return to the merking, and she wanted to do it before anyone would see her. She crept from her room and down the stairs and slipped out the door of the grange home, closing it carefully behind her.

She turned away from the door into the cool, shadowed morning. No one was out yet in the square, and the shops were all dark. She crossed the street to the park and entered at the nearest gate. She didn't have to go far into the trees before she found Strombidae. He sat on a bench and watched her approaching. Had he been up all night? Would he be angry?

Muri clung to Gray's words and to those of the woman who had helped her yesterday afternoon. Strombidae was dried out. He could no longer form a tail, and he could no longer be the merking. That meant she didn't have to follow his orders.

Could she disobey him to his face, though? Obedience to the merking had been ingrained in her for the past twenty-three seasons. It was expected of her, by him, and by all the merpeople.

But they weren't in Glorypool. From what she'd seen in the past day, women on land had standing in the community. She was safe from Strombidae's orders while she was here, and when she went home, he couldn't follow to harass her. He wouldn't be able to tell anyone she'd been disobedient.

She stopped across the path from him.

"Muri," he said, and his tone had changed from the previous day. Instead of commanding, he sounded wheedling. "I've never seen short hair on a mermaid before. It's quite becoming. How did you enjoy sleeping on a mattress with blankets?"

"How do you know where I slept?"

"Oh please, those old biddies at the grange home wouldn't have you on the floor. It was kind of them to take you in. They've never given me a bed."

"You apparently have a reputation, sir."

"'Sir'? What happened to calling me 'your highness'?"

"I know what's become of you. You can't return to Glorypool, can you?"

His eyes narrowed and she feared he'd become angry, but the glare came and went. "I see your new friends have been gossiping about me."

"Is it true?"

"It may be. But you're still my betrothed, and I expect you to honor that promise."

Muri's blood raced. Don't be rash, she told herself. Don't get yourself in trouble. But the nerve of Strombidae! She'd been marked as his, not asked. She'd never promised him anything.

"Tell me about your human bride," she said to avoid replying to his comment.

"Oh come, surely your fairy friends have told you all about her."

"I'm giving you a chance to tell your side so I don't have to believe the atrocities they told me."

"She was warped," he said. "She was under a fairy spell and couldn't see clearly. That's why she rejected me."

"Did you try to take her anyway?"

"Her father gave her to me."

"Did he know you planned to take her into the sea?"

"He wouldn't have cared."

"And you think that's right, to drag her away against her will when she probably couldn't even swim?"

"You know the humans don't feel things the way we do," Strombidae said.

Muri shook her head slightly. "I'm not sure that's true. Not from what I've seen."

"In all your seasons of experience?"

He was right. She'd been on land for only a day. Maybe the woman who'd been kind to her was exceptional. But what about Jack? He'd certainly seemed to feel things when he'd spoken about his parents. Or when he'd first looked at her. A shiver ran down her spine.

Muri glared at Strombidae and didn't answer.

Strombidae's head tilted. "You know, Muricidae, you haven't been behaving very well. You seem to have a lot of . . . opinions."

"So what if I do?"

"You're on land now, but you're going to be in trouble when you return home."

"I guess I'd better enjoy my freedom while I have it," Muri shot back. She bit her lip before she said more. Why was it so hard to behave the way she was supposed to?

Strombidae was watching her with narrowed eyes. "You always had that hint of rebelliousness, just like—" He stopped himself abruptly.

Muri waited, hoping he'd continue, but he pressed his lips together and lowered his head slowly.

"What do you plan to do?" he said instead.

"Lotti's expecting a report. I have to tell her what I've found."

"You're leaving."

"No. I have her shell necklace."

He leaned forward. "You do? Give it to me."

"It's not here. I lost it, but I know where it is, and I've got a plan to get it back."

"When you do, you bring it to me. I don't want you telling any of them what happened to me."

"What you did to yourself, you mean."

Strombidae stood abruptly and came toward her. "I mean it, Muricidae. If you tell—"

He cut himself off as Muri stepped back quickly. He let the threat hang in the air, but he stopped moving toward her.

"Lotti needs to know," Muri said. "What do you think will happen to her and the others when Bull takes the throne? They need time to make a plan."

Strombidae didn't respond for a moment. "What about that man with the flowers?" he asked. "He seemed terribly friendly toward you last night."

Muri's face heated. "He *was* friendly," she said, "and respectful, not like the human beasts I learned about in Glorypool."

"You can't trust them."

"Even so, I need him to get Lotti's shell back."

"And you'll speak to me before you do anything."

Muri hesitated. "Fine," she said at last. "But you haven't changed my mind. Lotti needs to know."

Before he spoke again, Muri stepped away.

She hurried away from the trees. Her shoulders tensed and she expected Strombidae to follow and grab her. She dashed toward the park gate and only when she reached it did she look back. The grass behind her was empty. She hurried out of the park and across to the grange home. The sky was brightening, and she didn't want to explain why she'd been out.

A few hours later, as Muri helped the grange residents clean up after breakfast (more biscuits and jam, as well as whole strawberries and boiled bird eggs—which were larger than the ones they found in nests on the island), Gray appeared, mentioning to the residents he was there for his "date in the gardens" with Muri. His arrival caused no small amount of fuss among the ladies, although it was different than it had been with Jack the previous night. With Jack, the ladies had been more reserved, at least until Jack left. With Gray, they squeezed his hands and peppered him with questions about the flower shop.

As Muri followed Gray out the door, Margery—who talked the most of all of them—called out, "Don't stay out too late, dear. You'll need time to dress."

"What's that about?" Gray asked as they departed the grange home and headed across the square. He was wearing a shirt dyed a lovely shade of purple—or maybe it was one of his illusions. It stood out among the plain whites and browns of the other villagers' clothes.

"I've no idea."

Gray turned his head toward her. "No idea. None whatsoever?"

"Well, Jack is taking me to a public house tonight."

Gray's face lit up. "Ah. That explains it. You'll want to look your best on your actual date."

"Is it an actual date?" Muri asked. She'd only wanted to spend more time with Jack—and get her shell back—and somehow she'd ended up embroiled in this human custom. "What does it mean?"

"Don't worry," Gray said. "Dating can mean lots of things. Like you might be courting someone to try to win them over so they'll bond—ah, marry you."

"*Marry* me?" Did Jack think she had asked him to the pub so he'd marry her? No wonder he'd been surprised.

"Or, so they'll have sex with you."

Muri's mouth dropped open. This was even worse.

"But it can also mean you just want to get to know the other person. Don't the merfolk have courtship rituals?" Gray asked.

Muri scoffed. "If you mean dragging a mermaid up to the island for a tryst or a spawning session, then yes."

Gray grimaced. "Spawning session? You did not just say that."

"What would you call it?"

"On land, it's 'tumbling' if you're being informal. Or 'making love' if you want to be romantic."

"But what if you're trying to reproduce?"

"Same."

"But surely Jack doesn't think I asked him to go to the pub so that we'd—you know, afterward?"

Gray grinned. "You asked him? Way to go, ocean girl." His grin softened as he regarded her. "Don't worry about Jack. He's a gentleman—he won't pester you for it if you're not interested. And he thinks you're a temporary visitor in town. He won't have any expectations."

A temporary visitor.

Gray led Muri around the edge of the park. Back against the trees, some people in bizarre colorful clothing were fussing with a set of poles and fabric. The woman's dress trailed behind her on the grass and was so tight against her chest and puffed out beneath it was hard to believe she could move in it. And the man had sleeves like a pufferfish but his trousers hugged his legs like skin, and his clothes had all the same colors as the woman's, as if they'd been sewn from the scraps. Gray didn't even glance at the couple, so they must not be anything unusual on land.

On the lawn, a mother tossed a ball with some children the same way a merwoman might—if Glorypool had any merchildren in its nursery. And another woman with the hump of a pregnancy sat on a blanket nearby, watching. Were some of the little ones hers?

Muri had never seen a pregnant person. Even when new babies *had* been allowed in Glorypool, pregnant merwomen had to stay on land—with legs—for the baby to grow. Supposedly there'd been huts in the jungle where they had stayed until they delivered. After that, they returned to the water, and the baby went to live in the nursery, where some of the older merwomen took care of them. But these days, the only ones using the nursery were mermen drunk on phyta who didn't want to pass out in the arena, where all could see.

Muri hadn't expected to see the community displayed by these mothers with their young. They seemed . . . playful. She'd pictured the humans nursing their young quickly and turning them out into the world. But these children were many seasons old and didn't look hardy at all. One of those cats in the lane could easily take one out.

Gray aimed for the flower shop. "Let's stop by the shop so you can say hi to Hyacinth."

Another bluebird perched on the shop's sign as Gray opened the door. Or was it the same bird? It let out a series of low-pitched tweets, and Gray looked up at it and rolled his eyes. Muri smiled at the bird as she passed.

Hyacinth was behind the counter with several buckets of flowers before her. She snipped the end off a stem and pushed it into a bouquet like the one Jack had carried to the grange last night.

"I've made the deliveries," Gray said.

"Thanks, Gray," she replied. "You all enjoy your visit to the gardens." Her fingers flashed as she snipped another stem. Muri stepped closer—Hyacinth wasn't using a blade like the knife Muri carried. The blade looked like a razor clam shell, of all things. Muri squinted. It *was* a razor clam shell. Hyacinth had two fingers under it and as she lifted her hand, the shell stayed attached to them, held snug against her fingers by bands of metal on the underside. Hyacinth slashed with her fingers, and the shell glided through the stems like they were made of loose sand.

Muri's eyes widened.

Gray leaned in. "Hy never uses human scissors. She feels more powerful chopping flower stems with a fairy blade."

Hyacinth frowned at Gray across the counter. "Scissors damage the stems and the flowers don't last as long."

"That blade can cut stone," Gray whispered loudly. "It's enchanted. And she uses it for flowers." Hyacinth was arranging the cut flowers in the jug.

"Can it really cut stone?" Muri asked.

Hyacinth pursed her lips at Gray.

He grinned and stepped to the door, leaving it open to the morning breeze as he went out. He returned with a small rock.

Gray placed the rock on the counter and grinned again. His green eyes still made Muri's skin crawl a tiny bit, but she was getting used to them. She remembered him towering over her at the wharf the previous afternoon and how scared she'd felt. He didn't seem dangerous at all now.

In fact, he seemed a bit like a friend.

Hyacinth cleared her throat. When Muri turned to watch, she pressed the edge of the shell to the rock. It slid slowly in, and the rock broke cleanly in two.

Muri stepped back.

"You'd better step back," Gray said. "She's dangerous."

"Oh Gray," Hyacinth said, turning back to her flowers. She addressed Muri. "I always secure the blade when I'm not using it. There's a protection spell."

She said some strange words—fairy words, Muri guessed. Hyacinth touched the edge of the blade. "See? It's not sharp anymore. You have to be wearing it and say the words for it to be sharp."

Hyacinth said the spell again and resumed trimming the flowers.

Muri could have watched Hyacinth slice flower stems with her magical razor clam shell all morning, but Gray took her arm and tugged her out the door. As the bluebird trilled behind them, they headed back into the square. The people with children on the grass had gathered into a crowd in back, where a banner now sagged between two erect poles. In the center of the crowd, the woman in the strange dress was sobbing.

Muri's steps slowed. The crowd watched the woman and no one offered to help her. A shiver went through Muri. This behavior was what she'd expected from the humans.

The man in the matching clothes yelled at the woman and she sobbed harder. And everyone else continued standing like rocks, watching, even the children, some held in their mothers' arms.

"Muri," Gray said. He had stopped walking, too. "It's not real."

"Not real?"

He stepped back toward her. "It's called a theatrical."

"A theatrical?"

"That woman crying—she's pretending."

"And they watch her pretend to cry?"

Gray smiled. "There's a story. They're telling a story. See that man"—Gray pointed—"he's probably her lover. And they can't be together so she's crying. But something else will happen so they *can* be together and it will have a happy ending."

"Oh."

"Or, her lover will be killed and she'll kill herself to be with him in the forever beyond."

"No," Muri said.

"Sometimes theatricals are tragic. But given the number of children watching, I'd guess this one will have a happy ending."

They watched another minute, and sure enough, the woman started kissing the man. Gray took Muri's hand and tugged on it until she came after him.

He led her down a lane away from the park and out of the village, opposite the direction of the wharf. The grand stone buildings of the main square ended and smaller cottages stood with gardens between them. Gray turned onto a small path between two cottages.

They left behind the buildings, and the path dropped between bushes with trees hanging above. To the left, between the budding branches, Muri glimpsed the ocean.

They exited the tunnel of bushes, and fields spread out around them. The tall spires of the castle towered on their right. Muri stopped to goggle. How had the humans built the castle? The towers reached to the sky without toppling, and the walls shone smooth as the inside of a shell.

She caught up to Gray and walked beside him as the path widened.

"So about dating," she began, and his eyes crinkled into another smile as he waited for her to continue, "you said sometimes the people just want to get to know each other. So *are* we on a date?"

"I should've been clearer," Gray said. "Sometimes the word 'date' gets used for friends getting together, like we're doing. But the concept of 'dating' is only for people who are *romantically* interested, or who are attracted to each other. You're getting to know each other to see if you want to take it further."

"So Jack will know I was attracted to him?" Maybe she shouldn't have stared at him.

"Muri, a sea slug would've known the two of you were attracted to each other. The air was crackling with it."

She grabbed Gray's elbow. "Wait, he's attracted to me?"

Gray rolled his eyes but wouldn't answer.

"So are you dating anyone?" she asked, trying to get him talking again.

"Not at the moment."

"Why not?"

Gray shrugged, biting his lip. "I thought I would," he said at last. He sighed. "I always had partners when the fairies lived in the caverns, but my last boyfriend decided to travel once we were free. And Hyacinth wanted to move to the village, and I wanted to stay with her. I thought I'd try somewhere new and see what the people in the village were like."

"And?"

"We've been here a few moons now, and I just haven't met anyone I really click with. The human women are, I don't know . . . a lot of them seem focused on amassing wealth and possessions. And having babies. None of which appeals to me. And the men are so macho. I don't seem to have anything in common with any of them."

"Could you go back to live with the fairies?"

He shrugged. "I don't really want to. I like the village, and I'm busy helping with the shop."

Muri touched his arm. "You'll meet the right person someday. Human or otherwise."

He smiled a little. "Maybe I should meet some merpeople."

Muri snorted. "If you think the human men are macho, you should see the mermen."

"They're that bad?"

"They're always ordering the merwomen around or dragging them up to the island for a tryst. I didn't want to be engaged to the merking, but at least it stopped the other mermen from bothering me."

"It sounds like the merwomen don't have any rights," Gray said, his tone growing serious.

Muri frowned and shrugged. "No. But it's always been that way."

Gray shook his head and whistled. "What a patriarchy."

"What a *what*?"

"A patriarchal society. A society where men have all the power." He continued along the cliff in silence.

A patriarchal society. Weren't all societies that way? Apparently not, from what she'd seen in Woodglen.

The land beside them dropped away in a rocky cliff over the ocean. The wind gusted at Muri, bringing the scent of the sea. Whitecaps danced across the rippling surface as the wind tossed her shortened hair. Home was out there under the waves—home, where she'd soon return. Where life consisted of catching fish and gathering seaweed and waiting on a merman to choose you. The thought soured in her stomach.

A tall stone wall appeared ahead on the path. A gate through the wall stood open. As they neared, Muri glimpsed a burst of color inside.

Gray held out an elbow toward her the way he had yesterday, but this time, he didn't force her to take it. She slipped her fingers into the crook of his arm, and together they strolled into the gardens.

Inside the wall, the wind died. And the colors were amazing! Before them spread a mosaic of flowers in beds with geometric shapes and paths between them—more hyacinths, and "tulips," Gray called them, like the ones in the grange's bouquet, in a tumult of colors, the stems swaying in the slight breeze. Thin bushes with tiny yellow flowers like four-pointed starfish grew in a wide bed down the center. Spiraling bushes, shaped like giant green turritella shells, stood sentinel at the corners of the flowerbeds.

She and Gray ventured deeper into the garden. Gray named the flowers for her, showing her the ones Hyacinth had planted. The yellow flowers were forsythia, and their bushes would spread to fill the entire bed. Apparently the human king, overthrown by Strombidae's would-be bride, had favored tropical flowers from other lands, but he'd had dozens of servants to care for them. Over the past seasons, since he had been removed, Hyacinth and other volunteers had planted more practical flowers and shrubs that didn't require as much care in this climate. The tulips and hyacinths came up spring after spring, but they were cleverly spaced so summer flowers would grow between them and the garden would bloom all season.

At the far end of the beds, a path through a gate led to a beach. Gray raised his brows, but she shook her head. She didn't want to go near the water.

He turned the other way, ducking through a tunnel in a hedge to enter another garden. Here, a few people knelt over a bed, lining up stones to make a wall. The castle towers rose beyond them.

A few hours later, they'd walked through all of the gardens—one of herbs, one where only purple flowers were planted, and many more. Other visitors strolled through the paths, too, and Muri and Gray passed gardeners pulling weeds and planting small plants that would bloom this summer—all volunteers, Gray said, organized by a committee overseen by the grange. How did the humans have time for something like this—to make a beautiful space that didn't produce food or provide anything useful? How would the volunteers eat? Did others give them food?

At last the gardens ended at a green lawn spreading far out to a stone patio, and behind the patio towered the massive castle. A fountain plashed at the edge of the lawn. Gray sank down onto the lip of the fountain and patted the space beside him.

"Unless you need to keep your distance," he said, jerking his head at the water.

"No," Muri said, sitting. "A splash won't change me. I need to be pretty much submerged."

"Well, if you fancy a swim . . ."

Muri winced. "I can see the posters in the village now. 'Killer Mermaid Causes Panic in the Gardens.'"

Gray laughed.

"Why are the humans scared of us? Like in that poster by the wharf?"

Gray pursed his lips and his brow wrinkled. "Humans are weird. Their first instinct is usually fear. If they see something new—like a mermaid—they become scared. I think it comes from not having magic. They had to be careful not to get eaten by monsters or other horrible creatures."

"Merpeople are that way, too, though."

"Same thing. No magic."

Muri frowned, but before she could contradict him, Gray continued.

"But from what I've heard by talking to the villagers over the past moons, to the humans, merfolk were kind of this mythical monster no one truly believed in. When people learned an actual merman had tried to drag Princess Rose out to sea, it caused a fuss. People got scared that more were coming and no one was safe." He looked over at her. "More aren't coming, are they?"

"Not that I know of. I had to sneak out of Glorypool to get here. Everyone there thinks it's the best place ever because we have a volcanic island that warms the sea, and they criticize everything about land dwellers. But I don't think anyone knows what it's truly like here."

Gray gave her a sly grin. "You mean, full of gorgeous men begging to tumble an attractive mermaid?"

"Ten seas, they'd never have sent me if they'd known—" Muri stopped.

Gray bent over laughing. He'd tricked her into admitting she'd had the same thoughts.

"Are the fairies scared of merpeople?" she asked.

He stifled his laughter and sat up. "Sort of. Ages ago, the merpeople would come to land and trade with the fairies. They'd bring things we could use in our spells—like plants growing under the sea. And the fairies made spells for the merpeople to take back with them to Glorypool. Or wherever. I've never been clear on how many settlements the merpeople have."

"Glorypool is the only one in the Cold Sea, I think. It would be too cold to live here without the heat from our island. Most of the merpeople live in the Warm Sea."

"Anyway, Queen Oleander—the mean one who Rose defeated—she came to power forty-some winters ago, and as things went on with her, the fairies weren't allowed to stray far, and eventually they weren't allowed to leave the caverns at all. So their relationship with the merfolk ended.

"I always knew about the merfolk, though. Some of the fairies liked them. But about ten winters ago, when I was a boy, something happened. I remember it like a hush going through the cavern, and no one would tell the children what it was about, but of course we listened when they didn't know it. The merfolk had killed a few humans but hadn't been caught doing it. I don't know why it happened or how the fairies found out. Maybe the birds told them. Some of the fairies are skilled with that kind of communication—communicating with birds and animals even over a distance. And after that, we had no news of the merfolk for ages. Until Murkel showed up here last spring."

Ten winters ago—that would mean merpeople she knew had been involved. Where had it happened? And why had the merpeople been near land? What if... Dread settled in Muri's chest. Jack's parents had mysteriously disappeared out on the sea ten winters ago. What if they were the ones the merpeople had killed?

Gray sighed and settled back on the fountain. He'd given her quite a history lesson.

"How long can you go without water?" he said at last.

"With none at all, I'd be dried out in a quarter-moon. But if I were drinking even a little, a moon or more. But I start to get uncomfortable after a few days with legs."

"Uncomfortable?"

"Itchy feeling. But over my whole body."

Gray grimaced. "Is that how Murkel feels?"

Muri shrugged. "I think it stops when you're dried out. Your body doesn't crave the water. It stops when you're pregnant, too."

"Because you can't form a tail when you're pregnant if you want the baby, so you're on land for nine moons."

"Right. How do you know all this?"

"We had lessons on merfolk biology. Didn't you learn about fairies?"

"We did, but all we learned was how treacherous you all are."

Gray grinned.

"I've only heard stories about fairies," Muri continued. "My people used to visit some of the smaller land villages, but I never got to go. They said it became too dangerous. But probably they just didn't want us seeing how good you all have it, with the food and everyone having fun." Muri sighed. "But anyway, no one gets pregnant in Glorypool anymore."

Gray's grin faded and he tilted his head.

"For the past twenty seasons. Since the lean times—the merking back then banned new merchildren. We can barely feed the people we have."

"I didn't know."

"Lotti always said—" Muri stopped, flushing hot.

"Said what?" Gray asked, nudging her.

"It's not true though."

"Tell me."

"She always said it was the fairies' fault we had so little—that they were selfish and betrayed the merpeople and cut us off from supplies we needed. Even Janthinidae said so, and she wasn't half as fanatical as Lotti. But because the fairies were trapped . . ."

"We couldn't communicate with the merpeople."

"For the past forty seasons."

Gray heaved a deep breath in and sighed it out dramatically. "That's how rumors get started."

"I'll tell them the truth."

"When you go back?"

Muri shrank a bit under his gaze.

"You don't have to, you know. You could stay here."

Muri frowned. "Jack said I should ask to see your tricks," she said to change the subject.

"My tricks," Gray said, squinting one eye. "I like the sound of that."

"So, *land boy*. What can you do?"

Gray rolled his eyes. "I can do invisibility, but I'm not terribly good at it yet. I only fade a little." He focused ahead as if concentrating, and his form blurred in Muri's vision. She started when the fountain appeared right through him as if his body were a mirage. His form resolidified.

"Yesterday," she said, "I didn't see you in the park until you appeared by the tree."

"That's because I was hiding behind the tree," he said. "Hyacinth communes with plants, and she's gifted with animals, especially birds, and she makes spells out of flower pollen. She can do anything with hyacinth pollen. She'll be out harvesting in a few days from the acres of plants she installed as part of her plot to take over the village."

Muri was starting to know when Gray was kidding. "What do you mean, 'gifted with animals'?"

"She can send flocks of birds to attack humans who disobey her commands." Muri didn't fall for his joke and waited for him to continue. Gray huffed. "She can communicate with animals like most fairies can, but birds will do anything for her. They love her. And butterflies, too, except butterflies aren't useful for much. Hy transplanted a field of milkweed last autumn and became the butterfly champion."

"What's a butterfly?"

Gray's brow crinkled. "You don't have those on your island?" He flapped his hands in front of him. "Pretty wings, flutter around, drink nectar from flowers?"

She shook her head.

"You should stick around," he said. "They'll be here in another moon. They flutter around the gardens and land on the flowers. I'd seen a few in the woods, but last summer we visited here for the first time, and the gardens were full of them."

Muri wished she could see them. "What other tricks do *you* have?"

Gray straightened. "*I* am a master at illusions. All this time you've thought I had brown hair, right?" He waited for her to nod. She blinked and his hair was bright blue. Muri's mouth dropped open. Gray lifted his hand and snapped his fingers, and at the sound, the hair color changed back to brown but without the usual white highlights, and his shirt turned into the off-white linen the fish-catchers wore. But something else was different.

"Your skin?" Muri asked. It no longer had the shine of moonlight.

"I'm a human," Gray said in a comical tone, and Muri laughed. "I have a date with a mermaid tonight, and I don't know what to wear." Muri swatted his arm.

"Wait, here's one for you." He focused a moment, licking his lips. His hair darkened and a green shadow spread from the top of his forehead. His nose grew, and his shirt faded into a ridiculously hairy chest. She gawked as his legs disappeared and a giant green-blue tail rested against the ground. The tail fins flopped up and down on the grass.

"Gray, that's incredible," Muri said. She was sitting next to a merman on the edge of the fountain. She leaned in close. The scales were tiny and perfect. They even had a pattern to them, creating whorls on the tail like she'd never seen on a real merperson.

"You can touch it," Gray said. "I'm not shy."

Muri reached out a finger and ran it over the rough texture of the scales. "But if it's not real, how can I feel it?"

"Your mind expects to feel it. Picture my legs and try again."

Muri pictured the trousers Gray had been wearing and reached her fingers out. This time, she felt the rough cloth instead of the scales. The tail faded away. She looked up to find Gray back by her side. His hair was dark black.

"Is that your real hair color?"

"Yes, but it makes me look like a goblin, right?"

"I don't know what a goblin is."

"An imaginary monster that comes out at night to eat children. It's just dark and gloomy. So I lighten it up a bit." The darkness faded back to his usual brown with the white streaks. For a moment, the white moved like shooting stars. All Muri could do was smile.

They sat quietly in the sun after that. Gray tilted his head back and closed his eyes. Muri copied him and exhaled, relaxing onto her seat. Sitting here felt like being on the island, peaceful with an ocean breeze and birdsong. Only the occasional human noise broke the impression, like a clink of metal on metal or the clatter of someone moving stones among the garden beds.

Now that they were resting, Gray's words about the killing returned. Ten seasons ago—she and her friends had been merchildren, but Lotti hadn't. Did Lotti know about the humans who'd been killed? What had happened? Had it involved Jack's parents?

He'd been fourteen when they died—that would make him 24 seasons old, right about her age.

A patriarchal society, Gray had called Glorypool. Where men had all the power. That description was certainly true. Glorypool had a king, and he could do as he wished. Aside from obeying their king, the mermen could, too. The merwomen did as they were told. They mended the fishing nets and wove the baskets for gathering. The mermen's only responsibility was a vague notion of protecting the colony. But truly, the mermen spent their days playing sport-games or lying about, eating the food the merwomen prepared or drinking the fermented phyta the merwomen made. Or taking merwomen up to the island for a tryst. Muri didn't care if Gray laughed at what she called it. "Making love" was too ridiculous a description for the rutting around of a merman. Even "tumbling" sounded more fun.

The one time the mermen's protection had been needed, they had failed. Something had snatched Janthinidae away. No one saw it happen, but the patrol found her necklace lying at the edge of the seaweed fields.

A few good-natured mermen did live in Glorypool, ones who would help her and the other merwomen carry in their baskets at the end of the day, although they usually did it when they were hoping to mate. But that behavior wasn't the norm, and most of the mermen laughed at the few who treated the merwomen better. And that was the way it had always been. The mermen in control.

A patriarchy.

But the village of Woodglen didn't seem to be a patriarchy, not with a woman directing male fish-catchers on the docks, that woman chastising Strombidae in the park, and Hyacinth running a flower shop. And if the humans didn't live under patriarchal rule, and the fairies didn't, why should the merpeople?

Well, there was one reason. The merking possessed magic and no one else in Glorypool did. But that didn't mean he had to lord it over everyone. And he was just one merman. It wasn't like all the mermen had magical powers.

Muri's belly rumbled. The sun was past noon and heading behind the castle towers. Gray reached over his head, stretched like an octopus, and opened his eyes. "Hungry?" he said, dipping his chin and raising his eyebrows.

"I could get some seaweed," Muri said. She didn't know how she'd gather it without getting wet, but she didn't expect Gray to keep feeding her.

But he stood and held out a hand to her. "Let's go back to the shop for lunch. Hy will have something. We can tour the castle another time."

"Talk about a patriarchy," Muri said as they headed back into the gardens. "Relying on your sister to make all the food. And to run the shop, from what I've seen."

"I help," Gray said. "It's just with you in town, I've been distracted. Hyacinth does run the shop, but I'm her little servant. I do the deliveries, and I harvest things she needs from the woods. Besides, you haven't tasted my attempts at cooking."

As they crossed the clifftops back to the village, he eyed her dress.

"That's the same dress you had on yesterday," he said.

"I've only got one," Muri replied. "It's not like we wear them in Glorypool."

"I'd forgotten."

"Is it really that bad to walk about naked on land?"

Gray busted out laughing. "Yes, I'm afraid it is. Please don't try it."

"I don't see why, when the sun is so warm."

"Just, no."

"Some of the humans by the docks had their shirts off. That's okay?"

"Yes. No, wait. That's okay for men. Don't you try it."

"*What?* That makes even less sense."

"Not everything makes sense. It's simply how it is, and it would be hard to change. You can be naked all you want in your own private, fenced-in garden."

"If I had one."

"Or in Jack's garden," Gray said, and he winked.

"Stop!" Muri said, nudging him.

"Seriously, though, you can't wear that dress tonight."

"Why not? Don't humans wear the same dress over and over?"

"It's not that. It's just . . ." He hesitated, then burst out with, "It makes you look dull."

"Dull?"

"They've hidden you beneath that sack of a dress, and all the color is washed out of it. It's all wrong for a date."

"There are different clothes for dates?"

"Yes. You wear your everyday clothes to work, and you have fancier clothes you wear on special occasions. To lure in the men."

Muri ignored the last bit. What a bother these clothes were! But she didn't want to meet Jack wearing something that wasn't right. "What should I do?"

"Don't worry. You're smaller than Hyacinth, so I can find you something of hers. She won't mind lending you something." His eyes glinted. "And I bet Jack won't mind it, either."

Chapter 7

୨୦ ✸ ଓ୧

Muri was sitting primly in the parlor of the grange home with five eager chaperones when Jack arrived to meet her for their date. At the sight of him, her heart flopped about like a fish pulled from the water, and she realized that, like the fish, she had stopped breathing. Thank the seas Gray had dressed her—Jack was no longer wearing a rough shirt and trousers like the night before, but sleeker, nicer clothing that fitted him snugly. His slightly damp hair was combed smooth.

He stopped in the doorway to the parlor and their eyes met, and for a moment, the parlor wallpaper and furniture faded as his gaze held Muri entranced. He smiled and entered the room, and the talking of the ladies resumed, and Muri gasped in a breath.

As her lungs expanded, the fabric of Hyacinth's dress pushed back against her chest. The dress was beautiful, with a floral design woven into the material in bright green threads. Gray had declared it "somewhat busy" but it fit better than the others, and when he saw her caressing the fabric and tracing the flowers, he laughed and told her to take it. It hugged her like another skin. Gray had shown her the trick for fixing combs in her hair, using two delicate combs decorated with abalone shell.

All day, she'd felt calm about the evening, but now that the date was here, her nerves jangled. It was scary enough that she was about to spend time with a man she actually might like—one who made her feel different simply by being in the same room. But a human man? A man she knew nothing about? And whom she couldn't trust with the truth of her identity?

And whom, she reminded herself, she was planning to steal from.

Jack finished charming the grange home's residents and assured them he'd bring Muri back safely. He offered his hand and she stood, and the ladies waved them out the door into the cool evening air.

The door thudded closed, cutting off the warm light from indoors, and Jack let go of her hand. Muri scanned the trees of the park and did not see Strombidae lurking in the twilight shadows. She sighed in relief.

"I thought they might watch us walk off into the evening," Jack said as he started down the square, "waving goodbye until we were out of sight." He was smiling as he said it.

Muri paced beside him. "They talked of nothing but our date all through dinner. Our date and my dress."

"You look lovely," Jack said, and Muri's cheeks flushed. His low voice sounded sincere and not suggestive at all—not like one of the mermen trying to win over a mate. She murmured her thanks.

Jack led her to the lane sloping down from the square toward the water. She couldn't think what to say, but when she peeked up at Jack, he walked along comfortably in silence. A flicker of motion pulled her gaze higher. One of the cat creatures watched them from over the edge of the rooftop. Muri stumbled.

Jack reached to steady her. "All right?"

"Yes. It's just the cats."

Jack followed her gaze. As they passed under the cat, its eyes shone like twin moons in the dark. "You don't like cats?"

"They're always watching me like they want to eat me. They seem to be hiding something."

He smiled. "They might be. Hiding something, that is. I've heard the village cats have some kind of secret communication network, the same way the fairies can communicate with animals through their thoughts. But they've never eaten anyone—the cats, I mean. Well, the fairies, too."

"Not that you know of," Muri muttered, but Jack only laughed.

Before they'd gone far, he turned into a side street. The nearest buildings had the swinging wooden signs that signified shops. Farther ahead were no signs, but the buildings had flowers out front, and a pair of boots and a wagon rested beside one door. Perhaps those were homes.

"The White Pony is here," Jack said, gesturing ahead. "I hope it's enough of a pub experience for you. The pubs down at the docks are a bit more exciting, but I'd hate for a fight to break out in the middle of our evening."

Muri didn't tell him she was used to fights breaking out when men gathered. "Why would a fight break out?"

"No reason. Just happens when people drink too much ale. Usually, they're friends again by morning."

"They don't hurt each other."

"Right."

They stopped at the pub Jack had indicated. A white horse pranced on the sign, with stalks of grain sprouting beneath its hooves. A thick wooden door was recessed in an alcove. Next to the doorway, a many-paned window looked into the pub. A small flame glowed inside the glass like a tiny beach fire. Muri squinted past the flame. People sat at tables inside.

"There's no outdoor tables like the pubs at the docks," Muri said.

"I'm sorry, no." His voice sounded concerned.

"I don't mind. I just wondered why not."

Jack tipped his chin toward the end of the street. "The residents wouldn't like the noise. It's not such a problem down by the docks."

"Why not?"

Jack considered. "I guess because the people who live down there are used to noise, so they don't complain."

He reached for the door and tugged it open. The sounds of chattering and laughter wafted out, along with a shrill noise—some kind of human music? She stepped through the doorway.

The public house was dark inside except for dim lanterns glowing behind a counter and more of the small flames, which were scattered around the room, one on each table. People sat at the tables and along the counter, drinking from mugs and talking loudly. The music came from a musician perched on a stool at the back, pulling a bow across the strings of a wooden instrument. The noise was terrible, but the humans must like it because in the corner beside the musician, a man and woman were kissing.

Jack stepped toward the counter. On the other side, a man wiped the surface with a towel—maybe he was the pub's owner. Another man came through a doorway with a dozen mugs gripped in his fists. He set them down on the counter and pecked the owner's cheek before heading back through the doorway.

The owner tucked the towel into his apron and picked up a few mugs, turning to line them up on the shelves behind the counter, where a few clear bottles glinted like jewels in the light.

When the man behind the counter turned back, Jack held up two fingers and slid him a coin. The man turned to a barrel and began to pour drinks.

Muri had forgotten all about coins to pay for their drinks. Humans paid for everything with metal coins, and she had none. "Do you need a coin?" she asked Jack. She could stop the pub man before he poured her drink.

But Jack replied, "My treat." Relief washed over her.

"How did he know what you wanted?" Muri asked as the man came forward with the two mugs. Jack thanked him and lifted the mugs, handing one to her. She gripped the handle and followed him to a table.

"Most everyone wants ale," he said as they sat. "It's cheap and it does the trick."

"What trick?" she asked, thinking of Gray's illusions.

Jack scrunched his brow. "You do know public houses serve alcohol, right?"

"Of course." Alcohol. That was like the merpeople's phyta. It made you behave differently. So humans came to pubs to have fun and get drunk.

"I meant they come to get tipsy," Jack said, "and to forget about work. Have you ever drunk ale? Or anything?"

Muri shook her head.

He gestured toward her mug. She lifted it and sipped. The sour ale stung her tongue and she winced. Did phyta taste like this? "This is what I've been missing?"

Jack laughed, lifting his own mug. "You'll like it more once you've had some. But don't drink it too fast. It might make you lightheaded."

They both sipped, looking at each other over their mugs across the table. Something about him made her want to smile for no reason.

"What does your family do up in Nor Bay—the family you live with? Are they traders?"

Of course he was going to ask about her. Gray had warned her. That's what humans did on dates—they got to know each other.

"Yes, my father's a trader."

Jack raised his eyebrows, waiting for more.

"Um, he mostly trades with the islands to the east. It's a small outfit."

"Do you help him, or do you have other pursuits?"

Why did he care about all this? Talking to Jack was hard—she had to invent more and more of a story for herself. She'd never before met a man who cared anything about her, and now that she had, she couldn't tell him anything true.

What had she learned from the stories about humans, about their occupations and habits? All she could remember was that they were brutes, which was starting to seem like one big lie.

Hyacinth flashed into her mind. "I like flowers," she said. That was true enough. She recalled the orchids and hibiscus growing on the island. "Some of the merchants bring me plants from the islands, which have a more tropical climate. I'm trying to find any that will grow here so we could sell them. But I haven't had much luck."

"Do you keep them in pots and bring them indoors in the winter?"

Now there was an idea. "Yes, that's the idea. How about you. You've always been a fish-catcher. Are you happy doing that?"

He shrugged. "It's not glamorous, but the villagers need to eat and I'm adept at it."

"What about when you're not on the water?"

"I mend the nets. Keep a garden. I help when someone's building a new cottage or when the grange needs something. It's not terribly exciting, I'm afraid." He smiled a flat little smile, as if he were embarrassed.

"What's an exciting job in Woodglen?"

He pressed his lips together. Muri had another drink of her ale. Jack was right—it didn't taste so bad this time.

"Maybe the person who gives tours of the castle?"

"Tours?"

"It's one way the grange makes money for its charities. The castle gardens are open, but you can pay a coin to go up in all the rooms and the towers. I've not been through all of it, but I hear the view is spectacular. You can even visit Princess Rose's tower, the one she climbed out of to rescue the castle servants."

Princess Rose again! Muri couldn't resist asking. "Tell me about Rose. I've heard she rescued the fairies, and she rescued the villagers, and that Str— Murkel was her fiancé. What's the whole story?"

"I'm surprised you haven't heard it. I thought everyone knew the story by now."

"I've heard this and that, but none of the stories in Nor Bay match. What do you think happened?"

"Well," Jack said, "I heard it from Ladi, and she heard it from Rose—she was even with Rose for part of it. So I believe it. It happened last spring."

Then he launched into the most fascinating story, weaving together all the bits and pieces Muri had gleaned since arriving on land. "Prince Murkel" had arrived at court to woo Rose at the same time as another suitor, Dustan. Murkel had won over Rose's father with lies about his wealth and paid chests of gold to have her. But when he'd tried to drag her into the sea, Dustan—who was actually the fairy prince Broadleaf in disguise—rescued her with the help of the sea creatures. Dustan had hidden her away in the forest.

"Murkel really dragged her into the ocean?"

"She said he formed a giant tail and his skin turned green, and he told her he was a king with multiple brides already, and he was going to keep her in a chamber of air at the bottom of the ocean." Jack frowned. "I hope that last part was said in jest." He paused to sip his ale.

Muri shivered. How had it ever seemed okay to keep a human locked up under the sea like that? She'd heard the story from enough people—and this time almost straight from Rose—that she no longer doubted what Strombidae had done. He'd tried to kidnap an innocent woman, to take her with violence, and to force her to marry him.

The same way he'd forced Muri into her engagement.

Jack lowered his ale. "Then Murkel's gold all turned to seashells. It was fairy gold, made with a spell."

The gold was another merspell, not a fairy spell, but Muri kept silent.

"The king began hunting Murkel and eventually they caught him, but Rose and Dustan had disappeared into the forest. Dustan had cast a love spell on Rose, but by now, he had truly fallen in love with her. So he removed his spell and set her free. He thought she'd forget all about him and he returned to the fairies. But she was truly in love with him, too, so she went after him to the caverns where the fairies lived."

Muri had leaned forward over her ale as Jack spoke, watching the words fall from his lips. This was turning into the most romantic tale she'd ever heard.

"Back then, the fairies had a cruel queen and she kept them trapped underground. She convinced them the humans were dangerous. And the humans had mostly forgotten about the fairies and thought they were only a myth, and that the forest was a deadly place. But Rose was secretly half fairy, and she found the way into the caverns and found Dustan, and they rescued all the queen's slaves. And soon after were the two rebellions."

"The human one and the fairy one."

"Yes."

Muri frowned. "If you don't have a king, who runs things?"

"We have a village council," Jack said.

"What's that?"

"It's a group of people chosen by the villagers. They make the decisions and if they do a good job, they'll be chosen again. And one person from each village council travels to the Council of Villages, which governs the entire continent of Sylvania. Someone from Nor Bay goes." Jack tilted his head. "Didn't you participate in the election?"

Muri shook her head. She vaguely knew she shouldn't risk asking more questions, but the ale made it hard to think. "Before the rebellion, this king . . . would you say he was patriarchal?"

Jack laughed and she wasn't sure why. "That's one way to put it. We've always had an equitable society, but the castle court seemed to run differently. And the king's soldiers were brutal. People were getting more angry and violent, and men's attitudes were changing. If the rebellion hadn't happened when it did, I'm not sure things in the village would have remained as peaceful and just as they are. As it is, we sometimes have incidents now. But the past summer and winter, since the soldiers' abuses stopped and the heavy taxes lifted, it's been a time of healing."

Jack stopped for a drink. The word "healing" echoed in Muri's mind.

"Do you think the merpeople are dangerous?" Muri asked. Words kept slipping out of her.

He didn't answer for a long moment. "There were always rumors of merfolk, even before Prince Murkel came. When my parents disappeared, people said it might have been merfolk who sank their boat."

Muri's eyes went wide.

He frowned. "I don't know why a merperson would do that. I don't want to scare you. It was just strange for them to disappear on the sea when they were such experienced sailors, and with no sign of their boat and no bad weather or anything. Boats don't sink that fast. And many other people were out fishing that day. For no one to see them . . ." He took a deep breath and let it out slowly. "When I see the posters about merfolk, I feel angry all over again. I thought I was past it, but something about all the turmoil the past spring and Murkel trying to take Princess Rose like that, it brings it all back. But then I think of Hyacinth and Gray."

"Hyacinth and Gray?"

"And the other fairies. They thought we were dangerous, but they overcame their fear and gave us a chance. They've helped the village so much in the past seasons. And when the fairies started venturing into the village, and everyone knew they could change their appearance or cast a love spell like the one Dustan had cast on Rose, they made people nervous. But they've only helped us. I'd hate to judge anyone without knowing them. It's just hard not to wonder sometimes, now that I know merfolk exist."

Jack nodded at her mug. "You want another?"

Muri hadn't realized she'd drunk the ale down to the bottom. "No, thank you. You can, though. I don't mind waiting."

"I'm fine," he said, and her heartbeat skipped. Was he going to take her back to the grange? Was this the end of their date?

"Do you want to go back?" he asked as if he'd heard her thoughts.

"No."

He smiled at her quick response, and she found herself smiling back.

"Do you—"

"Would you—"

They both stopped and smiled again. Jack gestured for her to continue.

"Would you show me your boat?"

"I would love to."

Jack took their mugs to the counter. As Muri stood, the room swayed a bit and she grasped the table. This dizziness must be an effect of the ale. When Jack returned, he eyed her hanging onto the table and offered an arm. She took it gratefully, and he guided her to the door.

"How bad are you?" he asked once they were out in the quiet street. After being inside, the night air felt fresh. Darkness had come completely, but lanterns on poles illuminated the cobblestones.

"Things are spinning a bit."

"Tell me if you feel sick."

"Sick?"

"Sometimes too much ale makes people sick."

Wonderful. She clutched his arm as they started off down the street. Beneath her fingers was solid muscle, and she started to run her fingers up it before catching herself. Her gaze trailed up his arm to his silhouette. She'd seen other humans around the village square and in the gardens, and Jack was finer to look at than any of them.

Why didn't he already have a wife?

"What's that?" he asked as they turned onto the main road and down the hill.

"I was wondering—" She stopped. What had she blurted out? Her impulsiveness had gotten her in trouble in the past, and with the alcohol making it so easy to talk, she was in danger of making a fool of herself. "I'm sorry," she said, looking away. "Sometimes I speak without thinking. I'm trying to curb it."

His hand covered hers. "I like that about you."

Muri looked up. He was gazing back and his face was serious. "You do?"

"People never say what they mean or speak honestly. I'd rather have you say it. If you still want to."

Muri couldn't meet his gaze as she said, "I was wondering why you don't have a—a mate. You seem, um, you seem quite handsome to me. To not have attracted several."

She risked a glance up at him. Even in the darkness, she could tell he was blushing.

"You don't have to answer," she said.

"No, uh, thank you."

She wished she hadn't asked, but once he started speaking, the awkwardness disappeared.

"I had a fiancée when I was younger but she left me. Everyone was struggling back then, with the king taking all our income as taxes, and she met a merchant who offered her more than I ever could. I didn't blame her but it hurt."

"Didn't you get over her?"

"I did, but I lost interest. Ladies in the village would get me out to the pub or the dances, but I'd go and wish I hadn't. I could never figure what they wanted—if they wanted me to talk to them or buy them things or just tumble them once and move on. It was easier to avoid it. And now they've all given up on me."

He looked at her. "I really do like that about you. You're straightforward, and you're interested in things—like asking about patriarchies. I don't think I've ever heard anyone say that word aloud."

"I learned it from Gray only today," Muri said.

They walked past a few shops in silence before Jack asked, "Do you have a beau?"

Ahead, the end of the street opened on the wharf. On the horizon, the line of the ocean was illuminated in moonlight. The line swayed back and forth, and she closed her eyes and stopped walking, pulling Jack to a stop. After a moment, things steadied and she resumed walking.

"Someone wanted to bond with me," she said quietly, "but I didn't want him. I thought I had to though, so I've been waiting all these seasons, dreading the day. But before I left Nor Bay, I told him I wouldn't go through with it."

"That sounds like it was hard," Jack said.

Her hand slipped down his arm until she found his hand. It closed around hers, his fingers twining through hers.

"I'm scared of what might happen when I go back. That I won't be strong enough to fight back."

He squeezed her hand. "If you ever need help, you only need to ask. You always have a place to go."

Tears threatened to spill from Muri's eyes. "Why would you help me?" she whispered.

"That's what friends do. Gray and Hyacinth would say the same to you, I'm sure of it. You're not alone."

Friends? Were Gray and Hyacinth her friends, just like that? Jack seemed to think so. He counted himself as her friend, and he'd known her only a day.

She wiped away the tears and murmured, "Thank you."

A full moon had risen over the harbor, and its golden light sparkled on the water and shone on the wharf as they came out of the lane. Raucous voices drifted over from the wharf-side pubs, but they walked on until they'd cleared the buildings and the noise faded. A breeze stole gently over them, bringing the salty scent of the water. As they neared the edge of the wharf, the slapping of the waves filled the silence.

Jack held Muri's hand firmly as he led her down the ramp onto the docks, which shifted slowly under her feet. Muri swallowed and held tighter to Jack. She was near the water. If she fell in, her tail would form, and there'd be no way to hide it from Jack. With the chance that merpeople had killed his parents, he could never find out what she was.

Jack's hand squeezed back. Hopefully he'd think she was clinging to him because she was drunk on ale.

The halyards of the fishing boats tapped against the masts as the boats rocked on the steady waves. Muri followed Jack down one dock after another until they were at the edge of the boats. Jack stopped.

"This is *Alina's Dream*," he said.

"*Alina's Dream*?"

"I was sixteen when I named it. Alina was my mother."

Jack's boat appeared the same as all the others—a smooth, curved wooden hull, one mast, and the sail bound around a crossbeam resting in the boat's central cockpit atop a pile of nets. Muri would have expected the docks to smell like dead fish, but she inhaled fresh ocean breeze. Jack's boat was spotless, as if he had cleaned it after unloading his catch.

"Would you like to step aboard?" he asked.

"I would."

Jack let go of her hand to step down into the boat. As it tilted, the moonlight glinted off an object at the base of the mast.

Her shell.

She'd forgotten all about it. She quickly averted her gaze.

Jack turned and held out a hand. When she took it, he gripped her fingers tightly and supported her as she stepped down into the boat. The boat tilted toward the dock and away. His other hand stretched out as if waiting to catch her. She considered falling into him as an excuse to have his arms around her, but she didn't want to pretend with him—not any more than she already was. When she found her balance, she nodded and he let go.

She stole another peek at her shell, which had its cord tied around the base of the mast, but Jack moved and her gaze drifted to him. She'd rather watch him than worry about the shell right now.

"I didn't expect a visitor; otherwise I would have cleared out the parlor," Jack said, moving a coil of rope. Muri didn't know what he was talking about, but she didn't much care. With the moonlight illuminating his body as he lugged his nets to the side, and the glow from the ale, happiness filled her. He extended his hand again and helped her to cross the boat, climbing over the sails. She sat cross-legged on the nets with the sail-wrapped beam against her back. She faced the water, with the moonlight dancing across its rippling surface.

He lowered himself to sit beside her and stretched his legs, resting them on the edge of the boat so his feet were out over the water. He leaned back and stared up at the sky.

"The spring star is up," he said.

"This season, it hangs over the island," Muri said.

"What island?"

Drat. She'd done it again. "Oh, nothing, just one of the islands my plants come from."

They were silent for a moment as the water lapped against the boat. His hands moved. He held a scrap of rope, twisting it into a complicated knot without even looking. He undid the knot. Muri was mesmerized. She found herself reaching to touch his hand.

He stopped moving. He was watching her. Ten seas, she wanted to hold his hand again, but he was staring like she had an octopus on her head and she was touching his hand for no reason.

"Show me what you're doing," she said.

He smiled and looked at his hands. He flipped one side of the rope over the other, and his fingers deftly twisted and pulled it through. "That's a bowline knot. I use that on the boat often."

"Show me how."

He undid the knot and repeated it more slowly before handing the rope to Muri. She flipped one side over the other and paused, holding the free end. Jack reached for her hand and gently pulled it in the right direction, helping her finish the knot. His fingers left hers. She undid the knot and formed it again on her own.

"Show me another."

He took the rope. "Give me your arm," he said.

She held out her arm and he wrapped the rope around it, crossing it in an X as it wound around her a second time. He slipped the end through and pulled it snug. "That's a clove hitch. You'll see it on the docks a lot."

Her free hand pulled the knot off. Jack extended his arm to let her try.

"Here's my favorite," Jack said when she'd finished with his arm. He came up with a second scrap of rope. Taking two of the ends, he flipped them over and around each other. When he'd finished, they were bound together.

He held it out to her. "It has such perfect symmetry," he said. "And the tighter you pull, the stronger it holds them together."

"What's it called?"

"A square knot."

"A *square* knot?"

"What's wrong with that?"

"It's ordinary. It should be called a lover's knot."

"No, this is a lover's knot," he said, undoing the square knot. "See, it's a simple overhand knot"—he tied a quick loop in one rope, not pulling it tight—"and then another overhand knot tied to it." The second rope slipped through the first one, and he pulled the knots together.

"It's two plain knots tied together."

He turned to her, his voice rising slightly. "But see, that's why it's the perfect symbol of love. It's two knots that work fine on their own, but together they form something truly special. But without each other, they still work. They don't just collapse into a loose rope."

A loose rope. Muri wouldn't want to be that. Not that anyone in Glorypool had that problem—no one could depend on anyone there. She'd always had to be her own knot.

Muri peered in his face. "Are you fine on your own?"

Jack looked down, and Muri couldn't be sure in the dim light, but he might've blushed. "I am now." He laughed and dropped the lover's knot into the boat. "Thanks for giving me practice with my knot tying."

"Like you need it."

"No, I guess not."

"Thanks for showing me."

"Anytime. How are you feeling?"

She squinted at the horizon, pausing to study it, and it stayed steady. "The ale's worn off."

"Good." When she turned back to him, he smiled. He leaned back and closed his eyes.

Muri tried to copy him, but he seemed relaxed whereas all her senses were alert. The boat rocked gently beneath her, and Jack gave off a nice smell, like wood smoke tinted by the ale. Above the water, smells were sharper and clearer, and whiffs of Jack kept reaching her. She began listing toward him.

She rested her cheek on his arm.

"Muri," he said in a low voice, "I might kiss you if you do that."

She closed her eyes and tilted her face up. He laughed, but before she could feel embarrassed at yet another impulsive mistake, his hand touched her face. His rough thumb smoothed over her lips. She held her breath, and his lips pressed into hers.

No one had ever kissed her so softly, as if it were about that moment and about only the kiss and not what came after. She leaned into him, inhaling his smoky scent and kissing him back, and his hand caressed her cheek and moved to support her neck. Somewhere down on the nets, his other hand found hers and closed around it.

After a moment, he broke away. Hadn't he liked the kiss? She opened her eyes. His face was shadowed, his eyes deep pools. Before she could speak, his lips parted.

"I like kissing you," he whispered.

He dropped her hand and his arms went around her, pulling her tight against his chest. His pulse pounded in her ear, faster even than her own, and waves of emotion rolled off him like heat shimmering off sand. Kissing her had affected him somehow that she didn't understand. She closed her eyes and stayed quiet, pressed against his warm chest and letting him hold her.

She must have drifted off, because she woke to someone gently shaking her. "Muri."

She snuggled into the warm body beside her, a contrast to the stiff breeze off the ocean.

"Muri."

She opened her eyes and remembered where she was. On the boat, with Jack. He still had one arm around her. The moon was higher, and the distant noise of the pubs was gone. She must have fallen asleep in his arms.

"I should take you home."

She rubbed her eyes. "Can I see you again?"

"I'd like that." He leaned forward and gave her a quick kiss on her temple.

He let go of her and stood, stretching, and turned to give her a hand. The boat had drifted, angling out into the harbor, and they had to climb up onto the bow to reach the dock. Jack went first. As she held the mast to balance herself, Jack stiffened.

Strombidae was on the dock a few paces back from the edge.

Muri's first instinct was to hide behind Jack. Then anger filled her. Why had Strombidae shown up here like this? Had he been following her? How long had he watched them? She stood taller and scowled at him from beside Jack.

Strombidae's face was impassive, but she caught the flick of his eyes away and back. He had spotted her shell. If she didn't take it, he certainly would after they left.

Jack stepped toward the dock. As he stepped off the boat, Muri reached down for the shell. She fingered the knot in the cord—a simple bow knot—and pulled it free. She snatched up the whole thing and slipped it into her dress pocket.

"Murkel," Jack said, eyeing the other man. "Can I help you with something?"

Jack didn't turn to extend a hand to help her off the boat. He wanted her to stay back, as if he were protecting her from Strombidae.

"I'm here for the girl," Strombidae said, and Jack jerked forward before restraining himself.

"You're not to touch her," Jack growled.

Strombidae's lips pressed together in a twisted smile. "You think I mean to bother her. It's nothing like that. Muricidae and I have a history together."

White hot anger flared up in Muri's chest. How dare he do this? Jack looked to her to deny Strombidae's words, but she couldn't. She gave a small nod.

"How do you know each other?" Jack asked.

"How about it, Muri," Strombidae said. "Why don't you tell him how we met." Strombidae's eyes gleamed in the lamplight.

He knew she couldn't tell Jack the truth. What would Jack think of her if he knew? Strombidae was toying with her, getting his revenge for how she'd treated him in the park.

"My, um, my adopted father came this way on business last summer. His horse was hurt on the road, and Str— Murkel helped him. My father asked me to visit with him while I'm here."

The story was inadequate, but it was the best she could come up with.

"She'd agreed to spend the evening with me before you stepped in," Strombidae said. "If your evening together is ending, I'd like a word with her."

Jack was watching her with a strange expression. Muri dropped her head, afraid to meet his gaze. He'd think she wanted this—that she wanted to stay here with Strombidae instead of leaving with him.

Jack finally extended a hand and helped her off the boat. He stepped in close, shielding her from Strombidae with his body. He spoke quietly so only she could hear.

"Do you know what he wants?"

"No. But I'll hear him out and go home."

"Muri, are you sure? I don't like leaving you with him. He has a reputation for bad behavior around women."

She couldn't look in Jack's eye. "I'm not scared of him. Please, Jack. It's best if you go."

He hesitated with his hand on her arm, continuing to watch her face. She felt sick about turning him away when it was the last thing she wanted to do.

His hand loosened. "If it's what you want. But please, if you need help, please tell me."

"Okay," she whispered.

Jack stepped back. He gave a curt nod to Strombidae and headed up the docks. Muri watched until he had climbed the ramp to the wharf and disappeared behind the buildings.

"Satisfied?" Muri hissed at Strombidae.

He had the nerve to smirk at her. "You like the human."

"So what if I do?"

"You're still my fiancée."

Something inside Muri snapped. "I'm not and you know it. You can't make me marry you when you can't even return to Glorypool. And you never even asked in the first place. You ordered it."

"Merwomen don't get a choice."

Muri stuck up her chin. "This one does. It's over."

He glowered at her. "At least give me the shell."

"I don't see why. You know you can't use it."

"What do you mean? Of course I can."

"Only a merperson can use it. That's how the ancient merspells work."

To her surprise, Strombidae laughed. "Merspells. I'd forgotten about that." His smile faded. "There are no merspells. Only fairies are able to perform spells."

"Fairies?"

"The merking's magic is a hoax. It's a dwindling supply of fairy spells."

"What?"

"You heard me. Merpeople don't possess any magic."

The merking had no magic? Muri tried to grasp it, but how could it be true?

"All our spells and magical objects came from the fairies, once upon a time," he continued. "But the greedy fairies stopped sharing the magic with us. They betrayed us and left us to starve. We have almost none of their magic left."

The fairies hadn't intended to cut off the merpeople, but Strombidae wouldn't care if Muri tried to explain it. "Why are you telling me this?"

Strombidae shrugged. "I can't benefit from the hoax anymore. The secret is no longer important to me. Now give me that shell. I can use it the same as you."

"What are you going to tell Lotti?"

"It's none of your business."

He didn't move toward her. Why did he hesitate? Why didn't he come at her?

Because she could escape into the water. And he could not.

Muri gripped the shell tighter as a power filled her. Strombidae had trapped her earlier and forced Jack away. He'd ruined her date and her night—the happiest she'd ever felt in her life. No way was she giving him Lotti's shell.

"Lotti gave it to me. And you ruined my date. I don't feel much like obeying you anymore."

"Ruined your *date*? I thought you were seducing the human to get the shell. Now you've got it."

Muri didn't answer.

Strombidae's eyes narrowed. "You're not to see him again."

Muri's face heated, but it wasn't a blush. Her anger boiled over. She'd had enough of arrogant mermen for a lifetime. "It's none of your business if I do," she said, holding back her rage. "Now. Good. Night."

She stalked away from him along the docks, daring him to follow. She would push him in the blasted water if he bothered her. But he didn't grab her. When she reached the wharf, she glanced back. Strombidae stood where she'd left him, staring out to sea.

Chapter 8

ಬ☀ಛ

MURI WOKE WITH THE SUN the next morning. She lay in her small room in the grange home, studying the light outside. Now that she was used to the stillness of a human bed, she found sleeping in one peaceful. Sounds on land were sharper, not muffled like in the steady hum of silence below the water. But when the human world became quiet, it seemed even more quiet as a result. She listened hard and could hear only a bird singing through the open window and the clock in the hallway ticking.

Was Jack awake?

Muri groaned, remembering Strombidae's arrival on the docks the previous night. She and Jack had shared such a special moment—at least she'd thought so. The way he'd held her after they'd kissed . . . it warmed her to think of it. No one in Glorypool had ever held her like that. The closeness and caring she felt with Jack made her want to stay on land forever, to see if he wanted to keep courting or even become mates. Jack had seemed to like her, too, hadn't he?

And then Strombidae had appeared and ruined everything. What must Jack think? Had he known she was lying—on the docks or earlier? Her cobbled-together story about how she knew Strombidae, and all the answers she'd given Jack while she was drunk, hadn't been as well thought out as the lies she'd practiced about visiting from Nor Bay to meet her cousin. She hadn't expected to be talking to land dwellers enough that her story would grow the way it had, and the lies were getting out of her control.

Sleep wouldn't return. Muri pushed back the covers and sat up in the cool room. The breeze blowing in had been a lot warmer when she'd opened her window last night. She rubbed the crust from her eyes—an odd result of sleeping in air—and went to the window to see the sunrise.

The tree branches in the park glowed faintly. Beyond them, the sky shone pink with the approaching sun. The shadowed cobblestones below were deserted, except for the bench across from the grange home, where a man sat leaning with his elbows on his knees.

It was Jack.

Jack was here! Muri almost called out but stopped herself and stepped away from the window. She pulled Hyacinth's dress over her head and combed her fingers through her hair. She fumbled with the combs Gray had slid into place so easily. At last she got them in. She tiptoed from her room and down the stairs, keeping quiet to avoid waking the other residents.

Jack looked up as soon as she opened the door. He stood and came to her as she slipped out. She wanted so badly to smile—but would he be angry about how their date had ended?

He stopped in front of her and neither of them spoke. Jack smiled but looked away. "I hope I didn't startle you, sitting outside like this."

"No. I'm glad you've come." Muri bit her lip, embarrassed. "I'm sorry about last night—about Murkel. I wish he hadn't come." The bitterness inside her tinged her words.

"He didn't misbehave after I left, did he?" Jack asked in a low voice. "He didn't . . . try anything you didn't want?"

"No. He just talked."

"Was it okay?"

"It was nothing important. I think he just wanted to interfere with my evening since I went with you instead of him. I spoke with him a moment and made an excuse and left."

"I wish I could have walked you home," Jack said.

"So do I."

A silence stretched between them.

"Are you going out on the water soon?" Muri asked at last.

"I could. But I wondered if you had plans. Has your cousin arrived?"

"My cousin? Oh, no, there's been no word. I don't have plans."

"Would you like to spend the day together?"

Joy blossomed inside her. Jack wasn't angry with her. And he wanted to spend more time with her.

"I would love that."

He smiled, warm and caring. "I'll come back when the sun's up in the square." He hesitated another moment before turning away.

He ambled toward the lane down to the wharf. If he glanced back, he'd see her gawping after him. She ducked her head, then remembered Strombidae and quickly surveyed the park, but he wasn't lurking in the trees as far as she could tell. She slipped back inside the grange home.

Muri sat in the parlor to wait for the others to wake. Her hand curled around the shell in her pocket. She had to tell Lotti what had happened to Strombidae regardless of what he wanted. Only four days remained before Strombidae lost the throne. Could Lotti and the others still be hoping he'd return? Surely they knew something must have gone wrong and that Strombidae wouldn't be returning. Lotti might cling to the past and send Muri on this foolish mission, but the other wives would know better. Surely they'd make a plan to . . . to what? Even if they knew Strombidae would never return, it wasn't like they had anywhere to go. All they could do was align with one of the new contenders for the throne.

Still, she owed it to them to send a message. She should have done it last night after leaving Strombidae. She could have returned to the water's edge and done it. But if she had, she'd have had her tail to deal with. She'd have had to dry it and get dressed and back to the grange home before dawn. And perhaps Strombidae would have caused more trouble.

And now Jack wanted to spend the day with her.

She wanted to be selfish and spend the day with Jack and put off her task as long as possible. Had anyone in Glorypool ever put her first? Would they give up a chance to feel as wonderful as she'd felt last night, to help her? Not likely. She'd contact Lotti later.

Muri rose and returned to her room. She hid the shell under the pillow on the bed.

The house remained quiet but she couldn't sit any longer. She went to the kitchen and got out the plates for breakfast, as she'd seen the ladies do the previous morning. She'd seen them heat water for tea, but she didn't dare work with fire while inside a building like this. She filled the kettle and got out the mugs and the dried herbs and waited. Finally, Margery shuffled in. She passed Muri a bowl and basket of eggs to crack and moved to the hearth.

Margery appraised Muri from the side as they worked. "You seem happy. Does that mean your date was a success?"

Muri broke into a smile. "It was wonderful. And he's coming back today."

"Even better. Perhaps we'll see more of you even after your visit with your cousin."

How long could Muri pretend her cousin was coming to visit? Maybe Gray could help her send a letter to herself, which could arrive, stating that her cousin wasn't coming, but that Muri wasn't needed at home and could stay in Woodglen another—

"Here, dear, could you hang the kettle for me?" Margery said. Muri put aside the bowl of eggs to lift the kettle onto the rod that swung over the fire.

Soon everyone was up, and Muri had to answer a hundred more questions about her date with Jack and where they might go today. Where would they go? Another pub? It would be nice if they could go somewhere quieter with only the two of them, the way it had been on his boat the previous night. And somewhere Strombidae wouldn't find them.

Maybe Jack would take her out on his boat! Muri felt a simultaneous longing to have him all to herself and a terror of being out on a boat where she could easily fall into the sea.

As they finished eating breakfast, a knock sounded on the front door. Muri started to get up, but Margery placed a hand on her arm.

"I'll answer," Margery said. "You take a moment and compose yourself. Then step into the hallway like a grand princess." The ladies tittered around the table. The woman called Hilda squeezed Muri's other arm.

Margery hobbled out and greeted Jack. The low rumble of Jack's voice in reply sent thrills up Muri's spine and back down it, warming her throughout. She exhaled, willing her pulse to stop racing. The faces around the table nodded and smiled at her, so she rose and stepped into the hallway.

Jack stood framed in the open doorway, his broad shoulders filling it and his head ducked under the top of the frame. He carried a basket like the kind the merwomen stored fish in, but made of sticks instead of kombu strips.

He turned her way and smiled.

"You're going on a picnic?" Margery asked.

"If Muri is feeling up to it."

"Oh, she is," Margery said. Muri hoped Margery was right. She had no idea what skills a picnic required.

As Margery ushered her out the door after Jack, Muri scanned the park for Strombidae. Wherever Jack was taking her, she was determined not to let Strombidae know about it.

Jack was also watching the park. He smiled down at Muri. "I'm hoping we can avoid being followed today."

"Me too. I don't see him. Where are we going?"

"We could go to the beach, or up along the cliffs."

"The cliffs," Muri said to avoid the possibility of swimming, although the weather seemed cold for humans to swim. She longed to ask what a picnic was, but she didn't dare in case it was something common in the human world.

Jack headed up the road out of the village. The cottages petered out into wide fields, and the castle towered in the distance to their left. To the right, also in the distance, were scores of trees—the forest. Most of the fairies lived in the forest. It was a place of danger, Muri had been taught, but now she didn't know what to believe. At least Jack hadn't said they were going there.

The road from the village ended at a cross road, and Jack turned to the right toward the forest. The cliff's edge at the sea was far off across fields. Jack glanced behind them and said, "We're taking a roundabout path to the cliffs. To make sure no one is following." Muri glanced back too. The long stretch of road behind them was empty.

They walked along the new road a few hundred paces before Jack cut across the fields. The land had appeared flat from the road, but once they were crossing the fields, the land rolled gently up and down. The edge of the village slipped out of sight. Even if Strombidae had been watching them from behind a cottage on the outskirts of the village, he would lose sight of them as they walked down the gentle slope. By the time they arrived at the edge of the cliffs, up the coast from the village and with the buildings small in the distance, Muri felt certain Strombidae wasn't following. They were farther along the shoreline than she had been when she'd first arrived. The tiny sails of the fishing boats dotted the bay.

They turned onto the barest of footpaths. Jack walked along the edge of it on the grass so Muri could use the path.

The wind whistled by. Muri held up her hand and the air rushed through her fingers toward the sea. "The wind," she said. "It changes direction. It was blowing in from the sea last night." She'd never been on land long enough to notice a change.

"Yes."

"I wonder why."

Jack moved the basket to his other side, leaving empty space between them. Muri glanced down at his hand, then up at him shyly, smiling.

He grinned back and held out his hand, and she took it.

"The wind blows out to sea in the morning and back in to land in the afternoon. I think it has to do with the temperature."

"The temperature?"

"Yes. You know how in winter, when you have a fire in your hearth, the top of the room will be hotter?"

Muri knew no such thing, but she nodded.

"And on a sunny day, you can feel heat rising off the ground? But when the cold comes, it lingers around the floorboards. So hot air rises, and cold air sinks." He let go her hand and made a motion in the air, his hand rising and falling in a cycle. "And if air is rising here, and falling here, in between it would be moving sideways. I think that's what causes wind."

"That's brilliant. You figured that out."

Jack blushed. "I think about things like that when I'm on the water. I'm usually fishing alone with lots of time to think." When he dropped his hand, he took hers again.

"So why does it blow out in the mornings?"

"The seawater is cold in spring. It's been cold all winter, and it won't warm until late summer."

Muri had only ever known the sea to vary slightly in temperature, colder in the depths while warmer near the surface. Without a volcano to warm the water, perhaps the water temperature changed with the seasons.

"But the land warms up each day in the sun," Jack continued, "and cools at night. In the morning, the land is chilly and the air sinks and moves out to sea. But by the afternoon, the land will be hot and the air rising over it, and the wind blows in." He squeezed her hand. "We'll have to watch this afternoon and see if I'm right."

Muri grinned up at him. She liked the thought that they'd still be together later in the day. She started to say they'd have to watch later in the season as well, but she caught herself. She didn't want him to think she was making assumptions. Besides, by the time summer came to Woodglen, she'd be long gone to the darkness of Glorypool. How she hated the idea.

The footpath led them up and down along the grassy clifftops. The wind gusted fiercely as they left the bay and faced the open ocean. Closer to the village, crops had covered the fields, but now that they'd left the village far behind, the land was rocky and wild. The high points offered glimpses of the distant forest far inland. The walking and the wind left Muri slightly breathless, so she was glad Jack seemed content to walk in silence.

About an hour after they'd left the village, Jack stopped. He indicated a large boulder alongside the path. "That's the marker I use to find this place. Follow me."

He dropped her hand and started down the steep hillside toward the water. Muri followed with her arms out for balance. As they dipped out of sight of the footpath, the wind calmed. Jack stopped. Next to him, a narrow path ran along the face of the cliff. Below, waves crashed into the rocks.

"Can you manage this?" he asked. It would be scary to walk here if you feared falling down into the foaming sea, but crossing was easy for her. Not that she wanted to fall—if she did, her tail would form and she'd have to let Jack see it, or let him think she had drowned. And knowing Jack even as little as she did, she guessed he'd jump into the water to try to save her and risk drowning himself.

Across the narrow space, the path widened and came around the rocky wall onto a wide lawn. The wind had completely died in the shelter of the cliff walls. The cliff rose up so steeply that the top was not visible. The space was entirely hidden except for the view out to the ocean. The distant crashing of the waves sounded from below.

Jack set the basket down on the grass.

"What is this place?" Muri asked. "Is it secret?"

Jack smiled. "You could say that. My parents used to bring me here on picnics, and we never told anyone about it. I've never seen anyone else here."

"I won't tell."

He knelt down and opened the basket. A folded blanket filled the inside. When he pulled it out, a giant biscuit and other foods rested below. A picnic must be about eating.

Jack threw open the blanket, letting it spread in the air. As it sank to the grass, he pulled it to lie flat. Muri caught the nearest corner and helped. They sat on the blanket and he moved the basket between them and unloaded the giant biscuit, a jar like the one with Hyacinth's strawberry jam, and a cream-colored block of something solid that Muri had no idea about. He also had small cups and a gourd filled with cold tea.

He poured two cups of tea and handed one to Muri. Then he sliced the edge off the block and offered her a piece—cheese, he called it.

Muri sniffed the cheese. It smelled odd and somewhat unpleasant. "Do you know how this is made?" she asked. She didn't dare ask what it was because probably all humans knew what cheese was. Hopefully cheese-making wasn't so simple that everyone knew how to do it, too.

Jack gave a brief description. Apparently, cheese was made from rotten animal milk left to sit and get more rotty and moldy, and you could eat it on bread, which was the name of the giant biscuit, or as a snack on slices of fruit, or put it on salads or stews or just about anything. It sounded like the humans ate a lot of cheese.

Muri couldn't believe they wouldn't get sick from eating it, but if Jack was willing to eat it—he actually seemed enthusiastic about it—she would, too. Once she was chewing a piece, the foul smell diminished. The bread was dry and scratchy, but it didn't have the slimy texture of the biscuits. Covered with jam, it was even quite tasty. The jam was darker than Hyacinth's and made of blackberries.

As they ate, Muri asked Jack questions about Woodglen. She

wanted to prevent him from asking questions about her, but she also wanted to learn as much as she could about the village. After they ate, they leaned back on the blanket, sipping their tea in the stillness. The sun shone onto the secluded spot, warming them. This was a picnic? Lounging on the ground and talking and eating? Was that all there was to it?

Muri glanced across at Jack's profile. Her eyes moved down the length of him. A few more things they might do during a picnic came to mind, and all they'd need would be the blanket on the ground. Or not even. She wrenched her gaze away so he wouldn't catch her studying him.

"I was thinking," Jack said a few moments later, "about the poster in the village. The one about the merman sighting."

Muri swallowed. "Mm?"

"Avianna and some of the other women have been learning to fight."

"Fight? Like with swords?"

"Not exactly. They're learning to defend themselves. So if someone like Murkel were to bother them they could get away. Not that he's much of a danger, I don't think. But say a stronger man were bothering you. Or another one of the mermen came ashore and threatened the village. You could fight him off. Not like a fighting match to win, but to knock him over and give you time to run away."

She remembered how scared she'd been when Gray had grabbed her arm the first time they'd met. Having skills to get away? "That sounds smart."

"You've not heard of anything like that in Nor Bay?"

"No."

"I thought you might like to learn."

Would she! Human men weren't much of a threat, but once she was home . . . How wonderful it would be to not feel defenseless around the mermen! Although if she ever dared to fight back, she'd be in for it. But who knew? Things could change. If they did, she would be ready. She nodded eagerly.

"I could find out when the women are meeting, if you're still in town. Or I could show you some basic moves."

"You could? I mean, I would like that."

"What, you think I don't know how to fight?" Jack narrowed his eyes and lifted an eyebrow, and somehow, even though he wasn't serious, his confrontational expression made Muri hot. As if they were talking about something other than fighting. But they were talking about fighting—Jack was, anyway. Focus, she told herself.

"You just don't seem, um, aggressive."

He smirked. "There's generally not any reason to be. But if something happens, I know how to fight."

"But usually you don't need to."

He shook his head.

She believed him. The interactions between humans that she'd witnessed in the village had been docile. The crowd reading the posters had been agitated but only because they were scared of mermen invading their village. Otherwise, everyone had been getting along. The human gatherings completely differed from gatherings in Glorypool, with their constant competition and bravado, and alliances forming and breaking, all to control one another.

"I didn't have any siblings to fight," Jack said. "But my father and I used to wrestle. It's useful training for escape moves."

"Escape moves." Muri liked the sound of that. She grinned at Jack. "Can you show me now?"

He grinned back. In one smooth motion he sat up and pushed himself to his feet. He towered over her, holding out a hand.

She took it and he pulled her up beside him. Muri's insides crawled in delighted anticipation. He led her away from the picnic blanket and onto the lawn.

Jack's thumb rubbed over Muri's fingers as he turned to face her. "I'll start with the first thing my father showed me. It's a handy move if you face someone bigger than you."

"It's hard to imagine you facing someone bigger than you."

Jack laughed. "I was only twelve when he showed me. I was small." He lifted her fingers in his and squeezed them before dropping her hand. "Okay, imagine someone is coming at you. If you try to resist them or to stop them, you won't be able to because they're bigger than you. Instead, you can use the attacker's motion to help yourself."

"I'm not sure I understand."

"It would be easier if I could show you. I won't hurt you, but it might startle you."

"So I'll attack you, and you'll . . . ?"

"I'll use your motion to pull you off balance and onto the ground. But I'll be careful."

"Okay."

Jack stepped away from her and motioned her toward him. "Run like you want to attack me."

Attack him? Muri imagined running and jumping onto him and sinking her fingers into his thick hair and kissing him. Before she could start blushing, she leapt forward. Jack's arm went up. In a blur, she was on her back on the ground. Jack knelt over her, holding her wrist. His other hand was beneath her. It had cushioned her fall so she hadn't even felt herself hit the ground. The move had been effortless.

Muri sucked in air. Jack hovered overhead. He was going to lean down and kiss her.

Her heart beat once, twice, and the moment passed.

"Are you okay?" he said.

"How did you do that?" She tugged on his hand and he pulled her to sit up. She scooched back to get him out of kissing distance, before she tried to kiss him and embarrassed herself.

He stood and pulled her to her feet. "Try again and I'll do it in slow motion."

Do it in slow motion? Ten seas, he was killing her.

This time when she moved slowly at him, he reached out and waited for her. He took her wrist as she neared. His hips twisted as his other arm came around her back, and he pulled her in the same direction she was moving. Her feet came off the ground and she rolled over his hip. He stopped with her hanging horizontal in the air, resting on his hip.

"I use my legs, see?" His hip nudged her as if to make her aware of it—like she wasn't already keenly aware of his hipbone digging into her belly, a hand's width higher than where she wanted it. Her trip through the air resumed and she began to fall. He caught her and lowered her to the ground. She gazed up at him. Being thrown was even better in slow motion. She could do this all day.

"Of course if you're being attacked, you don't need to worry about providing a gentle landing," he said, standing and pulling her up again. "Your turn."

"My turn?"

"To throw me."

"You want *me* to do *that*?"

He nodded.

"To you?"

He nodded again.

"But you're . . . so big."

"You can do it. I promise. Try grabbing my wrist to start."

They practiced a few times with Jack running at her and Muri grabbing his wrist and pulling. She could see that if she kept moving, pulling him along, he'd follow the right trajectory. But to get her hip under him and lift him in the air? She was strong, but she doubted she was *that* strong.

"That's good," he said. "Try the whole thing this time. It'll help if you're angry. Think of something that makes you angry. Or something you really want. And gather all that feeling and when I come at you and you grab my arm, let it all out as you pull. Shout if you want to."

Muri bit her lip. Strombidae made her angry—that was easy. She had wanted to kiss Jack again last night, and Strombidae had shown up and ruined it. She should have been walked home by Jack and kissed goodnight on the doorstep. She was sick of oppressive, controlling, selfish mermen and merkings who ordered the merwomen around and she was sick of her whole stupid kingdom, and Jack was moving and if she didn't get to kiss him again she was going to—

"Aaaahrrr!" Muri shouted and twisted her hip into Jack's body and rolled him over her hip as she gripped his wrist and yanked his arm down, and he sailed past her and thumped onto the ground. Muri froze. She'd done it. She'd known she was strong, but it wasn't like she went around lifting people or dolphins or tree trunks. And Jack was wide as a date palm.

Jack lay motionless with his eyes closed. They flickered open.

She dropped to her knees by his side. "Oh Jack. Are you okay?" Her hands gripped the front of his shirt.

"That was quite a throw," he gasped, staring up at her.

"I'm sorry. I didn't mean to hurt you." She couldn't stop her hand from touching his face, gently as if she'd break him further.

A smile split across his face. "You didn't hurt me. That was . . . impressive. I'm just catching my breath."

Did he mean it, or had she embarrassed him? She bit her lower lip, waiting on him to recover.

"I can't remember the last time someone tossed me to the ground like that." He reached for her fluttering hand and wrapped her fingers with his own. "Not since my father, anyway."

With one hand trapped, her other hand took its place, as if she couldn't stop touching him.

"I really did it."

"You did."

"If I can throw you, I can throw anyone."

"You could win a prize at the harvest festival with a throw like that."

"A prize?"

"What would you like?" He was still smiling at her, but his voice had dropped a notch, from encouraging to teasing to something else in the space of four words. His hand was rubbing hers gently, pressed against his cheek. She trailed her free fingertips along his cheekbone to his ear and into his hair.

"I'll give it to you if I can," he whispered.

She leaned down and pressed her lips onto his.

Kissing him was as wonderful as it had been last night. Better even, because this time she wasn't terrified with wondering if he liked it. And this time his lips tasted like blackberry jam instead of ale. He dropped her hand and reached to caress her face.

Kissing him made her want more. Muri caught herself. She broke their kiss and drew back enough to look at him. Her hands rested flat on his chest.

His eyelids drifted open as he stroked back her hair. "I've never seen anyone with hair the color of yours," he said. "Or eyes as gold as the moon. It's enchanting."

"Is that what you like best about me?"

His hand stilled. "Oh Muri, of course not."

Emotion swirled up in Muri's throat, and she fought to hide it while Jack continued to gaze at her as if he'd do it the rest of the day. "No one's ever wanted me the way I am," she said. "They've told me I have to behave, to stop speaking out of turn, and they say I'm short, and I'm weak, and—" She stopped herself, shaking her head. Jack didn't need to hear a list of her failings.

But he kept holding her face as he sat up. His gaze came level with hers. "I think you're perfect the way you are. The more I get to know you, the more I like you. And even if there were something I didn't like, I'd still like *you*. That's how it works. You don't pick and choose the parts of a person you want. You take the whole person, and sometimes you adjust things to make it fit."

But what if that person had a secret? And a tail?

He leaned forward and kissed her one more time.

"I think you've had your prize," he said, teasing. "Now you have more work to do."

He pulled them both to their feet and had her practice throwing him a few more times. Putting her energy and emotions into the throw made all the difference. He showed her what to do once her attacker was on the ground and how she could incapacitate him temporarily and escape. It wouldn't work so well on a merman under the water, where bodies floated and it would be harder to render him unconscious, but maybe she could adapt it somehow. Jack showed her weaknesses to exploit, like kneeing a man between his legs—again, not useful with a merman in the water, but she could poke his eyes or bite his ears . . . . She'd never have thought to do any of this.

Of course, if anyone in Glorypool saw her fight back against a merman, there was no telling what would happen. Merwomen didn't fight back. But what if all the merwomen knew how to fight? What if they all resisted together?

Jack's arms closed around her from behind. By now, she was hot in the sunlight, and his body was hot behind her. "See if you can escape."

"I don't want to escape, though."

He kissed behind her ear. "I want to know you're safe when I'm not around," he murmured. "Just two more moves, I promise."

"And then what?" She pressed back against him. His body told her he wanted her.

He nuzzled her ear, nibbling on her earlobe. "You can claim another prize." His arms tightened, holding her prisoner.

Muri focused on escaping his grasp, the exact opposite of what she wanted to do. She dropped all her weight onto Jack's arms, forcing him to hold her up. She searched for a weakness but found none. She'd have to make one. She bit Jack's wrist.

Of course she didn't bite it as hard as she could have, and probably he didn't have to react, but if she ever needed to, she could bite harder to free herself from someone who meant her harm.

Jack's grip loosened enough that she could wiggle her body. She dropped her weight again and pushed against his wrist and hand instead of his massive arm, and a moment later she was free.

She whipped around, grinning. "Prize time."

He rubbed his wrist but his eyes twinkled. "I said two more. That was one."

She stepped up to him. "What's the other?"

His arms came around her again, and before she could fight back, he'd swept her feet from beneath her and carried her to the ground. His body pressed her into the grass like it was a boulder. Only her arms and head were free. She looked up into his face, squinting against the sun behind him.

"I *really* don't want to escape this one," she gasped.

"Try."

"I would poke your eyes out."

All his weight pressed on her as he reached out and took both her hands. He brought them above her head and pinned them to the ground. "Now what?"

"I'd knock my head into your face and break your nose."

"Good." He lowered his face into the side of her neck and began to kiss her. "Now what?"

His kisses made her blood race, and his erection pressed into her thigh. He nuzzled behind her ear again, licking her. She squirmed, but her entire body was trapped.

"I want you," she whined.

"Free yourself and you can have me."

His grip on her arms was a vice. Her forehead could reach only air. There had to be a way to escape his hold. All she could move was her head. Her only weapon was her teeth. And the only thing she could reach was—

She bit his neck. His head jerked up and she twisted her face and caught his ear, stopping short of damaging him. But she had him. He'd have to let her go or risk losing his ear.

"Good." His hands slid off hers.

She let go with her teeth. Her lips were against his ear. "I liked your hands on mine," she whispered.

He began kissing her neck again, and his hands found her arms and smoothed up them to hold her hands again. His fingers tangled in hers and pressed them into the grass. "You like this?" he asked.

Muri couldn't explain it. She'd always hated feeling powerless beneath the mermen. She licked her lips. "Only because it's you. I like being near you. And I know you won't hurt me."

"I won't hurt you," he said. "And you can always stop me. You know that, right? I won't be angry if I try something you don't like and you stop me."

She shivered, all her nerves on end. What would he try? "I want you to try something."

He lifted himself up to look into her eyes. "And you'll tell me if you don't like it?"

"Yes."

He moved to whisper in her ear. "Can I take your underpants off?"

"I'm not wearing any."

Jack cursed softly, and she could swear he got even harder against her thigh. "Close your eyes," he whispered.

She lowered her lids and waited, breathless in the sparkling darkness. His fingertips skimmed down her arms and lifted off her, and the pressure of his body lifted off hers as his knees sank down between her thighs. She waited, anticipating. Where would he touch her next? His hands landed on her collarbone and slid lightly down her body, teasing over her breasts and encircling her waist, only to continue lower. For a moment they framed her center, where she ached for his touch, but they maddeningly moved on.

He reached the hem of her dress and touched her skin. His fingers were warm, but her skin was hot from the sun. His touch moved back up her legs, taking her dress with it.

The grass tickled the backs of her thighs as her dress tugged up beneath her. Sunshine warmed her bare skin, up her legs until it warmed her right between her thighs. The faintest breeze washed over her. She'd never felt the sun and the air between her legs like this. There had always been a cold damp merman on top of her. Jack's fingers were dancing across her skin, and she willed them to touch her between her legs.

At last he did, rubbing her gently back and forth. But his hands were still on her thighs. Was that—?

His lips pressed against her.

The touch of his lips sent tremors through her body. Her hips twitched, but his hands had settled under her thighs, holding her in place with her body against his mouth.

No one in Glorypool had ever done anything like this.

He kept on kissing her down between her legs, and the more he kissed, the more the pressure inside her built. When the tip of his tongue flicked over her, she quivered, about to explode.

"Jack," she gasped.

His lips closed over her skin, sucking on her, and her body jerked beneath him. Waves of pleasure rolled through her, and he kept them coming with his gentle force. She lost all sense, crying out and digging her fingernails into the dirt. She bucked against his hold on her legs. He held her down as she trembled, wringing herself out against him, until at last he wore her out. His lips let go and blew gently across her, causing a final shiver to work its way up her body. When she settled into the grass, he let go of her legs.

Tears had rolled down the sides of her face. She wiped them away as Jack crawled up the grass beside her. She turned into his chest. More tears were coming.

He rubbed her back. "Okay?"

She nodded vigorously and burrowed deeper against him. She didn't know why she was crying. Only that he'd done something she'd never experienced before. She knew sex could feel pleasant— Lotti had said so, and Muri had felt hints of it with different mermen in her times on the beach. But never had it been like this, full of passion and with the other person being so generous. Jack held her until she stilled.

She burrowed against his neck before pulling back to look up at him. What would he want from her? Tenderness was all she saw in his deep brown eyes. He brushed her hair back and smiled at her.

"Do you want me to . . . ?" Muri dipped her head toward their feet.

He caressed her face. "I just want to look at you."

She slipped her fingers under his shirt and tugged the fabric until she could slip her hand in and touch his skin. "Can I do this?" She bit her lip and grinned at him.

He smiled again. "Please," he murmured, his eyes half closing.

He settled back as she unbuttoned his trousers. His lashes rested on his cheeks. She pushed away his clothing and wrapped her hand around his penis, still rock hard. His lips parted but he didn't move, letting her do as she liked.

She slid his foreskin up and back. She did it again and again and listened to the catch of his breath. She worked him faster. His hand slid into her hair and tightened into a fist and his breathing grew ragged, but he let her stay in control. The power that he surrendered to her and watching what she could do to him made her hard all over again. She stroked him faster, closing her eyes to listen, and she knew the moment before he came from the change in his breathing.

Jack jerked in her grip. She found herself panting with his seed covering her hand. She pulled her dress back up and touched herself without thinking, needing another release. Jack pressed his forehead to hers, watching her face with his fist still tangled in her hair. She rubbed herself faster, smearing his stickiness over her sensitive skin, until a few heartbeats later she was writhing again. Her hair tugged against Jack's fist but he didn't let go.

When her body calmed, Jack leaned up to kiss her forehead.

They lay staring into each other's eyes in silence. Tumbling, the humans called it. Making love. Now she knew why. The hot sun kissed her calves and made her drowsy, and the breeze tickled against her bottom. She closed her eyes, wishing to stop time, but the crash of waves against the base of the cliff intruded. The sea reminded her of where she belonged. But she wanted to stay here—on land. Glorypool held nothing for her, not when Jack was here.

Chapter 9

❦

THE AFTERNOON GREW LATE AS Muri and Jack walked back to the village. Jack had his arm circled around Muri's shoulders the entire way. She leaned in against him with her own arm tight around his waist. The wind had shifted as Jack had predicted, and it brought in the salty ocean smell as they ambled along the grassy clifftop. As they traversed the edge of the harbor, the sailboats on the water headed back to port.

They walked alongside the water until a rocky chasm forced them inland. Across the chasm, Muri glimpsed the place she'd climbed up the cliffs from the sand. The outermost cottage of the village where she'd met the dog was beyond. It had been only two days, but she felt like a lifetime had passed.

As they walked into the fields, Jack gestured across the gap toward the cottage.

"That's my home," he said.

She pulled back to tilt her face up to him. "That cottage?" Of course she'd known he lived somewhere, but what were the chances his home was the first place she'd come across?

"My parents built it."

Muri had to stop herself from telling him she'd been there, peeking in his windows and patting his dog. "It looks cozy," she said, snuggling back into his side, and his arm tightened around her. He kissed the top of her head.

The sun radiated over the waving grains as they crossed the fields toward the village. It sank lower, dipping toward the forest and casting long shadows beside them. Its heat faded as it sank. In spite of Jack's body warming her, Muri was glad they'd be in the village before the sun set and the temperature dropped further.

What would Jack say when they parted? She wasn't sure how human courtship went—would he return her to the grange home, or take her to his cottage to ravish her all night? Somehow she suspected it would be the former. Jack didn't seem to rush into things.

They continued past the chasm toward the main village and at last came to the road. This late in the day, the road to town was deserted even as they entered among the cottages. Jack pulled her in for another kiss atop her head. She stopped walking and hugged him with both arms, and together they stumbled to the edge of the road. They were beside a cottage, not yet to the village square. Jack tugged her into the adjacent yard and up to a broad oak tree that shielded them from the cottage windows. He backed her against the trunk until she was trapped between it and his arms. He leaned down, and they were kissing again.

"I could spend the whole night doing this," Jack murmured between kisses.

Muri twisted her face away to break their kiss and gazed up at him hopefully. He laughed, smoothing his thumbs over her eyebrows before planting his hands on her shoulders. He squeezed, looking away.

"It scares me a little," he said, "how much I feel for you."

She didn't know what to say so she waited.

"It's like I'm in two worlds, the usual one where I'm a fish-catcher who works alone every day, and this new one where the only thing is you. And I want to give in to the new world but I know I need the old one, too."

"I understand." She was between two worlds, too, only for her, the old world wasn't worth saving.

She didn't understand what he needed. But she trusted him to figure his thoughts out.

"I need to check a few things on my boat," he said. "I thought

I might do that tonight. And I should go out on the bay tomorrow. We could see each other again tomorrow night. Would that be okay? Unless your cousin arrives, of course."

"I'm beginning to think she's never coming."

"I hope she's all right." He regarded her again.

"Whether she comes or not, I want to see you again. Whenever you're ready."

"Will you be all right on your own tomorrow—with the ladies in the grange? Or with Gray and Hyacinth? I know you will. I just hope it's not strange I'm not spending the day with you."

"Jack, it's fine. Whatever you need."

He kissed her forehead, and then they were kissing again as the light drained from the sky. By the time Jack left her at the door to the grange home, her lips felt swollen and the village was dark.

The evening passed slowly. All the ladies wanted to hear about her picnic. They made her what they called a "spring salad" since she had missed their dinner. The salad had delicate green lettuces and strawberries and cheese they'd made from goat's milk and nuts called pecans they'd gathered the previous autumn. Muri made herself eat, although her appetite waned each time she remembered what she had to do later.

She couldn't postpone any longer—she had to let Lotti know what had happened to Strombidae. After dinner, she passed a few minutes with the grange home residents before pretending to go to bed. In her room, she sat in the dark and waited until the house went quiet.

Then she waited even longer. The village square became silent, and the pale light of the streetlamps reflected only bare cobblestones. Finally, when the large, lopsided moon appeared over the trees in the direction of the wharf, Muri slipped from her room.

She made her way through the village in the pale moonlight. The White Pony was quiet, though lights flickered inside. On the lane down the hill, she passed a man, and when the lamplight caught on his skin, it had that shimmer to it, like Gray's. Her pulse accelerated. Another fairy! But he only nodded and continued past, carrying a stack of papers like the ones tacked up outside the pubs. Hopefully they weren't all about the dangers of the merpeople.

And of course, she spied two more cats watching her from above. She shuddered and hurried past. Jack said the cats didn't eat people, but they certainly ate fish so it was questionable what they'd think of eating her.

At the bottom of the lane, Muri surveyed the wharf. Voices came from the pubs off to her left, but the wharf was clear and nothing moved on the docks. She didn't want to run into Jack if he was still working on his boat. She crept along the closed storefronts as far as she could, scanning for any sign of activity on the docks, but all was silent. She moved out into the open, maintaining a normal pace to avoid drawing attention should anyone be watching. She reached the docks and hurried down the ramp.

She stopped again to scan for movement. The boats swayed slightly on the water, illuminated in the moonlight. A breeze ruffled her hair, blowing in off the water but gently. Out at the far end of the docks where *Alina's Dream* was tied, nothing moved. Muri exhaled. Jack must have finished his work and gone home.

Muri walked out on the docks. Probably she should do this farther from the village—maybe at the beach where she'd first come to shore—to be absolutely sure no one saw her with a tail. But she wanted to be back at the grange before anyone noticed her absence. And walking to and from that beach would take all night.

She could hear Lotti chastising her—she shouldn't be going back to the grange at all. She should be swimming back to Glorypool now that she'd found Strombidae and couldn't do anything to help him.

But she didn't want to go back.

Muri walked all the way out to Jack's boat. She would climb into it after her swim to wait for her legs to form. If anyone came along, she could hide beneath the sail. Her plan wasn't logical, but being near *Alina's Dream* made her feel safer.

"I've been waiting for you."

Muri started at the voice, but she recognized it immediately.

From the shadows of a barrel on the docks, legs stretched out, and Strombidae leaned forward where he sat behind the barrel. He'd known exactly where she would come.

"I have to tell Lotti what's happened," Muri said.

Strombidae leaned on his arm and pushed himself upright.

"Yes, I see that. But you don't have to tell her the whole story."

"What do you mean?"

"Tell her I'm not coming back. Tell her I'm happy on land, living in the castle with my bride, and I don't want to be king of Glorypool anymore."

Muri's mind went blank with anger. Her mouth dropped open as she struggled for words. "How could you suggest that?"

"They never have to know what's become of me. It would be better that way—remembering me strong and powerful, making a choice—"

"Better that way?" Muri spat out. "It would break Lotti's heart!"

Strombidae didn't reply. His head hung down at last and his shoulders sank in defeat.

"Then let me tell her."

Muri hesitated. If she gave him the shell, did she trust him to go through with it?

"I've told you," he said, "there's no merking magic. I can use that shell as well as you can. Anyone can."

"You have to use it underwater," she said. "How will you manage that if you're all dried out?" He winced, but she didn't care if her words smarted. He'd brought his fate upon himself with his selfish desires and cruelty. Wherever Princess Rose was, Muri hoped she knew she was safe from "Prince Murkel" and his sinister air chamber.

Strombidae remained silent and Muri pressed her advantage. "Besides, if there's no merking magic, if it's all stolen fairy spells, the merking has no greater power than anyone else. All the—the *tyranny* in Glorypool. There's no reason for it. There's no reason why—"

A hiss broke across Muri's voice and she jumped, startled into silence. Strombidae peered down past her. Something moved in the water, in the shadows between Jack's boat and the dock.

"Well," a voice rasped, and Muri's eyes widened. "Look who's here."

Bull's face appeared over the edge of the dock. His fingers curled into the wood.

Bull's protruding eyes leered up at Muri as she backed away. She glanced at Strombidae to find him already gone, halfway to the ramp and limping hurriedly away.

This was bad. Had Bull heard everything? Or had he watched them from beneath and surfaced only after she had spoken?

What would he do? Would he ask what she was doing on land or simply force her to go home? Probably the latter—Bull wasn't much of a talker. And no one could reason with Bull. If he got her into the water, he'd drag her all the way back to Glorypool.

Could she fight him off? Jack had said to run from a fight. Could she reach the wharf before he caught her?

Fear rooted her to the spot as Bull's strong arms lifted him up. His long hair was tied in a knot on his head. That was a bad sign. The mermen always wore their hair loose unless they planned to fight. He hoisted himself onto the dock.

He had a tail.

Of course! He had a tail. Until it dried, he wouldn't be able to chase her. Muri turned.

"I'm your king, Muricidae."

She froze.

"You know I'll be your king soon. Disobey me and you'll pay." His voice sent shivers over her skin.

Muri swallowed and faced him, backing slowly away. "You're not the merking yet. Strombidae has four days left to return."

"But he can't, can he?" Bull used his arms to propel himself forward along the dock after her. "What were you two talking about before I appeared? Why does he avoid the water? He's dried out, isn't he?"

Muri staggered back, keeping herself clear of his arms. "Even if he is, one of the other mermen might best you."

Bull scoffed as he hitched himself forward again. The breeze off the ocean whistled across his scales, drying the droplets clinging to him.

"I don't think that's likely."

"I don't have to go back at all," Muri said, and now she did turn and walk away. "I have friends here. And even if I didn't, I'd rather labor in a human house or work in their fields than return to Glorypool."

"You belong to Glorypool. You owe allegiance to your king."

"I renounce my citizenship as a resident of Glorypool," she tossed over her shoulder, and she ran for the wharf.

She had to get out of sight before Bull could follow her. She reached the first turn on the docks, retracing her steps from earlier. All was silent except the panting of her breath. She rounded the next turn. The ramp was before her.

Something banged behind her, and she risked a glance.

Bull was vaulting himself over the boats like a monkey, heading straight toward her. He had legs, and her quick glance registered his menacing scowl and his naked body. What would he do to her? What if he went after a human?

Muri bolted for the ramp and bounded up it to the wharf. She dashed toward the buildings. Lights shone from the pubs. If she could get in a pub door, Bull would have to stop or face a crowd of humans. She was halfway across—

Bull grabbed her arm, yanking her to a stop as he clamped his other hand over her mouth. She struggled against him as his clammy skin pressed into her back. And suddenly she thought of

Princess Rose. Rose must have been in this same situation with Strombidae. And she had fought back.

So would Muri.

Jack's lessons came to her. Don't waste your strength, he'd said. Find Bull's weakness. She had human shoes on and Bull didn't. She lifted her foot and stomped as hard as she could onto his bare toes. Bull cursed and his arms loosened. She threw her head back, cracking it into Bull's nose. One arm left her, and she twisted in the other and brought her knee up into his naked crotch, ignoring the sick sensation of his body squishing against Hyacinth's beautiful dress. He released her at last and doubled over, moaning. She ran for the row of pubs.

Someone was running to meet her.

Jack! He sprinted across the open wharf. When they met, she grasped his hands and tried to drag him away from the water. But he resisted, pulling toward Bull.

"Go, Muri. I'll stop him."

"Please, Jack, don't." She tugged on him.

"He could threaten the village. I can't let him escape until we've had a chance to talk to him."

"He's dangerous. You have to run." But Jack pulled free and strode toward Bull, who limped a step forward and stopped, watching Jack approach.

Jack was expecting a fair fight with moves like he'd taught her—punches and kicks. Maybe he could even win against Bull's strength. He was adroit at fighting. But Bull wouldn't fight fair. He'd do something awful. As Jack neared him, slowing and calling out a question, Bull sneered and leapt forward. Jack met him the way he'd taught Muri to do, pulling Bull forward and knocking him off balance. But Bull caught himself and stayed upright. The men grappled on the wharf. Bull freed himself. He stumbled away, straight toward the edge, before turning. This time he waited for Jack.

Bull was leading Jack to the water.

Muri started toward them. She had to keep Jack on land, even if it meant she was the one pulled under.

Jack moved closer and Bull circled, maneuvering Jack to the edge of the wharf. Muri ran. But as soon as Jack's back was to the water, Bull charged forward.

"No!" Muri screamed. Bull crashed into Jack and both of them hurtled toward the water. Together, they toppled off the wharf and disappeared.

Muri ran to the edge. The glimmering water churned, but the men had disappeared. Jack would be no match for Bull, not below the surface. Muri couldn't let him be killed. She had no choice.

She dove into the water after him.

Chapter 10

༶ ✸ ༶

As Muri hit the water, she exhaled the air in her lungs and sucked in seawater. Her legs stitched together in an instant, and she swished her tail, propelling herself downward after the trail of bubbles left by the men. Her eyes adjusted to the undersea gloom.

A moment later she spotted them. Bull had Jack locked in his arms on the seafloor. Jack's eyes were panicked as he struggled to break free.

Bull looked up at Muri as she approached. And then he smiled. He turned his body until Jack faced her. She knew the moment Jack recognized her because he froze, his eyes wide.

Muri shot forward, prepared to rip Bull's arms off to get Jack free. But Bull released Jack and pushed him toward her. Before Jack could react, Muri had her arm around his chest and was surging toward the surface and up into the air.

Jack gasped as Muri hauled him above the surface and swam straightaway for the docks. He twisted against her arm but she didn't let him go. Even if he could swim well enough on his own, she couldn't risk Bull pulling him under again. With her powerful strokes, she had him beside the boats in two flicks of her tail. She pulled the side of a boat down and lifted Jack as he clambered onto it. She hefted herself in beside him.

He turned to Muri, and for a moment they stared at each other. His eyes moved down to the hem of her dress where her tail curled against the bottom of the boat.

He scrambled away from her, out of reach of her arms, his eyes wide and panicked. He backed up until he hit the front end of the cockpit.

Bull had let Jack go so easily . . . because he'd trusted Jack's fear and anger to keep him away from her. Bull had known that Jack would fear her. And she'd lied to Jack, even while she was kissing him—of course he'd be angry. Tears welled up in her eyes. She blinked them back and folded her hands in her lap, resisting the urge to follow him across the boat.

"I'm sorry," she whispered. "Please, Jack . . ."

"You're one of them?"

"I won't hurt you."

"What do you want with me?"

"Nothing. It's not like that. I didn't plan to like you."

"What did you plan?"

"Nothing."

"Then why are you here?"

Her mission had been a secret. But she no longer cared what Strombidae thought, or Lotti or any of the others. She'd tell Jack everything. But Bull knew the truth now. Muri had to contact Lotti and warn the merwomen of what had happened.

Where was Bull? Had he started back to Glorypool to claim his victory?

"I can explain," she told Jack, "but I have to do something first. That merman you saw, Bullidae. I have to warn the others he might be coming."

"The others?"

"The merwomen back home. They won't have any protection when he arrives now that he knows the truth about King Murkel. It'll take but a moment. Will you wait here?"

Jack sat up. "Where are you going?"

Why was he asking? He cowered away from her, but his wide eyes also looked . . . concerned? Her tears returned as emotions spiraled inside her. Maybe Jack hadn't given up on her.

She drew the shell from her pocket. Jack jerked and twisted to check the base of the boat's mast as if he'd forgotten they weren't on his boat.

"It's mine," Muri said. "I lost it when I arrived in Woodglen. I can use it to talk to Lotti in Glorypool. It's part of a pair, and she has the other shell. But I have to go into the water to use it." Jack's lips parted but he stayed silent.

As she rested her hands on the edge of the boat, Jack reached for her.

"What if he's down there?"

"I'll be careful."

Muri hitched up the dress and flipped herself off the boat. She sank down a few hands deep. Nothing moved in the darkness anywhere around her or below. She held the shell before her and focused.

"Lotti?" she whispered.

For a moment, nothing happened. Was Lotti there? Lotti had to sneak into the merking's vault to use the other shell. She was trusting the merking's magic not to harm her since she was entering the vault in service of the current merking. Of course, Muri knew the truth now—no merking magic existed. But Lotti must be terrified entering Strombidae's vault without him. She'd promised to go every night to wait for Muri to call to her.

"Lotti?" Muri said again, louder. The shell warmed in her palms and Lotti's voice swirled in the water around her.

"Muri, I've been calling for you. Bull is coming to land."

"I've seen him. Lotti, he may be heading back. You have to get ready."

"Did you find Strombidae?"

"Lotti—" Muri had to force the words out, knowing how they would hurt Strombidae's first wife. "He's dried out. And Bull knows."

She felt Lotti's gasp as a tremor along her arms.

"Bull only just left here. You could swim away."

"There's nowhere to go."

"Lotti, you and the others could come here. It's different than we thought. The humans are—"

"Bull has the perimeter guarded," Lotti said. "I barely got into the vault tonight without being seen. We'd never get away. We'd never survive crossing the ocean."

"I did," Muri said. "I didn't see a single creature bigger than a dolphin all the way across."

"And where would we go? You can't really think we'd live among humans!"

"But what will you do?"

"I don't know. When you get back, find us in the grove. We'll make a plan."

Muri hesitated. She closed her eyes and took a steadying breath. "I'm not coming back yet."

The shell went still and cold. Lotti's voice crept over her skin.

"You're a mermaid, Muricidae, not a human. You belong to Glorypool. I don't like the change in ruler either, but we have to make the best of it."

"I don't belong to Glorypool. I don't want to come back. Nothing's like I've been told. The humans aren't beasts. Even the fairies have been kind to me. And Bull's already threatened me if I return."

"Muricidae, you don't have a choice."

"I'm sorry, Lotti," Muri said, "but I do." She lowered the shell, glancing one last time around the depths. She pushed herself up to the surface.

When she flopped into the boat, Jack winced before he exhaled and slumped back against the mast. Muri shifted herself to the stern of the cockpit, leaving an open space between Jack's feet and her tail. His eyes kept darting toward it, and he had his legs folded up against his chest with his arms tightly around them as if he were scared of touching it. Muri wasn't cold, but Jack shivered in his damp clothes. The hour was well past midnight, and the spring air had chilled.

He was never going to kiss her again. How could he, when he

knew she wasn't even human? He'd be repulsed by her now, the way she'd felt when Lotti had first described the humans to her. Once again, she'd jumped in where she shouldn't have. Getting involved with a human! Of course that would end badly.

It had almost ended far worse than she'd ever have imagined. At least Bull hadn't damaged Jack, as far as Muri could tell. But Bull wanted her to return to Glorypool. If she didn't return, what would Bull do? Would he really let her go this easily? She was determined to stay on land even if Jack never wanted to talk to her again.

Lotti's words echoed in her mind, telling her she had to go back and that she didn't have a choice. As if living in Glorypool was her duty just because she'd been unlucky enough to be born there! But the other mermaids, especially the young ones like Caly, would be stuck in Glorypool. Muri wouldn't be there to watch out for them. Guilt crept up inside her. How could she enjoy life on land, going on dates and wearing a dress and smelling the flowers, while her sisters lived in what she now recognized as a horrible patriarchy?

Not that she'd have another date now that Jack knew the truth. And once the other humans found out what she was, would they let her walk in the gardens and live in the grange home, or would they drive her away? Once again, she'd gotten herself into a mess.

Lotti had chastised her time and again for rushing headlong into things and being a fool. Muri would never have been claimed by Strombidae if it weren't for her impulsive nature. It had happened one day last spring, right before he'd left to go to land to court—or kidnap—Princess Rose.

Muri had been out in the current with the other merwomen, gathering green seaweed, when Angar had swum by. Angar was young but already a brute, and he'd begun eyeing Caly. Caly had not yet been to the island, and Muri didn't want her first time to be with someone like Angar. So when Angar had swum forward, Muri had put herself between him and the young mermaid and refused to move when he ordered her.

Word had gotten back to the merking and he'd brought Muri before him. She'd expected one of the usual punishments, but instead, he'd studied her as she'd tried not to squirm, like an arrow worm exposed on the seafloor and waiting to be snatched by a fish. And he'd declared her to be his next bride as soon as he returned from his trip to land.

In spite of the praise Lotti and the others had given her, being claimed by the merking had been worse than any quick punishment. She didn't want to lie beneath Strombidae on the beach or at the royal hot spring where he took his wives. And, should the ban ever be lifted, she especially didn't want to carry his babies—producing more arrogant mermen and subservient mermaids.

Of course, if the merking hadn't claimed her, she never would have been the one sent to land to find him. She never would have met Jack.

She risked a glance at Jack as he cowered at the far end of the cockpit. He was still watching her tail. She tried to keep it stationary, but her fins had a habit of flapping when she was nervous. Jack hadn't said a word since she'd climbed back into the boat.

He caught her watching him before she could look away. He cleared his throat. "When will it change?"

"When it dries," Muri said, avoiding looking directly at him. "It depends on the humidity."

He didn't reply.

Muri bit her lip. Everyone knew how merpeople's tails worked. "Did you mean, how long will it take? Maybe a few hundred more heartbeats?" Her left fin twitched. Hyacinth's dress was plastered to her skin and her wet hair hung limply with the combs half out. At least she hadn't lost those.

"Do Gray and Hyacinth know?" Jack said. "About . . ." He nodded at her tail.

"Yes."

"Do you have a cousin from Sar Bay?"

"No."

"Do you have a family?"

"Not like a human family. Merpeople raise their merchildren communally."

Jack rested his forehead on his knees.

"I'm sorry I lied to you," she whispered. "I understand if you hate me."

He leaned back and stared overhead. "You saved my life."

"The danger was my fault in the first place. He was only trying to get me."

Jack didn't reply.

"Why were you here at the wharf? I thought you'd gone home."

"It was the cats." Muri worried his brain was addled, but he continued. "I went to the pub after working on my boat. And one of the cats came in and jumped on my lap and wouldn't stop meowing and clawing at me. So I followed him outside—he kept turning back at me and crying, like he wanted me to follow—and he led me to the wharf, and I saw you fighting."

Muri would never criticize the cats again. If Jack hadn't come, Bull would have caught her and dragged her back to Glorypool. But still, Jack could have died.

"I'm sorry," she said again. "I only pretended to be human because I believed I'd be in danger on land if people knew I was a mermaid. But then I met you, and I liked you, and I worried that if you found out what I was, you wouldn't want to see me anymore. And I was going home soon so you'd never have to know.

"But instead I put you in danger. None of this would have happened if I hadn't tried to court you. I wasn't supposed to get involved. I was supposed to complete my mission and leave without ever interacting with any of the land dwellers. But I . . ." Muri was so embarrassed, she finished in a whisper. "I just really wanted to talk to you more."

"What was your mission?"

"To find out what happened to Strombidae—I mean, 'Prince

Murkel.' Strombidae is his given name. Murkel is the honor title of the merking."

"Murkel really is the king of the merfolk?"

"He was. But he's been gone from Glorypool almost a full season. If he's not back in four days, he'll forfeit the throne and all the mermen will begin fighting over who gets it next. I was sent to find him."

"By that merman?" Jack asked.

"Bullidae? No. He wants the throne for himself."

Jack winced as he asked, "Was Bullidae your fiancé?"

"No."

"Why was he threatening you?"

"He wants me to go back to Glorypool."

"Are you going to?" Jack asked quietly.

Muri looked up, forcing herself to meet Jack's gaze. He huddled at the far end of the boat, but his face was less rigid. Less angry.

"I don't want to," she said. "But I feel guilty leaving Lotti and the others while I'm here going to the pub and— and being happy."

Jack paused before asking, "Who's Lotti?"

"She was Strombidae's first wife."

"Wife?"

"A wife is what merpeople call a mate. But it's used only for females, and you can have more than one, and sometimes the bond falls apart."

Jack's face tightened. "How many 'wifes' does he have?"

"Eight."

Jack kept one arm wrapped around his knees, but he lifted a hand to run through his hair and his lips parted.

"Rose was to be nine," Muri added quietly. Her voice dropped even further. "And I would have been ten."

Jack's head jerked up, his eyes flashing. "But he's three times your age!"

"That's just how it is in Glorypool."

"Are his other mates that young?"

"Not Lotti. But the newer ones, yes."

"Patriarchal," Jack muttered. "Now I see why you asked about the word."

"I don't know how long Bull's been watching me. He wasn't supposed to know I was here. If he saw us together, that alone would get me punished. We're forbidden from talking to humans, much less . . . much less doing . . . the things we've—"

"Kissing?" Jack lifted his eyebrows.

"Yes." Muri's throat had gone dry. She swallowed. "And the parts that come after."

His eyes narrowed. "So the mermen are allowed to kidnap humans and keep them as mates, but the merwomen aren't even allowed to talk to humans? Is there a reason why it's forbidden? A good reason, I mean."

Muri's brow wrinkled. "A good reason?"

"I mean, if we were to . . . be together . . ." Jack ducked his head, and his arms finally let go of his legs. He rested one hand on the edge of the boat, then brought it back to his knee. "Would it work? Or doesn't it work with a human?"

Suddenly, Muri understood why he'd become awkward. He was talking about sex. About tumbling her, as Gray called it.

"It works," she said. She also ducked her head. Had he been thinking of it, too, on their picnic that afternoon? Had he wanted to do more with her? Gray had informed her that people who went on dates ended up having sex.

Gray had said Jack wouldn't pester her for it. But Gray hadn't said that Jack wouldn't ask politely. Maybe if they'd gone on another date, he'd have asked.

Maybe Jack hadn't wanted to tumble her, though. Maybe he was simply wondering about how it worked with mermaids in general.

The wind skipped over Muri's scales, and they crinkled as they dried out. Her tail faded away.

Jack stared out at the water, his hand on the back of his neck. She was too nervous to speak. When he looked to her at last, his eyes dropped down to her legs and he drew in his breath. After a moment he let it out.

"Can you walk right away?"

Muri flexed her ankles and nodded.

He sat up. "Let's get you home."

"Home?"

"To the grange, I mean."

Emotion swelled inside her. "You're going to walk me home?"

Jack stilled. "You're not . . ." He gestured at the water. "You can't go back there, not if they treat you this way."

Muri looked down, too overcome to speak.

"What is it?" he asked.

"I didn't think you'd be my friend anymore. I didn't think you'd trust me to sleep at the grange."

Jack's lips tightened. "Gray trusted you to stay there and he knew who you were. And I know you wouldn't hurt those ladies."

"I would never."

He looked down. "Could we talk more tomorrow?"

"You still want to talk to me?"

"Shouldn't we? I want to understand this."

"Oh Jack." Her emotions overwhelmed her again but this time she nodded.

With his hands on the beam wrapped in the sail, Jack carefully stood. His whole body shivered as he held on and stepped across the boat. Muri hated seeing him so fragile. No matter what he said, he wouldn't be in this state if he hadn't been spending time with her—if he hadn't challenged Bull to protect her. She climbed after him onto the dock before he could offer her a hand.

"Your feet are bare," he said.

"I lost my shoes in the water when my tail formed. I don't much like wearing shoes anyway."

"You must be freezing."

"I'm more worried about you. I can take the cold. You should go straight home and get warm, Jack. I can get myself back to the grange."

"I'm not leaving you while that merman's out here."

Giving in seemed the fastest way to get Jack moving. She touched his arm to start him walking and together they headed up the docks.

The wharf glowed in moonlight, but the moon was in the west now. As they crossed the empty wharf and entered the lane, the buildings blocked the light. Between the streetlamps, they passed through dark shadows. Muri's vision adjusted to the blackness. No one was out this late.

Jack trudged up the hill. She wanted to support him but he might not want her touching him. They walked the rest of the way in silence. The streets were deserted.

When they reached the door at the grange home, Jack said, "Do you know how to bolt the door?"

Muri shook her head.

"I'll show you. Bolt it after I'm gone. Just in case."

They entered quietly. The clock in the hallway ticked as Jack closed the door and carefully demonstrated the door's lock. It scraped when he slid it back, even though he did it slowly, and Muri winced, not wanting to wake any of the residents. Jack looked to her to be sure she understood.

He opened the door to leave and she looked up at his face, and for a moment she hoped he might lean in and kiss her.

"Tomorrow," he whispered. He stepped out and pulled the door gently closed.

Chapter 11

ஐ✹ଓ

"So how was your date?"

The next morning, Gray perched on the edge of a chair in the parlor and fixed his green eyes on Muri. "Or should I say, dates? I came by yesterday and learned you were out again."

"Wait'll you hear this," Margery said from across the parlor, where she was pulling the wilted flowers out of Hyacinth's arrangement. Muri was glad the whole house wasn't awake. Telling Margery she was a mermaid had been hard enough. Although, the woman hadn't reacted with shock. Her eyebrows had lifted and she'd leaned in closer, studied Muri, leaned back, and said, "Huh."

Gray turned to the older woman. "Are those flowers wilting already?" he asked.

"Only the tulips."

Gray huffed. "I'm so embarrassed. I'll tell my sister."

Margery turned on him. "Don't you dare!"

"The Fairweather Florist can't sell flowers that die before three days have passed. I'll just tell her to leave out the tulips."

"Young man, she includes tulips because she knows they're Hilda's favorite. Just because something lasts only three days doesn't mean it's not worth having."

The words rang true. Muri would never regret kissing Jack and lying beneath him on the grass, with his hands and lips and tongue on her, even if she never got to touch him again.

Margery turned back to the flowers, and Gray turned back to Muri, rolling his eyes. He fixed them on Muri again. "Now tell."

Muri recounted what had happened on the docks with Bullidae and Jack. Gray's eyes widened until he was clutching his chest with his mouth gaping. But before she could finish, he shook his head and waved his hand to stop her.

"Wait wait wait," he said. "Go back. How did we get to mermen fighting on the docks in the middle of the night? What happened on the date with *Jack*?"

"We went on our date and had a good time. And the next day he came again and we went on a picnic."

"A picnic."

"Yes—you sit on a blanket on the grass. With cheese and things."

"I know what a picnic is," Gray said, rolling his eyes again.

"Then why are you asking?"

"You were on a blanket on the grass." Gray lifted his eyebrows.

"Yes." Muri felt herself blushing.

Gray leaned in. "But did you *kiss* him?"

Muri blushed harder.

"That's exactly what I asked," Margery put in without turning from her work.

"You don't even need to tell me," Gray said, a smile stretched across his face. "I can tell how spectacular it was by how embarrassed you are."

"But Gray, I nearly got him killed. Bull showed up and tried to drag me home, and Jack defended me, and Bull pulled him into the water and almost drowned him. I pulled him out but when he saw my tail, he was scared of it. He looked like he thought it might curl around him and squeeze him to death."

"Can you do that?"

"No!"

"What happened next?" Gray leaned toward her, his eyes shining.

"Once my date was able to breathe properly, you mean?"

"This Bull fellow is gone, right? And Murkel scurried off. So it was just you and Jack?"

"We waited for my legs to form and Jack walked me home. He said we could talk today."

Gray settled back. "See? It's fine. The mermen are gone, you're both safe, and now you'll talk and everything will be fine."

"Unless he never wants to see me again."

"He wouldn't have asked you on another date if he never wanted to see you again."

"It's not another date! He said we need to talk."

"It'll be a date by the time you're done, kitten." Gray winked.

If only she shared Gray's optimism. Muri retrieved Hyacinth's hair combs and dress, which had somewhat dried after she'd washed it under the pump in the park early that morning. She had hung it on a line outside where the morning sunlight reached it. She asked Gray to apologize to Hyacinth for its state. She wouldn't let him lend her any more of Hyacinth's clothes. Maybe it would be better if Jack saw her in her shapeless sack of a dress. She didn't want him to think she was trying to seduce him to make him forget she'd lied to him.

"Chin up, ocean girl," Gray said before he left with the dress over his arm. He had to get on with his errands for the shop. "Let me know if you need anything."

After Gray left, Margery showed Muri something called "dusting," and she spent the next hour at work in all the common rooms. They didn't have dust in Glorypool, although sand had a way of getting into everything. Maybe dust was the land version of that.

Each time a resident came down the stairs and went to the kitchen, Margery's voice would carry down the hall: "Muri's date was wonderful, but you should know she's a mermaid." Soon the whole house knew, and no one had reacted with anger or fear.

When would Jack come? Had he changed his mind? Muri tugged open a window and shook out the dust rag. The bits of dust sparkled in the sun and drifted away on the breeze. Dust was so pretty. The hour was going on lunchtime. Would Jack—

A knock sounded on the grange door.

Muri startled to attention. She came into the hall as Margery opened the door.

Jack was on the step, framed in sunlight. The sight of him tied her in knots. He stood tall and the color had come back into his face. Thank the seas he had recovered from Bull's attack, at least physically. He wore his usual work shirt and trousers.

He greeted Margery and looked past her, his gaze settling on Muri. He didn't smile, but she was staring back at him without smiling either. She tried to smile but her face wouldn't work.

Margery turned back and forth between the two of them. "Well you two, get on with it," she said, and stepped away from the door.

Muri jerked into motion, her bare feet carrying her toward Jack even as her nerves twisted with fear that he might reject her, now that he'd had a night to think about it. As she passed Margery, the other woman eyed her dress.

Heat rose up Muri's neck. "It's all I have," Muri whispered.

"No matter—he'll like you whatever you wear." Margery tugged the dust cloth out of Muri's hand.

Jack stepped back from the doorway as Muri came out. He glanced at her bare feet but didn't comment. He didn't take her hand or offer his arm. They headed across the square toward the path to the castle gardens.

"Are you feeling better?" Muri asked as they came out on the oceanside cliff. The fleet of fishing boats was far out in the bay.

"Much better. Are you all right?"

"I'm fine."

"Can we sit on the beach?" he asked, and she nodded. They continued in silence. They followed the path across the windy clifftops until they reached the castle wall.

She followed Jack through the garden gate. Only two days had passed since her first visit, but already the petals were dropping off the tulips. The hyacinths stood taller. Maybe they had an advantage, given it was Hyacinth watching over them.

Jack walked all the way through the gardens, but instead of turning toward the castle, toward where Muri had sat with Gray by the fountain, he turned through a small gate in the opposite direction. A sand dune blocked the view but Muri sensed the ocean immediately. The stones of the garden path gave way to beach sand, hot in the sun beneath the soles of her bare feet. Jack led Muri around the dune and onto the deserted beach.

He chose a spot where the dunes rose up, sheltering them from the cool breezes as they sat. They could view the water, Muri noted, but they were as far from it as they could get on the beach.

Jack stared at the water. Muri hugged her knees and watched him.

"I don't know where to begin," he said at last. "You're going through so much, and I don't know how to help you. I don't even know if I understand everything you said last night. It was hard to think straight."

"Want me to start from the beginning?"

Muri told him everything. About being chosen as the merking's next bride and the unrest when the merking didn't return from his trip to marry the princess. About being chosen by the merwomen to find the merking and sneaking away from Glorypool to do it, and her fear of the humans and fairies. About losing her shell necklace, and running from Gray the first time they met, and discovering Strombidae was dried out, and knowing she had to alert Lotti. And about meeting him and discovering he had her shell.

"You call your home Glorypool," he said.

"I don't know why Strombidae made up the name Merlandia. Maybe he worried someone would have heard of Glorypool."

"That shell," Jack said. "I thought I saw someone in the water right before I found it. But I told myself I must have imagined it. I saw you, didn't I?"

She nodded.

"How did your shell end up in my net?"

Muri's face heated as she remembered how Jack's net had caught her. How she'd been spying on him from below the water. "Oh, um, about that."

Jack's eyebrows lifted.

"It was me who put the hole in your net. I'm sorry I ruined it and lost your fish."

"I can mend a net. But I don't understand. Were you trying to help the fish escape?"

"I was trying to help me escape."

He squinted, confused.

"I got caught in your net before I came ashore. I was watching the boats instead of paying attention around me, and suddenly the net was around me."

"You were in the net?" he asked. "With all the fish?"

"Can you imagine if you'd pulled me up before I escaped?"

"I might have fallen overboard in shock. How did you rip the net?"

Without thinking, Muri pulled up the hem of her dress to show him the knife belted at her waist. When she looked up, he was staring at her bare leg, and she remembered that humans were odd about nakedness. She lowered the dress and smoothed it down. "Sorry, I forgot. Gray told me I can't go around naked here."

Jack swallowed. "No." He pointed at the knife's location. "You got to your knife and cut your way out?"

"It was much easier to reach the knife before I had a dress on. I only put the dress on once I came ashore."

"Oh." Jack looked away, his eyes wide, and swallowed again.

Muri bit her lip, again remembering how the humans were about always keeping their clothes on. "I imagine you'd have been even *more* surprised to pull in your net and find a *naked* mermaid."

At last a smile broke across Jack's face. "I don't know if 'surprised' would accurately describe how I'd have felt." His smile faded. "When I saw you under the water last night, I was trapped by Bullidae. And then you had me—how did you get me away from him?"

"He let you go," Muri said. Jack scrunched his face in confusion. "He thought you'd reject me once you knew what I was. He thought I'd have to come home after losing you. So he let you go." Muri gazed out at the water, trying to keep herself from trembling.

"You haven't lost me," Jack said softly.

His words made her melt with hope. "I haven't?"

"No."

"But I hid what I was."

"You had to. You're right about people being dangerous—if you'd come ashore looking like a mermaid, you'd have scared people and they might have reacted badly."

"But I could have told you once I knew you were nice. I seduced you under false pretenses."

Jack halfway smiled and lifted his eyebrows. "You seduced me?"

"It wasn't right to get close to you while I had such a secret."

He sighed. "I suppose. But knowing it now, I wouldn't change what we did."

"You wouldn't?" she said in the tiniest voice.

"No."

"I thought you'd hate me."

"No."

"But you do hate my tail."

"I don't hate it."

"You flinched when you saw it."

"I'm just . . . not used to it. When I saw you coming for me I was relieved, and then I realized you were—you had a tail, too, and maybe you were coming to help him. When you pulled me to the boat, I didn't know what to think."

"You thought he was going to drown you," she said softly. "Like your parents."

He looked down.

"You said once it might have been merpeople who killed your parents. The posters made you angry. And now Bull's almost drowned you. I wouldn't blame you if you hated all of us."

"That was a rumor about my parents."

"Maybe not." Muri twisted her hands together. "Gray told me something. He said ten seasons ago, when he lived in the caverns, he overheard the older fairies talking about an incident. About some merpeople killing humans. But he never heard any more about it."

Jack had gone rigid. He inhaled slowly, in and out once. "It's no matter," he said in a quiet voice. "It's nothing to do with you."

Muri bit her lip to stop herself saying more. If she ever got a chance, she'd ask Lotti about the rumor. But until then, she wouldn't keep discussing it when it obviously upset Jack.

"Isn't it hard to go out on the water every day?" she asked instead.

"Yes."

"Couldn't you be a farmer or something else?"

"I didn't want to run from my fear. And fishing was what I knew how to do." He sifted sand through his fingers, staring at the ground.

Muri frowned. Did she run from fear? She didn't ever want to go back to the cruel mermen and the groveling, obedient merwomen of Glorypool, even if it meant running away from her fears instead of facing them. She almost wished she weren't a mermaid.

And it came to her. The way to solve their problem.

"I can stay human," she said, defiance flaring up in her chest. Jack jerked his head up. "I can dry out my tail and be done with it. You wouldn't have to see it ever again, and they couldn't make me go back to Glorypool."

Jack's mouth opened, but he didn't speak.

"I don't want to be a merwoman. All it brings is suffering. I hate it there. I want to stay here."

Jack pursed his lips and swallowed. "They could still take you. You wouldn't be able to defend yourself."

Muri didn't reply. The thought of Bull dragging her into the water and of not being able to swim—or breathe—stole her courage. Strombidae's air chamber popped into her mind. They could keep her locked in it, if she dried out.

"Besides," Jack said. "I can't believe that's healthy for you. I never saw Murkel before he was kept in the dungeons and . . . and 'dried,' but Avianna insists he was handsome—taller and stronger. She said his strength was unnatural. And now he's shrunken and frail. That change could be from losing his merman nature."

"Who's Avianna?"

"She lived in the castle with the princess. The rumor is she, uh, tumbled Murkel when he first arrived. While he was courting Rose. Avi lives in the village now. She runs things at the docks."

Muri remembered seeing the woman on the docks when she'd arrived in the village. She must have been the same woman who'd helped Muri in the park when Strombidae was grabbing her—Gray had called her Avi. She'd tumbled the merking?

"But if I could stay here," Muri said, "maybe it would be worth it. I don't want you to shudder when you see me."

Jack reached out his hand and lightly touched the back of Muri's. She slid her fingers into his, and he held them tightly.

"I don't shudder when I see you," he said quietly. "I think you're beautiful."

Tears smarted in Muri's eyes. No one had ever told her she was beautiful. They would call her small, or lucky to have been chosen by the merking, or impulsive. Never anything positive. But Jack had called her lovely and perfect and now beautiful. He'd said he liked her impulsiveness.

"But then I feel guilty about being with you," he continued, "like what if I don't know what I'm doing and can't give you what you need? What if I don't understand merpeople enough and can't do things right?"

"I feel the same about the humans."

"I want to know the real you, all of you. You're a mermaid, and you'd be one whether you could form a tail or not. I don't want you living a half-life because of me."

He gazed at her. His eyes were such a deep brown, like the kelp that grew only on the slopes nearest the island, and he watched her with resolve. "I want you to be a mermaid. I just want to *not* be nervous about it."

"Would it help if you spent time with me in mermaid form?"

"I'd like that."

Muri watched the gentle waves. "We could go sit in the water, but you'd be cold."

"I know you said the merman left, but he could come back. It doesn't seem safe in the water."

"You could stay here and I'll go in and change and come back to sit by you. We'll have some time—"

"It's not safe for you, I meant."

"Oh."

"Does it have to be seawater to change you?"

"Any water will do as long as there's enough of it."

"I have an idea but you might think it's strange."

"What is it?"

"Can I show you? It's hard to explain."

"Okay."

Jack pushed himself onto his knees. "We have to go into the castle," he said, standing and holding out a hand to help her up.

Did he mean the fountain? Surely he wouldn't expect her to swim somewhere so public. Was there some kind of cistern in the castle basement? Or . . . or a giant water tank? She remembered the air chamber in Glorypool and the water tank she'd imagined by comparison. But she was with Jack. He wouldn't put her in anything awful. She took his hand and let him pull her to her feet.

Chapter 12

⊱✳⊰

Muri and Jack left the beach and walked through the gardens toward the castle. Away from the wind, the warm sun continued to beat down, now heating the stones beneath her feet and caressing the flowers. Among the dying tulips, new green buds emerged from the soil.

They passed the fountain where Muri had sat with Gray, but Jack kept walking. Muri stepped onto the grass. It was soft and moist, and she had the strangest desire to lie down and roll in it. Each time she took a step, her foot sank into the cool blades.

They crossed the wide green expanse as the castle loomed closer and closer overhead. When they were beneath the towers, they climbed wide steps onto a patio. The stone floor was hot from the sun, searing the soles of her feet as she hurried across. A door stood open and beside it, Hilda sat reading some papers in the sunshine with a hat shielding her face.

"Good morning," Jack said, and Hilda's head jerked up.

"Morning," she said, putting aside the pamphlets. "I didn't hear you approach."

"Do you work here, Hilda?" Muri asked.

"Three days a week. Now, how can I help you—do you want the basic tour or the deluxe tower tour?"

Jack had said working as the castle tour guide was the *exciting* job in Woodglen. Somehow Muri hadn't pictured the job being held by Hilda. She peeked in the open door beside Hilda, but relative to the sunny outdoors, it was too dark to see anything inside the castle.

"I was hoping to show Muri what we've been building upstairs."

"Oh Jack, you go right on up. You know the way."

"Thank you." Jack reached for Muri's hand, but the moment he touched her, he stiffened. He looked down at her, unsure. Muri took his hand, and his shoulders relaxed as he pressed back. He stepped into the open doorway.

"I'll make sure no one else goes up," Hilda said. "Not much business today. I might as well close early." She smiled slyly and shooed them in the door.

Jack led Muri into a parlor ten times the size of the one in the grange home. Sunlight streamed in through tall windows. The wooden chairs had seats made of a shiny material and came in all colors like the flowers in the gardens. Wooden tables lined the walls along with glassed-in cases containing shelves covered with dainty dishes and vases and other objects. Muri couldn't even imagine why anyone would need all this.

"They've mostly left the rooms as they were during the monarchy," Jack said as they crossed the room. "Although, some of it was sold to fund different projects."

"The castle had more than this?"

Jack shot her a knowing look. "Uh-huh."

They exited the parlor into a darker hallway. Here, no windows opened to the outdoors, and the stone walls and floor radiated cold. Enough light filtered in from open doorways along the hallway to help them see. Jack took her to one end and through a door, down another hallway, up a few steps, and through more doorways. They passed by tapestries and walked under ironwork chandeliers that would provide light when the candles were lit. The castle was extreme. Muri couldn't imagine what it had been like filled with people.

And it was so much compared to Glorypool. How had Strombidae felt when he'd arrived and seen all this opulence? Muri pressed her lips together. She felt awed by it, but knowing Strombidae, he'd probably seen himself as better than the humans, regardless of their magnificent castle.

They started up a stone staircase, spiraling up like the inside of a shell. Narrow windows let in light at each of three turns. At the top was a door Jack pushed open. A breeze burst in Muri's face. They stepped out the door and onto a rooftop.

Muri squinted into the sunshine. They were up near the treetops on a narrow stone patio. A crenelated wall rimmed the edge. Beyond the wall spread the patterns of the gardens below, and beyond the far garden wall, the sea stretched blue to the horizon. She turned. Towers stood on either side. Another stone wall lined the back of the patio, overlooking a courtyard inside the castle. Behind the courtyard, more stone walls and windows and sloping roofs rose up even higher than the terrace where she and Jack stood. And over all that, tall towers rose into the sky.

Jack led her along the patio. They walked under the branches of a tree with pale green buds blocking the view to the gardens and beside the wall of a tower, leaving them in a sheltered space with the tallest branches reaching overhead.

The patio ended ahead of them, and a giant basket made of wooden boards was placed in the middle of it. It came up to Muri's chest. Inside was empty save for a scattering of dead leaves and a broom. What on earth was it for?

Jack stepped onto a stool beside the wooden tub and sat on the edge. He swung his legs over and dropped down inside.

He began sweeping up the leaves.

"What is this?"

"It's part of a rain catchment system." He gestured up with his head, and she followed his gaze. A wooden tank coated in thick black pitch perched above the tub Jack stood in, with a conduit leading from the tank's bottom to the edge of the tub.

"We built it to collect the rainwater off the castle rooftops. A network of gutters funnels the water into covered tanks like that one. When we need it, we can let it out into the tubs, and people can take it away in buckets. Or they can bathe in it."

"Bathe in it?" Humans had to take baths since the dirt of land could build up on their skin. But they used small basins like the one in her room at the grange home, not giant tubs like this.

"Mostly the water is for emergencies, like if a fire breaks out or we have a bad drought. We've built smaller systems on cottages, but the castle has such wide rooftops it seemed a waste not to use them. We'll have a cart to carry the water where it's needed. This pipe drains the water to ground level.

"But I had this new idea for the grange to make income from the castle by offering deluxe hot baths. The pitch that seals the tank also absorbs sunlight and heats the water. But we haven't tried it yet. The tank only filled with the recent spring rains. So if you're willing to test it . . . ?"

A human-style bath with warm rainwater in a giant tub? Muri couldn't imagine it, but she nodded.

Jack had swept the bottom of the tub clean. He climbed out, put aside the broom, and reached up to a sluice gate over the tub. "Here goes."

He opened the first gate and another at the side of the tank, and a moment later, water gushed out the spillway. It splashed against the bare bottom of the tub until it covered the bottom and the level began to rise. As the tub filled, the water caught the colors of the sky, shimmering blue and green like the tree branches. The bottom of the tub disappeared in the reflecting colors.

When the water was high enough, Muri reached in with her fingers. The water was like hot sunshine. She plunged her hand in, watching as the water level crept up her arm. It was at least ten hands deep, plenty deep to cover her. A hot bath! The island had a hot spring on the far side where the land sloped up, but she'd never been taken that far. The spring was only for the merking and his wives.

She pulled her arm from the water.

Jack grinned at her. He nudged the stool toward her. "You look game."

Muri grinned back. In one motion, she pulled the loose dress over her head and dropped it on the patio stones. She untied her knife belt and dropped it on top, stepped on the stool, and vaulted herself in.

The water closed around her, delicious and warm, like lying in the sun but with the familiar press of the ocean at the same time. Lying in the hot bath was the best of everything. She churned her tail around the spacious tub. She exhaled the air from her lungs and inhaled the water, warming herself from the inside. The water tasted different without the salt of the sea but was easy to breathe. As the bubbles she'd made cleared, the tree branches and sky waved overhead, the greens and blues blending with the wooden sides of the tub.

She surfaced, flicking the ends of her hair off her face and expelling the water from her lungs. The air on her cheeks felt cool, so she stayed low in the water as she turned to find Jack.

He stared up at the branches. His skin was flushed so dark Muri worried he'd gone ill. She looked down at her dress on the stones.

"Oh Jack, I'm sorry! I forgot!"

His gaze darted down as if checking her state before settling on her face.

She reached an arm out of the water to touch his shoulder. "I forgot you don't like naked bodies."

His lips pressed together, suppressing a smile. "I like naked bodies. I just didn't want to embarrass you. I forgot you don't mind."

"So you want me to show myself?"

He smiled and covered her hand with his. "Why don't you stay in there and enjoy your bath while the water's hot."

Muri tilted her head. What was Jack thinking? He'd seen parts of her naked. And look what had happened—they'd ending up grabbing each other like a pair of mating octopuses. Was it true what she'd learned about human men losing control around naked bodies? Nothing else she'd learned about humans had been true. And she'd been every bit as out of control as Jack had.

"It's *not* your animal lust, is it?" she asked.

Jack stepped back, dropping her hand. "My *what*?"

"The merpeople say . . ." Before the words were out, Muri's cheeks heated at how silly they sounded. "In their stories, they said human males lose all reason when they see a naked female, even just a breast, and they can't stop themselves from mating." She peeked over the edge of the tub. "That's not true, is it?"

Jack moved back to the tub and curled his fingers over the edge next to hers. "I think you should probably forget everything the merpeople told you about humans."

"Why is it you won't look at me? If you know I don't mind and it doesn't drive you mad with lust?"

"It's not that I don't want to. I'd like it very much." Jack bit his lip. "It's part of courtship here, at least for some people. Like kissing or touching each other. I wouldn't have kissed you before talking to you and knowing I liked you. Seeing each other naked is another step, but it usually happens along with making love."

Muri opened her mouth but bit back her words. She'd almost blurted out that they could make love, too. But if Jack wasn't ready to see her naked, she should probably hold off on trying to tumble him. Tumble. She liked the human words better when it came to Jack. She'd only known Jack a few days but she could tell he would be a thousand times better than any of the mermen she'd been with. With him, it really would be "making love."

"You wanted to see my tail, though, right?" she asked.

"Yes, if you're willing."

Muri patted the edge of the tub the way Gray had done to invite her to join him on the edge of the fountain in the gardens. Jack flattened his hands on the edge and pushed himself up, twisting to sit there with his back to the water.

Muri hooked her right elbow over the edge of the tub, careful to keep her chest below the surface. She backed away from him enough to make a space for her tail. She floated her tail up to break into the air and rested her tail fins on the edge next to Jack.

"It's a bit overwhelming," Jack said, looking along her tail. "I've been handling fish my whole life. And your tail looks so similar. And I'm not sure I ever really believed the merfolk were real, even after learning about Murkel, until I saw it last night. Uh, is it bad to compare you to a fish?"

Muri shrugged. "I guess that's probably what we're related too."

"Why isn't your skin green? Is that part not true?"

"I used clay to hide the color. Look." She scrubbed hard at the back of her left wrist, digging in with her fingernails, and the color darkened as the green tint showed through.

Would Jack still think she was beautiful when her skin was tinted green like eelgrass?

Jack held her hand and ran his thumb over the spot. He looked into her eyes. "I can't wait to see you green all over."

Muri wanted to lean in and kiss him.

"Is your tail fragile?"

"No. You can touch it if you'd like."

Jack let go her hand. Gingerly, he reached out until his fingertips grazed over her scales. Her body thrilled in response, her muscles clenching. Jack didn't appear to notice. He was too busy studying her tail. His hand was stroking up it.

"You know I can feel that, right?" she said, panting.

He looked at her, startled.

"It's the same as if I had legs and you were running your hands up them."

His hand jerked off her. "Of course. I'm sorry."

She grabbed for his hand. "Don't be sorry. I just wanted to make sure you knew." She placed his hand back on her tail and spread out his fingers one by one.

He smiled, watching her. She grinned down at their hands. When she removed hers from his, his eyes crinkled with mischief. He began to move his hand again, this time more slowly and deliberately. It moved up her tail, disappeared under the surface of the bath, and withdrew, washing water over her exposed scales. She closed her eyes.

"Does that feel good?"

"Yes."

He did it again, this time moving farther along her. She wanted him to keep going, to caress her all the way up her body, but again his hand moved away.

He stroked both sides of her tail fins. Her tail fins! How had he known? They were so sensitive, and he was petting them like she was a baby seal. She might explode with the bliss of it. She gripped the side of the tub, trying to stay still as his fingers smoothed over the skin.

"How about this?" he asked, stroking.

She opened her lips to respond but a moan came out.

"That sounds like it's good," he said.

"Yes," she panted. "Especially there."

He had one hand under her tail fin, the other stroking the top. He scooped a handful of warm water over her with his next stroke. She gasped his name.

"Hmm?"

"Kiss me. Please."

His lips pressed against her tail fins.

She pulled her tail into the water, launching herself toward him. "No, I meant—"

But he was waiting when she pushed herself up out of the water on the edge of the tub. His fingers closed around her arms and his lips met hers.

All her longing flowed out in the kiss. She didn't want to scare him, but he kissed her back as hard as she was kissing him, somehow staying balanced on the edge of the tub. He let go of her arms and instead reached to pull her body against his. She combed her fingers through his hair and curled them into fists in it. He held on tighter as he abandoned her lips and moved to her neck.

When he kissed her neck, he did it in a way that felt as marvelous as having her tail fins stroked. She focused on the pull on her skin and a shiver went through her body, and when Jack wobbled, she almost pulled him into the tub.

But she stopped herself and pushed him upright with a quick thrust of her tail. His head came up, and they stared into each other's eyes.

"Please come in the water," Muri said.

He swallowed and loosened his grip.

Muri sank down, peeping over the edge as he stood and pulled his shirt over his head to reveal his broad tanned chest. His torso narrowed as her gaze drifted downward over muscles to his belly, where a thin trail of hair led down into the trousers he was fumbling to undo. The trousers dropped and he stepped out of them and glanced at her. He still wore a pair of undershorts. Muri lifted her hands and covered her eyes, smiling. A moment later, he splashed into the water.

Muri turned to face him. He'd backed against the far side as if he'd become scared of her again. He slouched against the tub wall with only the tops of his shoulders above the surface.

She floated toward him.

"Okay?" she whispered.

"You're just . . ."

She tilted her head, hoping he'd continue.

He spoke so quietly she barely caught the words. "When I see you, I feel so much inside."

She drifted closer until she could reach out and touch him. His arms were straight down in the water. She ran her hand down one arm and found his hand below the surface, clenched in a fist. She worked her fingers into his.

"Can I try kissing your neck this time?" she asked.

He nodded, straightening a little.

"Will you touch me?"

In answer, his tight fingers unclasped in hers. She pressed her lips against his neck right at the waterline, and beneath the surface, she brought his fingers to her breast.

His breathing hitched as his hand made contact. He pressed his palm against her, smoothing it over her nipple before bringing it back and closing his fingers around her. His other hand found her other breast, and he softly squeezed. She bit his neck in response, holding back a cry as he slowly kneaded her.

She reveled in his touch a moment longer before twisting away. His eyes were closed and his head leaned back on the edge of the tub.

"Can I touch you?" she said.

He nodded without opening his eyes.

"Anywhere?"

One side of his lips twisted lazily up, and he slowly nodded again.

Muri sank under the water.

She grinned. He *had* removed his undershorts before climbing into the tub. She hadn't been sure he would. She loved that he didn't form a tail. His skin was pale where the sun didn't reach it. Her lips curved wider at the sight of his erection—as big as Bull's or any of the other mermen's, something every merman in Glorypool would deny. If she ever went back, she'd tell everyone the human men were just as big. Bull would be livid.

She reached out and ran her fingers gently up its length, watching it wave in response like seagrass in the ocean current. The soft skin under her fingertips made her practically climax, tail or not. She moved closer, planting her lips on his belly and pressing herself so his hard shaft knocked against her breasts. Her fingers curled around his bottom, digging into him and pulling her body against his. If only she could see his face to see how he was reacting. His arms had disappeared above the surface, holding him up on the edge of the tub.

She worked her way down his belly, kissing and biting and sucking on bits of him, with her hands clenching the backs of his thighs and her lips always moving closer to his erection. When she reached it, she kissed her way from the base to the tip before she took him in her mouth.

Muri had sucked on a merman's penis before but never because she had actually wanted to. She'd instigated it when she wanted to be done with him quickly, or when it seemed easier than having him thrusting about on top of her. And also, she hated when they told her to do it. If she suspected things were heading that way, she'd jump in and start it herself. It made her feel less out of control.

But it was different with Jack. She loved exploring his body and knowing she could bring him pleasure. She felt no pressure from him to do anything, as if he had no expectations of her. She wanted to give herself to him.

She curled one hand around his base, working it along with her mouth as her other arm hugged his thighs. Her rhythm grew faster, until his hand fisted in her hair and drew her face away from him. He jerked in her grasp, and as she watched him come in the water, a delicious shudder ran through her from his fist in her hair to the tip of her tail.

He let her go and she sank to the bottom of the bath, taking a moment to watch him above her before she surfaced.

Chapter 13

❧ ✻ ☙

The fishing boats were returning to the docks when Jack and Muri left the castle.

Jack had drained the tub using a spigot on the bottom that led to a channel that carried the water away to the ground. As he'd rinsed the tub with the last bit of rainwater, he'd commented that he'd never expected it to be used for *that*.

"The grange could probably make a lot more money," Muri said as he closed the spigot, "if they sold turns in a hot tumbling tub instead of hot baths."

Jack grinned.

They'd climbed down the steps and left through the parlor, where Hilda sat snoring, slumped on a divan.

Jack slid his arm around her shoulders as soon as they were out in the open. She leaned into him and couldn't stop her hand from resting on the muscles of his abdomen.

He shot a look down at her, one side of his lips curling, before removing his arm and taking her stroking hand off him.

"I don't want to end up tumbling you in the bushes," he said.

Muri grinned up at him. He laced his fingers through hers and continued holding her hand as they walked.

As they crossed the clifftop back to the village, Jack kept looking out at the boats.

"Did you miss being out today?" Muri asked.

He squeezed her hand. "When I could spend the day with you? Hardly." He looked out to sea again. "Something doesn't seem right. All the boats are returning together, and it's late in the day. Usually some are in by now."

A weight settled in Muri's chest. Somehow this would involve her.

When they reached the village square, Jack asked if she'd return to the grange, but she wanted to accompany him down to the wharf to make sure everything was all right.

They arrived at the wharf as the first of the boats were docking. The boats darted in off the sea like they'd crash into the dock, but at the final moment, they'd turn to glide up alongside it, and the sail would flap and drop into the boat. Avianna, the woman who'd helped Muri on her first day—the one who'd supposedly consorted with Strombidae—was there. She hurried from one boat to the next, gripping her tools tightly to her chest. Even without her words clear, her voice rang with alarm.

"There aren't any fish," Jack murmured.

"What?"

"The boats are empty."

Muri's dread grew as she followed Jack down the ramp to the docks. They approached the cluster of boats that had arrived.

"What's going on?" Jack called out, and Avianna turned to him.

"None of them have caught anything. They've been out all day and not a single fish." Avianna's voice was bewildered, and she turned back and forth as if looking for an explanation. The fish-catchers on the docks drifted between boats, talking in low voices with frowns on their faces.

Muri slipped her hand onto Jack's arm and he turned to her. As soon as he did, understanding dawned in his eyes.

"Avi," he said. "I'll get Hyacinth. She may be able to find out if something has happened under the water."

"Thank you, Jack," she said. She gave Muri a curious glance and smiled before turning back to the boats.

Jack and Muri hurried back across the wharf. "Do you have any idea what this is?" he said.

"It feels like a threat," she said. "But no, I've never seen anything that could make something like this happen. What can Hyacinth do?"

"She can ask the sea creatures what's going on."

Muri remembered Gray's jokes about Hyacinth directing flocks of birds to attack. Could she really communicate with other creatures? Jack wouldn't think so if it weren't true.

They jogged up the hill in silence.

Hyacinth was working on a bouquet when they entered her shop. Her smile faded the moment she saw them. "What's wrong?"

"We need your help at the docks, Hy. Please. Something is wrong in the bay."

Hyacinth slipped her enchanted blade off her fingers as she said the spell to protect it. She gathered the stems of the flowers lying on the counter and dropped them into a bucket. She reached for a shawl and came out from the back.

"Gray's making deliveries. I'll have him meet us there."

"Can you send him messages like you can the birds?" Muri asked, wide-eyed.

"Not exactly. I can ask the birds and others to pass on messages to other fairies. Gray isn't . . . experienced with animals, but since he and I are twins, it seems to work."

Hyacinth ushered them out the door. She rushed them through the village square, moving faster than Muri had imagined possible. They were halfway down the hill when Gray popped out of a side lane. He had a bucket of flowers in one arm and an empty bucket swinging from his other hand. He joined them hurrying down the hill.

"Causing trouble, Muri?" he said, but Hyacinth shot him a look and he grew serious. "It's that bad?"

"Something's definitely not right," Hyacinth said. "The gulls are saying they caught nothing in the bay since dawn. But the ones that headed out farther found plenty of fish."

Muri scrutinized Hyacinth. Was she making it up or could she really communicate with seagulls out in the bay? Jack's and Gray's faces grew grim.

They arrived again at the waterfront. Things had grown more frantic. All the boats were in now, and word had gone around that the fish-catchers had no fish. The townspeople who'd come to shop were crowding the fish market, trying to get answers. Avianna stood at the top of the docks with an older man, blocking anyone from going down to the boats, where the fish-catchers were rolling their sails in silence.

Muri, Jack, and Gray trailed Hyacinth to the edge of the wharf. She lowered herself to sit on the edge with her legs dangling off. She went silent, staring out at the bay with her eyes focused in the distance. Avianna joined them without saying a word.

Hyacinth blinked a few times and turned to the others. "There were mermen in the bay," she said. "They scared the fish away."

Avianna's hand went to her chest. "Mermen? Like Murkel? How do you know?"

"A dolphin saw them." Hyacinth looked down at her lap. She wasn't telling them everything.

"Are they still here?" Avianna asked.

"I'm not sure."

Gray stepped forward. "We might be able to ask the creature to speak to them and find out why they're here. We'll find out what's going on."

Avianna thanked them and hurried back to the docks. The others exchanged glances, but no one spoke. Beside her, Jack stepped closer, his warmth against her arm.

"Out with it," Gray said.

Hyacinth let out a long exhale. "The mermen came before dawn, the dolphin said. They made a line and herded the fish out to sea, and they've barricaded the mouth of the bay. She says they're swimming back and forth, chasing back any creature who tries to swim closer to land.

"I can't hear any other swimming creatures at all, only crabs on the sand. The dolphin says she's only in the bay where I can reach her because she skirted over the mermen when she saw them and swam away fast. She's been resting in the bay a few days and didn't want to leave."

"Can you really have her talk to the mermen?" Muri asked. "I've never heard of anyone in Glorypool speaking to the sea creatures."

"They can't," Hyacinth said. "And even if they could, we wouldn't ask them to. They're terrified of the merfolk." She turned to Gray.

"I was buying time," he said, shrugging. "I didn't want anyone to panic."

The crowd had begun to stir since Avianna had carried Hyacinth's news to the fish-catchers. Groups of people spoke together, and all around, eyes kept darting toward them. The villagers had already been fearful of the merpeople, based only on rumored sightings. This would put them over the edge. And if they found out she was one of them . . .

"I'll have to go talk to the mermen," Muri said.

"Muri, you can't," Jack said, and his arm went around her.

Gray extended a hand to Hyacinth and pulled her to her feet. "Let's just get out of here." He picked up his buckets from the ground and headed back into the lane.

Once they were away from the wharf, they stopped in the deserted street.

"I have to go," Muri said.

Jack slid his other arm around her and pulled her against his chest. He was so tall his chin rested on top of her head.

"It's not safe. They could drag you back to Glorypool and we'd never see you again."

"But if I don't, they could keep this up and starve the village.

They could do something worse." She hated to hurt Jack, but she had to make him see how dangerous the mermen were. She twisted her head to look at him. "What if they start tipping the boats, Jack, and drowning the fish-catchers?"

His arms tightened around her and he didn't reply. He was probably thinking of his parents.

"We have food other than fish," Gray said. "There are plenty of grains in the store sheds, and last autumn's root vegetables, and spring vegetables have been planted. The goats and things are about to give birth, so we'll have milk again soon. And some of the villagers hunt."

"We'd have to stop the fish-catchers from going out," Hyacinth said. "We'd have to tell them everything. I'm not sure how gracious they'd be." She didn't have to mention Muri's name.

"Margery and the others know," Muri said, "and the villagers will figure it out soon enough, whether you tell them or not."

"Just wait, Muri," Jack said. "Maybe the mermen will come back on land and we can talk to them. Or if you go to them, I could go out on the bay with you."

There was no way in the ten seas Muri would let that happen. She'd sink Jack's boat herself if he tried to leave the docks with the mermen lurking. But she didn't say anything.

"The villagers are sure to hold a meeting," Gray said. "They love meetings. We can wait to hear what they're saying."

"They won't welcome me when they learn the truth," Muri said.

"I won't let them hurt you," Jack said. "Just don't go yet."

"Okay," Muri said. She could wait a little longer. But she'd never let Jack go out on the bay, not with Bull and his henchmen out there.

But how could she stop the other villagers from going onto the water?

And what did the mermen want? The more she thought about it, the more the truth sank in. Bull was sending her a message: he wanted her to return home. She was one of Strombidae's chosen wives, to be returned to the pot for another merman to choose. If she left Glorypool and lived safely on land, the other mermaids might get ideas. Bull would never allow her to slip away.

The only way to stop the mermen was for her to leave with them.

At least all the fish-catchers had made it safely in off the water today. They were safe for the night. But come morning . . .

Jack released her from his arms, and the four of them walked slowly back up to the village square. Gray and Hyacinth left them at the door to the grange home. As soon as they were alone, Jack's arms went around her again. She snuggled her face in his chest and inhaled his scent.

"Come home with me," he whispered.

She clung to him, squeezing her eyes shut tight to stop her tears.

"Come stay with me."

She nodded.

Jack waited outside as she entered the grange home. Most of the residents were out in the park, likely dozing in the late afternoon sun, and Hilda might still be sleeping at the castle. Margery was kneading dough in the kitchen. Muri told her some of what had happened at the wharf—that the fish-catchers had had a poor day with no catch. She left out the bit about mermen surrounding the bay. She saw no sense in alarming the grange home residents when she planned to solve the problem by morning.

Margery grinned when Muri said she was going to stay with Jack and hurried her on. Muri gathered her satchel from her room. When she came down the stairs, Margery waited in the front hall. She held out a bundle of fabric.

"We wanted you to have a dress of your own," Margery said. "A nice one, that is. The ladies sewed this for you today."

Muri's eyes pricked with tears as she touched the fabric, woven with flowers as Hyacinth's dress had been.

"Put it on before you go, if you like," Margery said. "Let's make sure it fits."

When Muri reappeared in the hallway wearing the new dress, Hilda had joined Margery. They exclaimed over her. How had she ever believed the humans were beasts? She reached for the ladies and they shared a hug.

"I'll never forget you," Muri said.

"Of course you won't," Margery said, pulling back. "You'll be visiting us, I hope, even if you sleep at Jack's."

Hilda smirked. "You mean, even if she 'sleeps' at Jack's," she said. Muri blushed as the ladies giggled and hugged her again. They walked her to the door and let her out into the evening, where Jack waited.

Chapter 14

༄ ✴ ༄

Jack gripped Muri's hand tightly as they walked to his home. The village lane ended as the cobblestones gave way to the packed dirt path. It was the path Muri had walked when she'd entered the village—the path that passed the first cottage she'd come to, the one where Jack lived. The sun had sunk to the treetops as clouds moved into the sky, and the gusting wind off the ocean was growing chill.

They passed the scattered homes on the outskirts of the village until only the one cottage remained ahead. As they neared, a black spot in front of the door stirred, uncoiling itself into the dog. Without standing, he stretched and sat upright to watch them approach. Shadows covered the flat stones but they still warmed Muri's feet when she stepped onto the patio. The dog perked up one ear and thumped his tail, his fur ruffling in the breeze.

"That's all the welcome I get?" Jack asked softly. He let go of Muri's hand to kneel down and rub the dog's head. After a few strokes, the dog turned to her.

"This is Muri," Jack said, scrubbing his nails under the dog's chin. "Muri, this is Captain."

Muri knelt, too, and Captain lifted a paw and tapped her knee.

"He wants you to shake paws," Jack said, demonstrating. "It's a thing humans do with dogs."

After Muri had shaken the dog's paw, Captain lumbered to his feet, stretched again, and turned to the cottage door. Jack opened it, Captain let himself in first, and Jack motioned Muri in.

As she entered the cottage, the rushing sounds of the outdoors cut off. It had been quiet in the grange home, but the change was more noticeable here where the wind and ocean crashed right outside the door. The stone walls blocked the wind completely, and the last rays of sunlight pierced the dark interior through the western windows and shone on the far wall. A table stood at the back of the room with a hearth behind it. A loft stretched across the room over the back half, with steps up one wall to access it.

After Jack shut the door, Captain whined. Jack took something off a shelf beside the door and held it out. The object was some kind of animal bone. Captain took it gingerly in his mouth, walked in a circle on the rug inside the door, lay down, and began gnawing at the bone.

"Do you want something to eat?" Jack asked.

Muri shook her head. He came to stand beside her in the center of the room. The late sun caught on his hair and cast stark shadows on his face. Faintly, the sounds of the rolling sea seeped into the room.

Jack touched her arm. "I just want to lie with you. Would that be okay?"

Muri looked up into his eyes, the deep brown tinted orange from the sun. She nodded.

She followed him to the steps against the wall. They were steeper than the ones at the grange home, and without a railing, she could careen off the side. He stepped back to let her climb first, and when she clamped her fingertips onto the stones of the wall, moving slowly up, he put his arm out as if he would catch her should she fall.

At the top, Muri stepped onto the loft. A woven rug covered the wooden floor, and at the back under the sloping ceiling on the floor was a mattress covered with blankets—like the bed she'd slept on at the grange home but wider and without the wooden posts lifting it up. Other than a low wooden chest, the rest of the space was empty. A faint light reached in from the setting sun.

Jack came behind her and nudged her away from the edge with his hands on her shoulders. She let him walk her to the bed, where he had to duck his head to remain standing. He kissed the side of her neck before gently pushing her down to kneel on the mattress.

Muri crawled forward. Behind her, he wiggled out of his trousers and came after her on his knees. He pulled back the blankets, tugging them from underneath her, and she fell into the cool bedding. He followed her and pulled the blankets over them as they lay down together.

Muri nestled into his chest, and his arms held her. He was solid—his chest, but also his person. The way he didn't explode in anger or fight for dominance. The way he interacted with the other fish-catchers, how he deferred to Avianna at the docks, his friendship with Gray and Hyacinth—she loved all those things about him. And the way he treated her, like an equal. He was always considering her needs and asking to make sure she was all right. She wanted to stay with him. She wanted him to be her husband, or whatever the human word was—a forever mate.

But she couldn't have him. Bull would see to that.

She'd been on land four days. That meant in three more days, when Strombidae didn't return to Glorypool, his reign would officially end. Other mermen might fight Bull for the throne, but Bull would win. The mermen had already been taking sides before she'd left. No one wanted to hold out for Strombidae and risk offending the future merking. If Bull already had enough supporters to clear the Woodglen bay of fish, few, if any, would challenge him.

She didn't know what he'd do to her if she returned to Glorypool, but she had to go. She couldn't let him hurt the village fish-catchers. It wasn't only Jack she wanted to protect. The villagers had done nothing wrong—they didn't deserve to starve or to be pulled under the sea to drown. If any were killed when she could stop it, it would be her fault.

The humans were docile, not beasts as she'd been warned. She couldn't imagine them defending themselves from the mermen, especially not out on the water. And everyone she'd met—Gray and Hyacinth, Avianna, Margery—had been kind to her. She had to appease Bull to keep them all safe.

The blankets had warmed around her, and Jack gave off heat like molten lava. She tightened her arm around him. She liked his bed even better than the bath he'd put her in that afternoon.

His hand stroked her hair under the edge of the blanket and smoothed over the top of her head where it was exposed to the cool air, and he leaned in to kiss her forehead.

"I can't lose you," he murmured.

"You have me."

"I didn't think I'd ever care for anyone this way again," he continued, holding her close with his lips against her hair. "I didn't want to. I got up each day and went on the water. I went to the pub or came home to tend the garden and play with Captain. And then you showed up. You've knocked me off balance. And without you I don't think I'd want to get back up."

"It's the same for me," she whispered back. "There's never been anyone like you."

"You mean, anyone with legs?" She could hear from his voice that he was teasing.

She moved back enough to smile at him. They rested their heads on the pillow, facing each other. "The mermen have legs when they're on the island."

"You mentioned the island before. You said the spring star rises over it."

"Yes. Glorypool is under the water at the base of the sloping land, and above it, the island rises out of the sea. It was volcanic once. There are fissures below the surface where heat flows out, and somewhere up on the island is a hot spring, although I've never seen that. Only the merking is allowed to go there."

"Is the whole island warm?"

"Yes, it's a jungle. The flowers are different than the ones here—tropical plants like orchids and hibiscus. There are banana trees and vines strong enough to hang from. We cut them to use in Glorypool. And we harvest bananas, but they don't last under the water. You have to eat them on the island."

"What are bananas like?"

"They have a thick yellow peel, and you pop it open and peel it back, and the fruit is inside. It's long, like, um . . ." Suddenly, all she could think about was his erect penis, the way she'd seen it in the water that afternoon before she'd covered it with her lips.

Jack's lips pressed together to stop a laugh. "Like a carrot root?"

"Yes! Like a carrot. Only wider and softer and curved." Talking about bananas and carrots was making her flush. Muri tried to think of anything else. Something unpleasant, to stop her from reaching across to Jack and delving her hands down into his undershorts.

"Most of the mermen don't make it past the beach," she said.

"Why is that?"

"The merwomen do the harvesting so it's us who go into the jungle. The jungle's not bad but sometimes there are monkeys up in the trees. No one likes them even though they keep their distance."

"What's a monkey?"

"It's an animal. They're sort of human-like but with long arms and legs that can grip the trees, and they have fur all over, and they shriek like anything."

"Ugh."

"I know. They're awful. The mermen come to the island only to . . . well, to spawn. Gray says I shouldn't call it that, but that's what it is. They usually do it on the beach and return to the water."

"Do the merwomen have many children?"

"No. We still call it spawning, but for the past twenty seasons, no one has been allowed to have merchildren. Food is sparse and it's hard enough to get by. So the merking made a rule."

"How do you stop from having merchildren?"

"After the spawning, the merwoman returns to the water. Once she forms a tail, no merchild will result."

"You said the merwomen harvest. Fruits and nuts?"

"And seaweed. And we catch fish with nets."

"Do the mermen hunt larger prey?"

Muri scoffed. "Hardly. They play sports and drink phyta—like your ale—and fight each other. They say they offer protection, but now that I've been away from the settlement and across the Cold Sea, I suspect protecting the borders is hardly needed. I've seen no creatures that might harm the merpeople. I think the mermen offer nothing."

Jack was silent. What was he thinking? Was he disappointed to hear her talk about spawning? He must've known she'd been with mermen before.

His lips parted. "You can't go back to that."

"I don't want to. But I might not have a choice."

"We'll find a way."

"Jack," she said, looking in his eyes. "Tonight I just want to be with you. The way it's called here—tumbling." She whispered the last word.

His eyes crinkled in a smile. "You do, do you?"

"More than anything."

He stroked her hair back from her face.

She dropped her gaze and fiddled with the front of his shirt. "Do, um, do you want to?"

"Tumble you?" His voice had dropped low.

"Yes."

He leaned close to her. "More than anything," he whispered.

Muri smiled, pressing herself into him. He kept stroking her hair, and his legs rubbed against hers. She undid a few buttons and tugged on his shirt, and he leaned up to pull it off. As he settled back down, Muri ran her fingers over his chest, leaning in to kiss his skin.

He was watching her. "I have one request."

"Mm?"

"Please don't call it 'spawning' when you're with me. Whether there's a child or not, that's the wrong word for it."

She laughed before pulling on his arm, trying to roll beneath him. He resisted.

"Don't you want to be on top of me?" she asked.

"With our height difference, you'd have my chest in your face."

"It's okay. It can't be helped."

"Can't be helped?" Jack studied her face.

What was she missing?

Jack's lips pressed tight. "All these trips to your island. Were you on the bottom every time?" He did sound disappointed now.

Muri turned her face away.

But Jack's hand caught her cheek and turned her face back toward him. She stared at his neck. His voice softened. "I'm sorry I said it that way. I'm not angry with you, love."

Love.

"I just hate what's been done to you."

"It wasn't bad."

"But it wasn't good, was it?"

Muri risked a glance up at his face. His eyes shone. She shook her head.

Love, he'd called her.

"How else is it done?" she asked. "M-Making love."

He smiled. "Can I show you?"

Muri smiled back.

Jack's hand slid down her neck, down her body to her hip. He pushed her away from him, onto her back. Both his arms snaked around her and he pulled her over, turning her into him with her back pressed against his stomach. She couldn't imagine what was coming. Hopefully Jack could.

"This is called 'spooning,'" he whispered behind her ear.

"Spooning?"

"Uh-huh." His arm beneath her neck wrapped around her

front like an iron band, but his other arm let go and his hand landed on her leg. He kissed behind her ear as his hand slid up, pulling her dress up with it. When he tugged the dress's fabric up over her bottom, she felt him hard inside his undershorts against her.

His hand slid back down her leg, and he moved it inside her thighs and began slowly sliding it up again. "Is this all right?"

Muri tried to form a response, but his trailing hand made it hard to think. At last she just whimpered.

"Tell me what you want," he said, his hand slowing.

Muri moved her leg aside, giving him access. "Keep going."

His fingers moved up against her, touching her warm center. He rubbed on her in front first, in slow circles, and slid his fingers back where they could press into her. She felt how wet she was by how his fingers slid easily into her, opening her.

"Keep going," she murmured again.

His fingers slid slowly inside her and she shuddered. Her body closed tightly around them as Jack explored, massaging the inside of her one way and the other. But it wasn't enough. As far as he stroked, it wasn't enough.

"More," she said, unable to form coherent thoughts.

"You want more inside you?" He swirled his fingers and it peaked her desire.

"Yes."

His fingers withdrew slowly, leaving her empty and yearning, and he pressed his erection against her bottom. "You want this?"

"Yes."

He moved back only far enough to pull down his undershorts. His knuckles brushed her bottom with delicious promise. He held her tightly in his one arm, and the rough fabric of his clothing scraped her bottom as he pushed his shorts down. When he lifted up his hip to remove them, his hard penis pressed into the cleft of her bottom, and she couldn't help pushing back, trying to get him further forward. He chuckled as he kicked his legs to get the shorts off.

She tried to turn, to face him and allow him in, but his one arm held her fast. Then he was back against her, warm and soft and hard all at once. He guided his erection to the place where his fingers had been and pressed it against her. They fit together, with his tip pushed into her slick opening.

"Okay?" he whispered. It was more than okay. It was perfect. She pressed her bottom against him, and he slid inside her. Muri gasped as he filled her, solid and firm.

His arm came over her, pressing her belly and hugging her into him, and his fingers slid down her bare skin to land between her legs again. He curled his fingers into her, rubbing her as he began to work himself out and in behind her. The sensations built. She tingled from his touch on her front, satiated only by his erection pulling out and thrusting into her again, each time a shock inside her as he rubbed against places she'd never been touched.

His rhythm grew faster until his hand slipped off her front to grab her thigh, tugging it back to open her wider. He held her fast, driving into her until he cursed softly and his rhythm fell apart as he jerked against her. He panted behind her and went still.

But a moment later, he moved again, returning his hand to rest on her front between her legs.

"Sorry," he murmured into her hair. "I, uh, got a bit distracted. D'you still want this?"

She clenched her muscles around his shaft. "Yes."

He circled his fingers on her gently, pressing himself against her bottom to stay seated inside her as long as possible. With the stillness of him filling her, she focused on the sensations from his fingers. The way they danced over her was too light. She moaned softly and reached down to press them against her, and he pushed harder. She let the growing euphoria take her, building as her breasts tingled beneath the strength of his arm pinned across them. He shifted that arm so his hand landed firmly on her breast. She dug her fingernails into his arm, hanging on. He rubbed faster, a perfect pace and fast like the patter of rain on the leaves of the jungle. Heat swelled inside her. When he bit the side of her neck, she cried out in ecstasy as the sensations exploded. He kept biting her, his fingers rubbing her as she twisted against him, crying out as she spasmed in his arms.

When the spasms subsided, he wrapped her up tight. She lay with his presence around her, invading every pore of her skin. Her hot back was damp through her dress, and he stayed inside her, although not as fully as he had been.

"So that's one way," Jack whispered in her ear.

Muri forced his arms to loosen as she pulled herself off him, letting his penis slip out of her. She wiggled onto her back and gazed up at him.

"What's another?"

Jack laughed. His eyes glinted in the remaining light. "You're ready for another turn already?"

Muri blushed and tried to look away, but he was stroking her hair away from her face and held it toward him.

His thumb traced over her eyebrow. "Ten seas, Muri," he said, his voice tortured, "seeing you with that look on your face makes me hard for you all over again."

She nudged him down there with her knee, and he laughed again. But when she tried to pull his arm around her like it had been before, he resisted.

"This time I want you on top," he said, grinning at her. He rolled, pulling her with him until he lay beneath her, her belly pressed somewhere above his. He smoothed his hand down her body to her thigh and pulled her leg out to straddle his body. "Sit up," he said, but the way he said it was gentle, not a command. "I want to see you."

Muri pushed herself up to sit atop him. "Like this?"

"Just like that."

"But this is—" She didn't know how to finish. How could she tell him no merman would ever lie in such a submissive position?

"This is called 'going to market,' if you were wondering," he said, smiling up at her as if lying beneath her were the most natural position in the world.

"Going to *market*? Like, to buy fish?"

Jack laughed, rumbling under her legs. "I think the idea is, I'm a horse and you're riding me to market."

Muri nearly fell off him. "You're a *horse*?" He bucked beneath her a few times, grinning. "You don't mind?"

"Mind?" His head came off the pillow as he lifted his brow. "Why would I mind having you on top of me? Especially knowing how much you like pulling your dress off unexpectedly." He lay back, closed his eyes, and crossed his arms behind his head. The movement nudged his hips up against her.

Muri smiled at his feigned indifference. She undid the sash at the waist of the dress and reached around to undo the few buttons. She paused when she had it undone, until his eyes opened in slits. His pupils were deep with something, lust or hunger or something else she didn't understand. She lifted the dress up and over her head.

Her hand went to the knife belted at her waist. "I forgot about this. I'm glad it didn't stab you." She fumbled to untie the belt.

But his hand stopped hers. "Leave it."

"But—"

"It can't stab me from up there. And it makes you even sexier."

"Sexy? A knife?"

"Like you're going to ride me until you've had enough and then cut my heart out."

"Cut your *heart* out?"

His hands came to rest on her thighs. "No, I'm teasing. It makes you look like you're in control." His smile faded. "Like you're powerful, and I'm your servant."

"You like that?"

"Sometimes."

"I'm not used to being the one in control."

"I know," he said gently. "What do you think so far? You're certainly beautiful up there, and you look like a queen."

She blushed at his admiration. "I like it up here." Her fingers splayed across his flat stomach and curled around his sides as she leaned forward slightly. He was hard again—his erection bumped against her bottom. She lifted herself up, hovering over him and closing her eyes. Anticipating him inside her practically put her over the top. As she lowered her body, Jack's hand left her thigh to guide himself inside her.

Muri sighed as she sank all the way down on him. For a moment she reveled in how he filled her. Her eyes opened a sliver. Jack's head was back, with his eyes closed and his arms again folded behind his head. She was on her own.

"I've never ridden a horse," Muri said.

Jack smiled. "Do what's best for you," he murmured. His eyes slit open too. "Watching you feel good is half the fun."

"What if I'm not sure?"

"Try something and if it doesn't work, try something else. You can't do anything wrong, love." His eyes fell closed. "I promise." He stretched his whole body, bucking his hips again and pressing harder into her.

Muri closed her eyes and felt him inside her. She rose up on her knees, lifting off him and sliding back down. She smoothed her hands across his stomach until she held his sides. She pushed herself up with her arms this time and let herself sink onto him again.

She leaned forward on the bed until she found the place where she could rub her front against him as she moved up and down. It felt fine but not quite right.

Muri paused and followed her instinct. She moved off Jack, turned herself around, and climbed back on. This time when she slid onto him, he rubbed her right where she wanted it.

She began moving up and down with her hands pressed against his thighs, thrusting him into herself. Each time she stroked him inside her, she wound tighter. Ten seas, moving on him was magnificent, like every stolen moment of her life rolled into one. She kept going, almost over the edge but never all the way, until her knees began to tremble and she had to pause. She sank back, sitting on him with her knees bent at his sides.

Her attention returned to the darkened room around her and Jack's breathing rising and falling gently beneath her. She'd just about forgotten him.

"That's called 'going home from market,'" Jack said behind her. His fingertips touched her back and traced down her skin. He gripped her hips.

"Going home feels good," Muri panted, "but I'm about worn out."

He chuckled. "You want me to get us home?"

"Yes."

Jack sat up, keeping himself inside her. He twisted a bit, tucking his legs up and sitting back on his heels. She settled onto his thighs again with her knees outside his legs.

"Here you go," he said, and he gently pushed her down to sprawl over his legs. Her face dropped onto the bed and she put out her forearms to catch herself. His hands smoothed up her back to circle her neck. He leaned forward and kissed her spine as he slid his fingertips back down and reached around to cup her breasts.

"Do all the mermaids have short hair?" he asked with his face nuzzling her neck.

"No, I—oh!"

He'd begun kneading her breasts.

"Hmm?" he said. He planted kisses across her shoulder blades as his hips began to throb up and down, pushing him into her in time with his squeezing.

"We're not supposed to cut it," she panted, wriggling her bottom against Jack's belly. His hands were magic. "But I did."

He gave one final squeeze and sat up, bringing his hands to her waist. Her belt tightened and released and he dragged it off her body and tossed it aside. His fingers grazed over the place where her knife had been.

"You cut it off?"

She sighed in the pause of his gentle thrusts. "Yes."

His fingers dug into her hips. "I like it when you don't follow the rules," he growled, and he went up on his knees, carrying her body with him. As her body tilted, her weight shifted onto her arms. Jack held her hips steady. She leaned up on her forearms, bracing herself against the mattress and pressing her bottom back into him. Her knees did not quite reach the bed.

Jack nudged a pillow over with his knee, tucking it beneath her left leg. She sank onto it and he let go with one hand to reach another pillow, propping it under her right leg. His hands returned to her hips, pulling her back onto him tightly. With the pillows, their bodies lined up perfectly.

"What's this one called?" Muri asked.

"You don't want to know," Jack said, and he slid himself back and gently pushed into her again. "Are you okay down there?"

"Yes," Muri gasped, closing her eyes. "Just do it harder."

His laugh rumbled against the insides of her thighs as he pulled out and thrust back in. He drove into her again, setting up a cadence. He pushed her body away from him and pulled her back to meet his thrusts.

Lying with her face mashed into Jack's bed was awkward but also somehow wonderful. Her body held firmly in his grip was singing. When she cracked open her eyes and twisted enough to glimpse him towering above her, the sight of him unraveling as his thrusts grew faster peaked her arousal. A few more thrusts and she was thrashing against the mattress. Jack held onto her hips, driving with his steady rhythm through her chaos. He kept going even after she stopped, and she waited for him to fall over the edge after her. He did it with a soft moan, his fingers digging into her skin.

His grip slid down onto the front of her thighs, and he leaned over her and kissed the center of her back. He drew himself out of her body and helped her untangle herself and lie down. He knocked aside the pillows and lay beside her, pulling her into him.

"Sleep in my arms every night, Muri," he murmured against her hair.

Tears pricked her eyes. She held him tighter, hoping he'd think it meant yes.

Chapter 15

ఔ✱ఠ

Muri watched Jack's sleeping face in the dim light, hoping to sear it into her memory forever. She'd once told him memories were enough for her, but she'd have given a winter's supply of food to have some token of his, something she could hold in her hand to keep him with her.

A few raindrops pattered against the roof. Turning away, she eased herself off the mattress and crept from Jack's bed in the dark. She hadn't dared to sleep, fearing she'd doze off in his arms and not wake until the sun was high and the fish-catchers all out in the bay.

She found her knife belt and silently tied it around her waist. She crawled to the top of the steps and gently slid down them on her bottom, not trusting herself on her feet on the narrow stair. Captain lifted his head to watch her from his rug by the door.

Another patter of rain hit the windows on the ocean side. Moonlight shone in the opposite window, lighting the room enough to help her find her satchel. She pulled on the sack-like dress Lotti had given her in Glorypool. She'd left her beautiful new dress up in the loft where it had fallen when she'd pulled it off—when she'd been sitting atop Jack and he'd called her a queen. She shoved the thought from her mind—she couldn't think of their lovemaking. She'd intended to leave the dress as soon as Margery had given it to her—it would only be ruined in Glorypool.

And maybe, she didn't know how, but maybe someday she'd be able to return to Woodglen and wear it again.

Muri carefully opened the cottage door. A gust of cool wind

burst in the opening. Before it could blow into the loft and give her away, she squeezed herself through. She was barely able to fit without disturbing Captain. She shut the door behind her.

Muri stood on the patio in the wind and let herself sob once, tears spilling down her cheeks. She wanted to go back in—to climb up to Jack and crawl back into his warm arms where she belonged. This cottage could be her home, one where she'd be happy. She would never belong with anyone else.

But if she went back inside, he wouldn't let her go, and the entire village would be in danger. If she tried to leave later, he'd follow her out into the bay, where the mermen could harm him. By leaving now, she could keep everyone safe.

She took a deep breath to steady herself and wiped aside her tears. With one last touch to his door, she turned away.

Muri crept off the patio and hastened on toward the village. The moon was already in the western sky, moving toward the treetops as dawn neared. Moonlight limned the black clouds scudding across the starlit sky, and a few stray raindrops pricked her face. The horizon over the sea was dark as pitch and filled with storm clouds.

She followed the deserted lanes through the town, from the wharf up the hill and past the street where she and Jack had gone on their first date to The White Pony. Even the cats were absent at this hour—or maybe the hint of rain kept them hidden.

She came out in the village square. It felt like home here, and she had to blink back more tears as she skirted around the park on the side away from the grange home. Where was Strombidae? She hadn't seen him since he'd slunk away from the docks after Bull's arrival.

As she rounded the trees, the welcome light of the flower shop greeted her. Thank the seas they were up early. She'd hated the idea of leaving without telling anyone why she had to.

She hurried over and opened the door. The idyllic smell of the flowers overwhelmed her as she stepped inside. Hyacinth looked up from the pots she had lined up on the counter. She held a shovel of soil poised over them.

"Muri!" She lowered the shovel and came around to the front.

"I have to go, Hyacinth," Muri said. "I don't want to, but the mermen won't stop as long as I stay. I know them. They won't accept a mermaid leaving them for somewhere better. They won't leave your village alone until I go back with them."

Hyacinth frowned. She opened her mouth to speak, closed it, and shook her head. She pulled Muri in for a hug. For a long moment, they stood in silence as Hyacinth held her.

"Does Jack know you're leaving?" Hyacinth asked, stepping back.

Muri shook her head as her eyes filled with tears. This time she couldn't stop them. "I couldn't, Hy," she said, hiccupping as she sobbed. She wiped her cheeks but more tears came. "I love him. He'd never let me go. And they'd kill him."

"We could keep him off the water," Hyacinth said.

"But everyone's in danger. As soon as any of them go out today, they'll be in danger. Gray told me what happened ten seasons ago—that the merpeople drowned someone. I can't let it happen again."

Hyacinth rubbed Muri's arms. "Let me wake Gray. He'll want to say goodbye."

"Don't. It's too hard. Tell him goodbye for me. Tell him I'm so grateful for his help, and for his friendship." At the last word, she lost control, and Hyacinth pulled her into another hug as she wept.

When she'd calmed, Muri reached into her pocket and withdrew Lotti's shell. "Take it," she said, pressing it into Hyacinth's hand. "It was stolen from the fairies. And it would make me happy to know you have it—like we were still connected."

Hyacinth tilted her head as she took the shell.

"It's a pair," Muri explained. "The other is in Glorypool, and when you have them in the water, you can speak between them. I brought it with me to land so I could contact the other mermaids, but I lost it when I arrived and Jack found it."

Hyacinth cradled the shell in her hand.

Muri blinked one last time at her friend standing in the room filled with striking flowers. She turned to the door. She inhaled the floral scent and stepped out into the night.

She hurried down the hill to the wharf, not trusting herself to keep going if she stopped to think. She crossed the open space as the clouds rolled in from the sea and raindrops spattered on the ground. By the time she'd walked out to the end of the docks, the rain fell steadily, splashing off the water and dripping down the sides of the wooden pile that held the end of the dock in place. Muri stood by *Alina's Dream*.

She pulled the dress over her head and stuffed it into her satchel. For a moment, the moon cast her shadow onto the water, dark on the rippling light of the waves. Then the clouds swallowed the moon and its light went out.

Muri didn't look back. She dove into the water, filling her lungs as her legs disappeared into her shimmering tail.

She swam to the edge of the harbor and out into the bay. Her eyes quickly adjusted to the dim light as she dove deeper. Nothing stirred in the water, not a single fish, only the gentle waving of the eelgrass covering the sandy bottom. The sand turned into the darker muck of the seafloor as she swam farther. She skimmed the bottom for a while, searching for life among the rocks and streamers of seaweed reaching up from the deep. She moved closer to the surface, searching there, but the mermen truly had scared every last fish away.

Overhead, above the surface, the sky lightened. If only she could be back at the grange home, watching the light appear in the window of her cozy bedroom. Or back in Jack's arms as the sun came up—what would that have been like? Muri shook her head, shaking away the thought. She couldn't let herself think about what could have been.

Muri slowed as she neared the mouth of the bay. She scanned ahead, not wanting to be caught off guard. At last she spotted a figure hovering in the water halfway up to the surface. She moved in carefully. From the way his form bobbed slowly up and down, he was probably dozing. A beard drifted under his chin, and his long dark hair was shaggy as it floated around him. It was Turridae, one of Bull's followers.

Muri stopped twenty swishes away. She wouldn't be able to go back once he saw her.

She whistled, the piercing noise muffled by the water. How strange it all sounded, now that she'd been above the surface for days.

Turr's eyes opened, and when they turned on her, his lips pressed tightly. In a flash, he was beside her with his fingers clamped around her wrist. Muri's anger roiled inside at the way he touched her—how had she ever thought being grabbed that way was normal? But she held herself back from resisting his grip. She intended to return to Glorypool with the mermen. She'd do better if she didn't show any resistance. She didn't need to fight Turr over the way he grabbed her arm. She'd keep her knowledge about how to fight a secret.

"He knew you'd be back," Turr said with the deep, guttural sound of speech under water.

"Let me talk to him," Muri said.

Turr exhaled through his nose, narrowing his eyes. "Don't give me orders."

"Fine," Muri said, rolling her eyes. "Do whatever you want." She propped her free arm on her hip and stared into the distance, her tail fins flipping back and forth.

Turr hesitated. Muri guessed he didn't want to do what she'd asked, but of course that's exactly what he'd been ordered to do.

"Come on," he said at last and pulled her through the water after him. She made him drag her instead of swishing her tail to help.

When another figure appeared in the gloom, Turr called out

and the figure jerked awake. A moment later, Bull was with them. His dark eyes bored into Muri's as his hair swirled around his head. She didn't look away.

"Leave us," Bull said, not taking his eyes off Muri. Turr dropped her wrist, and the water churned as he swam away.

Bull eyed her warily as if she might attack. He wouldn't likely forget she'd fought back against him on the wharf. She'd have to be careful to avoid giving him any reason to watch her more closely. At least he wouldn't have told any of the other mermen about being kneed in the groin by a merwoman.

"I should punish you for your behavior," Bull said.

What had Bull witnessed? He'd seen her talking to Strombidae on the docks and nothing more. She'd refused to go with Bull, but he hadn't been her king when she did it.

"I haven't done anything wrong," Muri said quietly.

Bull didn't respond.

"Besides," she continued, "Strombidae told me the truth about the merking. He has no magic. The tricks in his vault are old fairy spells, and there's barely any left."

Bull's face glowered even darker, but he didn't argue. He must have heard Strombidae tell her the truth on the docks two nights ago. Otherwise, he'd be contradicting her.

"I could tell everyone," Muri said.

"Then I should kill you."

Muri's heart hammered, but she steeled herself against the threat in his voice. "If you kill me, who'll back you up when you tell the merpeople that Strombidae is dried out? No one will believe you when everyone knows how badly you want the throne."

"It doesn't matter what's happened to him. If he's not back in two days, he forfeits the throne."

"But you've been searching for him. I bet everyone knows that. Who's to say you didn't find him and kill him to stop him returning? That wouldn't go over well in Glorypool."

"I found him, and he was dried out," Bull said through his

teeth, his voice rising. His tail swished angrily back and forth. "That's the truth I need."

"Did anyone else see him?"

Bull frowned at her but didn't respond.

"He's hiding from you, isn't he?" she asked. "You can't find him to prove he's dried out. You need me. No one will believe Strombidae is dried out, not if you're the only one who says so."

"Fine. What do you want in return for your testimony about Strombidae?"

"I want you to leave the humans alone. And the fairies."

Bull's lips twisted into a mean grin. "I was right. You do care about them. What did you get up to there in the village, Muricidae, that you care about the humans and the fairies?"

"I saw enough to know I've been lied to. The humans are intelligent, and the fairies are kind."

Bull snorted. "It doesn't matter what you think. You're never going back there. You're a mermaid. You'll stay in Glorypool and serve your king."

Muri glared at him but kept her mouth shut.

Bull swam closer. "Whoever your king is. And if you think of leaving, remember what we can do. We can starve them. We can drown them." He pushed his face into hers. "We've done it before."

Muri shivered down her spine but she didn't ask what he meant. She'd wait and ask Lotti about it. Instead, she stayed frozen, staring at Bull but no longer seeing him. She waited, waited, and at last he exhaled and moved away. His call echoed out into the water, calling his henchmen, and he moved toward the ocean. She followed him out of the bay as the mermen moved in from both sides.

Chapter 16

ಬ✽ಜ

Fish darted away from the pack of mermen as they swam through the water. Muri hoped the fish would migrate toward the warmer waters of the bay now that the mermen were leaving. And the Woodglen fish-catchers would have a catch again today. Would Jack be out there with them? Or would he take a day off when he woke to find her gone?

What would he do when he woke alone?

After everything they'd shared, Muri had left him—just like his fiancée had left him when he was younger. He'd opened up to Muri, and she had hurt him all over again. That was the worst part of what she'd had to do.

Her hand settled on the knife in her belt, and she remembered Jack's expression as he lay beneath her. He'd regarded her like he adored her. He'd said she was certainly beautiful, that she looked like a queen. No one in Glorypool would ever see her that way.

Turr was eyeing her from the side. "Don't pull out that knife," he growled.

"I'll have to use it when I'm back at work cutting seaweed to fill your belly," she snapped. She dropped her hand and faced forward, hoping he'd leave her alone. Turr was loyal to Bull, but otherwise Muri didn't know much about him. He partnered with one of the other mermen and didn't spend time with the mermaids, so they'd never gathered much gossip about him.

The ocean shelf dropped away beneath them and they headed across the plain. On the journey in, Muri had stayed close to the surface to use the stars to guide her west to Sylvania. After a while, though, she'd found that each time she surfaced, she'd been swimming in the right direction, as if her body instinctively knew the way. When she'd focused her attention on the water around her, she'd sensed a faint pull from it, guiding her. By the time the sun had risen, she'd given up checking her direction, and she'd swum directly into the bay at Woodglen.

Now, the pack of mermen headed straight through the water. Bull led the way, and every few minutes one of his gang would surface to check their direction. The stars must be covered by clouds by now, but they could use the glow of the sun as it neared the horizon. Or maybe they also felt the pull of the water and land—but with the way they meticulously surfaced, Muri doubted it. And if Lotti knew of such a means of navigation, surely she'd have told Muri to use it. Did none of the merpeople sense it?

The pack of mermen stayed all around Muri as if they feared she might dart away. What made the mermen different from the people she'd met on land? Muri glanced at their rigid profiles. Was it something about merpeople that made the mermen aggressive and the merwomen meek?

Was she simply a fluke, the way she couldn't follow orders and obey? Or did other merwomen feel it, too? Janthinidae flashed into her mind, and Muri considered the old merwoman from a new perspective. Janthinidae had resisted in subtle ways. She had told the mermaids bits of history and lore that differed from the usual teachings. And she'd sometimes stashed away bits of food to share with the younger mermaids, aside from their usual ration.

And Janthinidae had disappeared . . . . What if she hadn't simply disappeared, though? What if she had left Glorypool? Or what if the mermen had driven her away—or even killed her?

The mermen surrounding Muri faced forward, following Bull's orders. Their eyes were hard and their lips set. Muri could imagine them driving Janthinidae out of Glorypool. She could imagine them tipping Jack's parents' boat and pulling them under. Bull had taken Jack under the water—what would he have done with Jack if she hadn't followed?

Again she wondered what made the mermen so hateful. All the ones in Bull's group had grown up in Glorypool. Like Muri, they were the youngest generation, born before the ban on merchildren had started twenty seasons ago. Their whole lives, they had existed in a shabby settlement with dwindling food and supplies.

But the older ones had come from Merianalis, where food and resources had been plentiful, and they were just as bad. The founders of Glorypool had learned about the volcanic island with its warm water and migrated with only the belongings they could carry. The merking's magic had supposedly helped them build the settlement.

Muri frowned. That last bit wasn't true. How much of the rest of their history was? Had the founders truly been oppressed in Merianalis, as Muri had always been told? Janthinidae had never disputed the story, but whenever she'd talked about Merianalis, she'd gotten a light in her eye that betrayed her fondness for her old home. Why had she ever left it?

Then, the story always went, some of the founders had traveled to the land to the west for additional supplies and befriended land-dwelling fairies, who helped them using their magic, supplementing the merking's. But the fairies soon betrayed the merpeople, leaving them to flounder, and life had been hard ever since.

In the stories, it was always the fairies' fault life in Glorypool was hard—that food was scarce and no one had materials to repair the huts or build anything new, and that they no longer had magical protections and lived in constant danger of attack from the creatures of the sea, requiring the mermen to patrol the borders of the settlement continuously. But now Muri was crossing the sea for the second time, and still she saw no sign of anything dangerous. She should have asked Hyacinth, who knew the sea creatures.

What if the sea were not dangerous at all, and the mermen had created the threat to keep everyone trapped in Glorypool? And to give the mermen an excuse to avoid the labor of gathering food?

The journey to Woodglen had been fearful and exciting, and the hours crossing the sea plain had rushed past. Now the time dragged as the group drove on through the water. The sky above lightened as if the storm had moved past. But much as she disliked swimming with the mermen, Muri dreaded arriving. Even if Bull didn't punish her, even if he forgot about her in his quest to be merking, nothing would be the same. Her life in Glorypool would be empty now that she'd known something better.

What if she resisted? What if she disobeyed and fought back?

She still wouldn't have Jack.

But maybe that was for the best. Her life was forfeit. She no longer cared what happened to her, not if she couldn't be with him. She could give her life to fight for the merwomen.

Would it be enough? Could one mermaid make a difference? Back on land, the princess they all spoke about—Rose—she had changed things for her people. She'd led a rebellion. Maybe Muri could, too. But would anyone join her?

The sun rose high overhead, filtering down to where they swam, and at long last, the first of the sea mountains appeared. As the group swam over it, more mountains appeared ahead, taller and taller until the mermen had to move near the surface to keep their straight path. The barrenness of the plain gave way to corals and waving forests of kelp, and fishes flickered among the rocks. The sunlight shone on the seagrass—if only she could break the surface and soak in the light. And walk on the land again.

At last the undersea slopes of the island appeared.

Bull headed around the island to the south and downward. They passed one group of merwomen harvesting seaweed, but none of Strombidae's wives were there. Find us in the grove, Lotti had said; Bull had mermen guarding them. Even the merwomen out harvesting were watched by a merman, who half-bowed at Bull as he swam by. The merwomen's baskets were full this late in the day. From behind the guard, a face peeked out staring at Muri—it was Caly. Muri stopped herself from lifting her hand to wave, but she held Caly's gaze as she passed.

At last they swam under the stone arch into the settlement and stopped. A dozen stone huts stood on the seafloor, their woven fiber roofs swaying in the slight current. Merpeople glanced up from where they floated near the sand. Older merpeople rested by the hut doors. Some of the merwomen wove strands of seagrass into baskets and satchels. Others prepared food for later, picking the meat off fish bones or grinding seaweed into paste.

Bull muttered to Turr and swam to Muri.

"I'll be king in two days," he said. "You'd better be ready to accept it and do your duty." He snorted, his lip pulled up in a sneer. His mermen floated in the water, watching from a short distance away. All of them made her sick.

Turr appeared by her side and grasped her arm. He pulled her away.

Turr dragged her through the huts as more merpeople came out to watch. He aimed for the entrance to the arena. Towering rock walls enclosed a sandy floor the merpeople used for sporting games—and fighting. Turr could have swum around the outside of the rocks to reach the grove, but crossing the arena floor was more direct. The space was mostly empty. High up among the rocks, a few merpeople watched them pass—couples who'd come to be alone, or friends gossiping away from the ears of their elders.

A second opening on the far side let them out by the entrance to the grove. The grove was also made of towering rocks and shared a wall with the arena. As soon as Muri was out of sight of any other merpeople, she wrenched her arm against Turr's grasp. It worked—she aimed for the weak spot of his thumb, and her arm popped out of his hold.

"I'm not going to escape," she said as he reached for her again. "Honestly, where do you think I would go? Glorypool is the only settlement in the Cold Sea."

Turr grunted but didn't take her arm.

"Is no one competing against Bull?" Muri asked as they swam along the towering stone wall to the gate.

Turr scoffed. "Hipp is making noise, but he'll quiet soon enough."

Hipponicidae. He was as big as Bull but not as mean. Still, maybe he could win in a fight. But Bull would have more support from the mermen, if only because he scared them into following him.

A merman slumped beside the gate, scratching his tail. He hadn't even noticed their approach. "Some guard," Muri muttered.

The guard startled as they reached the gate to the grove. While the grove's sides were natural rock, the gate and the front wall had been built of stone and had the flat, even appearance of human-made walls. Muri couldn't imagine how the early settlers had done it, until she remembered they had had magic to help. Fairy magic, she now knew. They had filled in the gap in the natural rocks to create a solid fortress with only one gate. A tunnel led through the wall into the rocks. Once you were inside, the space opened up, but the entire top had been blocked with nets woven of vines from the island. The merpeople used the grove to store fish and other creatures for times when food became scarce. Now apparently it was a prison for Strombidae Murkel's eight wives. And his one wife-to-be, or never-to-be, as it turned out.

Turr grunted at the guard and he pulled open the rusting metal gate. Turr reached for Muri's knife and slid it from its sheath before shoving her forward. She swam into the grove without looking back. The gate scraped closed behind her.

Eight merwomen huddled in the center of the grove. Some leaned on boulders, arms around each other. Lotti was watching as Muri entered, and as soon as she moved, the other merwomen all noticed and rushed Muri, their tails swirling. No guards were with the merwomen, but far overhead, someone floated above the nets.

"Muri," Lotti said, "what happened to your hair?"

Of all the things to ask, that's what Lotti asked first?

"I cut it," Muri said. "I had to. You know how it can snarl when it's dry, and all the humans were noticing. I couldn't hide it."

"Never mind. It will grow back," Lotti said, reaching to touch Muri's hand. "Thank the seas you've made it home."

Muri scanned the faces—Apl's and those of the other wives—all of them drawn with worry. "I think I was safer on land. How long have you been locked in here?"

"Bull came as soon as you'd left. We got you out just in time. He brought us here but he noticed you were missing. We said we didn't know where you'd gone and maybe you were up on the island."

"He showed up in Woodglen as I was about to contact you."

"Did he hurt Strombidae?"

Of course Lotti would ask that.

"No," Muri said. "As soon as Bull emerged from the water, Strombidae ran. I didn't see him again."

"He's really dried out?" Lotti whispered.

Muri nodded.

"What did they do to him? Those horrible people."

"No," Muri said. "They're not."

Lotti's brow furrowed in anger. "How can you say that? After what they did to his majesty!"

"They did nothing wrong," Muri said. "You don't understand. We've been lied to." Muri scanned the faces, all intent on hers. "Nothing on land is like we've been told. The humans are kind. They feel things the way we do. They helped me even though I was a stranger. They sheltered me and fed me. They even made me a new dress."

Lotti started to protest. Muri hurried on. "Strombidae's new wife had no idea he planned to bring her here—she didn't even know he was a merman. And she couldn't swim! He dragged her unwilling into the sea. She fought to get away and he almost drowned her.

"He'd have caged her like an animal in that air chamber of his. But the humans aren't animals—they're intelligent and caring. Imagine how you'd feel if a human kept you as a pet in a tank of water and you could never escape to the ocean or even leave your tank. That's how it would've been for her."

The merwives' eyes had widened. Only Lotti huffed, pursing her lips. "If that's true, why didn't Strombidae make it back here, with or without the human?"

"She had a lover, and he saved her."

The merwomen gasped. Even Lotti's eyes were wide. "A lover?"

"A *fairy* lover. He rescued her and stole away with her into the fairy forest. And when her father the king realized Strombidae had paid him with mergold seashells, he went after Strombidae, and that's how Strombidae ended up dried out—he was locked in the castle dungeon for cheating the king with mergold."

Lotti clutched her throat and reached for the nearest wall, but the other wives only pressed closer to Muri.

"There's something else," Muri said. "Strombidae himself told me."

Lotti looked up.

"The merking magic—it's not real. The merking doesn't have any special powers. He's a regular merman. He's a fraud."

"But the shell," Lotti said. "It works. You saw its power."

"The shell has a fairy spell cast on it. That's why it worked. All the merking's magic is stolen fairy spells."

"That's not true," Lotti said, shaking her head vehemently. "The fairies are tricksters. They'd tell a lie like that."

"Strombidae told me," Muri said. "Now that he can't be merking, he doesn't care what happens. He told me: Only the fairies have magic. And I met fairies, and they're not tricksters and liars. The ones in the village help the humans, and they helped me. We've been told the humans are like beasts, but I saw mothers playing with children and older folks who are taken care of.

"And I learned something else." She pinned Lotti with her gaze. "Ten seasons ago, merpeople went to the village and killed some humans. No one there knows why. Do you know?"

Lotti dropped her gaze to the ground. Her face was rigid and she didn't reply.

Muri turned to the merwomen crowded around her. "Don't you see? The merpeople aren't special. And if the merking's magic isn't real, there's no reason we have to listen to a king. He's no better than the rest of the merpeople. The way things work here isn't the only way. It's different on land. The men work, too, and the women have a voice. The men listen to them. And they—"

"Muri, don't cause trouble," Lotti said. "You know where it leads. You speak out, and you end up punished."

Muri paused. Lotti was right. Every time Muri spoke out or didn't do as she was told, she got in trouble. That was how she'd ended up Strombidae's fiancée, and how she'd ended up caught in a fishing net.

But that was also how she'd ended up in Jack's arms.

Jack had said he liked her outspokenness. He'd liked that she thought about things instead of simply accepting them. And Strombidae's unwilling bride, Princess Rose—if she had accepted her fate, she'd be locked in the air chamber and Strombidae would still be merking. Rose had fought back, and she'd freed her people and found happiness with the man she loved.

Maybe getting in trouble was a good thing.

If Muri was going to fight back, she could start with Lotti. And she could start with her own self-doubt.

"I end up punished when I speak out because I'm alone. Everyone stands by and lets me be punished. I'm only one mermaid. But if we all resisted together—"

"Resist?" Lotti laughed. "How? The mermen are stronger than we are."

"Maybe their arms are stronger, but we could fight back in other ways. We do all the work around here. They rely on us. We could refuse to feed them if they don't cooperate." Muri lowered her voice. "We could refuse to lie with them."

A few of the merwomen gasped, and others hid smiles behind their hands. But Lotti only grew more outraged. "I won't have you getting everyone here punished."

"You're just going to wait for Bullidae to decide all our fates?"

"Hipponicidae is challenging him. If Hipp wins in two days, he'll treat us kindly."

"And what if he doesn't win?"

"We have to wait and see. Now that's enough." Lotti held out her hand. "My shell?"

Muri dropped her head, biting her lip. Of course the shell meant something to Lotti. Her husband had given it to her, and she'd never see him again.

But Muri was glad she'd left the shell with the fairies. She met Lotti's gaze defiantly. "I lost it. After I talked to you, Bull appeared and he grabbed at me and I dropped it. I'm sorry."

Lotti lowered her hand, shaking her head, and swam away.

But no one else left.

"Tell us about the humans," Apl said, "and the fairies."

"They really aren't beasts?"

Muri hovered over the sand and her sisters backed away and settled around her.

"No," she said, "they're not beasts at all, not even the men. They're kinder than the men here." She thought of Jack and her eyes misted over, but the tears carried away into the ocean without a trace.

Apl was watching her. "What did you do, Muri?"

Muri smothered her smile as warmth flushed up through her face. "I met someone."

Everyone waited, motionless.

"He was kind to me. And gentle—but strong. He was taller than Bull even. When Bull showed up on land and tried to drag me away, he ran to defend me."

The merwomen sighed and smiled around her.

"He found out I wasn't human but it didn't matter. He still wanted to be with me."

"How did you meet him?"

Muri remembered being caught in Jack's net, but she didn't want to scare the merwomen. She smoothed her hands over her cheeks, willing away the sob rising in her chest.

"When I first arrived, I was scared. I had to walk through a crowd in the village, and I was trying to figure out where to find the merking. And someone approached me. He was a fairy and he knew I was a mermaid, and he challenged me." She smiled, remembering Gray.

"But he became a friend. He only confronted me because he was worried I'd hurt the humans, and he tries to protect them. They're all scared of merpeople because of what King Murkel did to their princess. The fairy worried I might be on land to cause more trouble.

"He told me the truth about the merking and took me home. He and his sister have a flower shop—it's like the other human shops, but instead of selling food or clothing, they sell beautiful bunches of land flowers. They had kinds I'd never seen before—tulips and hyacinths and forsythia. The fairies fed me and they found a place for me to sleep. In a human bed!"

Everyone stared.

"And while I was in their shop, Jack came in." She lowered her gaze. "The moment I saw him, my heart started pounding and I couldn't think straight."

"He was that handsome?"

"*I* thought so. The human men wear their hair short. And he was tan from being in the sun all day. And all muscles. And he was staring at me, too! I asked him to show me the village." She broke into a smile. "They call it a 'date' there. When two people go off together."

"To tryst, you mean?" Apl said. "Muri, did you—"

"It's not like that," Muri cut in. "You talk first and decide if you like each other and want to be together. And you have to both want to. Jack was always checking what I wanted the whole time we were together. And it all takes a lot more time beforehand. There's a lot more kissing and snuggling."

Apl's eyes narrowed and she smirked. "You seem to know a lot about it."

Muri couldn't stop smiling in spite of the pain in her chest. Someone had loved her, really loved her, and she'd felt that love back. Nothing would ever change that.

"Muri!" Lotti's voice boomed through the water. "Come help me."

The merwomen backed away to give Muri space to swim up from the group. Muri studied the circle of faces.

"It could be different here," she said. "The humans had an oppressive king, too, and they fought back. And do you know who led them? Their princess. The one King Murkel tried to steal. She escaped King Murkel, but she went back to fight against her own father. And now their people are free. And everyone works, the men and the women, and the women aren't bullied. It could be different here, too—if we banded together to resist."

She scanned the faces one last time. Lotti called again, and Muri swam away.

Chapter 17

☙✱❧

Two days after Muri's return to Glorypool, she joined the merpeople gathering in the arena. Merpeople perched on outcroppings or clung to the faces of the boulders, covering the towering rock walls, their tails slowly swishing to keep them upright. Low murmurs came through the water. The vast ring of flat sand at the floor was empty. This was where the mermen would fight to be merking.

How did the humans choose their leaders? Jack had said something about a council, a group of people who made the rules all together and who were chosen by everyone. And the fairies had chosen Rose as their queen because she was brave and kind. A system of choice made a lot more sense than the king being the winner of a wrestling fight. No wonder the merpeople ended up with such lousy kings.

Muri watched with the eight royal wives by a broad rock near the sand. Apl's hand slipped into hers and squeezed. Bull was swimming toward them.

Bull took Muri's arm and pulled her over the sand of the ring. His hair was tied up again, bobbing on his head like a dead fish at the surface. The murmuring voices quieted.

"Muricidae was on land." Bull's voice boomed out. "She has testimony to give the merpeople."

He flung Muri upward into the center of the arena. Everyone watched her.

"I went to land to find Strombidae Murkel. To see if he'd return," Muri said. The merpeople strained in her direction. She took a deep breath and projected her voice into the space. "He cannot. He is dried out."

The audience broke into murmurs of conversations. Below, Lotti cowered in the arms of the others, huddled at the edge of the sand.

Bull swished up beside Muri. "I've witnessed this, too," he said. "If Strombidae Murkel cannot return to Glorypool, he forfeits the throne."

The merpeople's voices rose to a din and a pounding began as the mermen smacked their palms on the rocks. Bullidae shoved Muri aside and began to circle the space. He didn't need to announce his intentions. Everyone already knew.

As Muri backed away, Hipponicidae stirred the water beside her. He glanced at her and acknowledged her as he passed.

Bull and Hipp circled each other in the arena. Muri sank down to join the other merwomen—the ex-wives. And the fight began.

The fight was like every other merfight she'd seen, and there had been many. Merkings were constantly under attack from their rivals. Umbraculidae lost his throne in a fight with Strombidae, who—in his nine seasons—had to fight many times to stay king. And unlike Lotti, Muri had little hope Hipp would win. The meanest merman always won.

But this time, Muri watched the mermen's moves and remembered what Jack had taught her. Jack's defense moves had been fluid and graceful, taking the opponent's motion and using it. Bull and Hipp were the opposite—they crashed together with their shoulders and fists, like two boulders bashing together in a rockslide. The fighting illustrated why the merpeople were strong compared to the humans—why she'd been able to toss Jack to the ground with barely any effort. Moving underwater took more strength than moving in air. It gave merpeople an advantage on land.

Muri had no practice fighting underwater. But she'd worked every day at hauling nets and harvesting seaweed. She had strength.

And she had Jack's technique. The mermen only pounded each other, trying to break instead of subdue.

Maybe she'd have a chance at winning if she ever needed to fight.

Hipp was flagging and blood drifted away from his face. "Stop," Muri whispered. "Stop before it's too late. Don't let your foolish merman pride get you killed."

Bull rushed Hipp again and Hipp slipped out of the way. His face was set. He raised both his hands in defeat.

The mermen roared. Muri clutched her fists, watching for Bull to hurt Hipp, but Bull followed the rules and allowed Hipp to withdraw into the crowd.

Bull circled the arena, spiraling upward from the sand to pass every face. "Are there any other challengers?" he crowed. The mermen cheered in response and no one came forward.

But Muri studied the merwomen's faces. What were they thinking? Did they support Bull? Or did they have a desire to resist, the way she did? She spotted Euli floating high up, and Caly hidden by a rock beside her. Or hiding intentionally perhaps—Caly was shy and always kept her head down, quietly doing her work. At least she hadn't ever had to spawn with Angar. After Muri's interference, Hipp had claimed Caly for a while. Hipp was about the best merman Muri could have hoped for as a partner for Caly, and he was strong enough that no one else had bothered her. But his defeat today might change things.

"No one challenges me," Bull bellowed. "I proclaim myself, Bullidae, King Murkel of Glorypool!"

Muri rolled her eyes at the familiar words, words she'd heard time and again in her 23 seasons. But deep down, a thread of fear squirmed inside her. She tamped it down and frowned. Bull circled the ring and brandished his fists at the crowd. Beside her, Lotti shuddered with sobs in Apl's arms. They were no longer royal wives but single mermaids like all the other merwomen.

Maybe Bull had forgotten about her. Maybe he'd keep circling the arena and pumping his fist and shouting until he grew tired and went to lie on a rock in the sun and drink phyta while the merwomen went back to work. Maybe—

Bull's head turned and his gaze pinned Muri to the floor.

Her heart pounded. Maybe she would get to fight after all.

When Bull swam down, Muri rose up to meet him. At least she could lead him away from the others. He took her wrist and pulled her away without a word, and her anger boiled up. Why were mermen always grabbing things? The whole lot of them were horrid.

She let him pull her out the top of the arena as everyone watched. He could tire out from hauling her through the water, while she'd save her strength. Whatever he wanted, whether he thought she'd lie with him or wanted to berate her more, she'd be ready. The sounds of voices faded into the deep silence of the ocean, broken only by the churning water of Bull's harsh breathing. They passed over the seaweed fields and up the slope of the island as the water lightened. Her scales warmed and a moment later, her fins brushed against sand.

Bull flopped onto the beach, dragging Muri beside him. He let go of her wrist at last. Muri pulled her tail from the waves, shaking off the droplets of seawater. If she could dry first, she'd have a moment where she could stand while Bull would be prone on the sand. He'd hate that.

The crescent-shaped beach was empty and quiet. Ripples of waves washed up and fell back beside her. On either end of the sand, mangroves stood in the shallow water. Greenery lined the back side of the beach, with a few waving palms and coconut trees poking up from thick undergrowth. The sun was high overhead.

Muri had always liked going to the island. She'd enjoyed the sunshine on the beach and the wind and warmth on her skin, so different from the nonstop chill and darkness below. And escaping the drudgery of harvesting seaweed and mending nets was always nice. Sometimes the trysting had even been fun. Around Bull, she could easily grouse about how awful mermen were, but if she had to be honest with herself, some of them weren't that bad.

But this time on the island was different—she wasn't here for fun. She was going to fight back if Bull tried to coerce her into anything.

Muri had imagined different plans over the past two days, but not knowing what Bull intended made it hard. Now she scanned the tree line for a break indicating the trail to the hot spring, but a thick wall of hibiscus bushes and low sea grape and tamarind trees filled the spaces between the trunks of the taller trees. She'd never been to the hot spring, but a trail from this beach led to it.

Bull panted beside her. Good—hopefully he'd worn himself out with all the fighting and fist-pumping and dragging he'd done. It wasn't like he'd had to drag her up here. She wouldn't have resisted. But she suspected he liked the idea that he was forcing her into coming to the island. She could use that against him.

Her scales tingled as they dried. The moment had come to see if she was a skilled enough actress to trick Bull. Her tail faded into legs and she scrambled to her feet. She was steady after spending days on land but she let herself sway a bit. As she stepped away, Bull grabbed her ankle.

"Where are you going?"

"To the—" Muri pointed but quickly dropped her hand and bit her lip as if she'd spoken by accident.

Bull tugged and she fell to the sand.

"Never mind," she said, sighing. She relaxed her shoulders and pretended to hide a smile. "We can stay here on the beach."

"What were you going to say?" Bull asked, squeezing her ankle. "You thought we were going somewhere."

Muri pressed her lips shut.

Bull yanked her leg. "Tell me or I'll force it out of you."

She cried out. "It's just I thought you'd want to go to the royal hot spring, your majesty."

If Muri guessed right, Bull had no idea where the royal hot

spring was. Neither did she, of course. The merking wouldn't have taken her there until they were married. In the past, it had been where wives stayed while they were carrying a merchild. After the ban, the merking had turned it into his private retreat, and Strombidae had particularly liked having a place all to himself. Once he took over, he'd allowed no one to go to the spring without the merking's blessing. He'd even tried to extend the threat of the merking's magic that protected the royal vault, saying it would harm anyone who tried to reach the hot spring without him.

But Bull hadn't defeated Strombidae to take the throne, so Strombidae had not told him the merking's secrets, like the location of the hot spring. Lotti and the other wives certainly wouldn't have told Bull, who'd left with Muri right after the fight.

Bull's tail faded into legs and he sat up, holding her ankle in his beefy fingers. He considered her, his head tilted. "You don't want to go there."

Muri froze, staring at the sand.

"You should never have been there. Strombidae hadn't married you."

"He didn't wait, your majesty," Muri whispered.

Bull huffed. "Why would he take you there? Why not just take you here on the beach?"

Muri didn't answer, twisting her hands together. Acting nervous was easy. All her nerves were on end.

"Why don't you want to go there? Tell me!" He squeezed her ankle harder.

"It scared me!" Tears welled up in her eyes—real tears. If only the merpeople had theatricals like the humans. Muri could perform instead of gathering seaweed all day.

Bull smirked. "What would scare you about hot water?"

"You don't understand!" Muri let her voice get hysterical. "You don't know what it's like there. He—" She broke down in tears. Hopefully Bull wouldn't press her because she had no idea what she could make up to justify her terror.

But Bull released her ankle and grinned. He scrambled to his feet and yanked her up after him. "Show me," he said. He pulled her a few steps across the sand toward the trees and stopped.

Muri scanned the edge of the jungle. From what the other mer-women had said, the trail to the hot spring started at one end of the curved beach—but which end? She recalled Jack's theory about the wind. Hot air rising, the wind gusting toward it. The wind always gusted a little on the eastern end of the beach. She headed that way with Bull trailing behind her.

A few palm trees leaned out over the sand. She stepped into the cool patch created by their shadows. Near the end of the beach, up from where the mangroves began, a break in the undergrowth suggested the start of a trail. Muri made for it.

"Wait," Bull ordered.

Muri stopped. She shuddered when his fingers touched her hip. He undid the knot of her knife belt and dropped it to the ground.

"You won't have any harvesting to do on this trip," he said, "and I don't trust you with a knife."

Muri didn't respond. She could get it back when she emerged from the jungle. Alone.

She led him into the trees, and thankfully a footpath appeared before her. If it ended abruptly, what would she do? Hopefully it led to the hot spring. Thoughts spiraled in her head with panic never far off. Muri tried to rein them in. Suggesting the hot spring had gained her time to think. She needed to plan her next move.

As they left the beach, the swish of waves and whistle of the breeze faded. Birds called in the treetops, and overhead, fronds scraped together lazily in the steady wind. But on the trail, the air was humid and still. Her footsteps were silent, but Bull thumped behind her, panting again.

She pushed through a branch across the path and let it go. It snapped back at Bull's face.

"Are you sure this is the trail?" Bull swatted the branch away.

"I think so, your majesty. I was here only once, but I think so.

It's been a full season since anyone passed this way, so it's bound to be overgrown."

Muri took deep breaths to slow her racing pulse. Okay, think, she told herself. She'd have only one chance to defeat Bull. She had to succeed, or he'd be on guard around her and she'd never beat him—if he even left her alive. No merwoman had ever fought back that Muri knew of, but she wouldn't be surprised if Bull reacted with anger and aggression. But would he kill her?

Better to imagine beating him in a fight than what would happen if she didn't. For the hundredth time that morning, she recalled the moves she had practiced with Jack. Jack, lying on the ground beneath her. She squeezed her eyes shut. Don't think of Jack; think of what he taught you. She imagined Bull coming at her. She could get him to the ground. She'd need to press the way Jack had taught her until Bull was inert. That was the part that scared her most because she'd never practiced it on Jack. And once Bull was unconscious, she would bind his arms with vines. She began watching for vines in the trees.

The footpath continued, winding deeper into the jungle and sloping upward. Birds screeched high in the canopy. A flash of brown moved between trees, and a true jolt of fear shot through Muri. She stopped and Bull knocked into her.

"Monkey," she whispered, pointing.

Bull didn't reply. Even Bull was unable to maintain his bravado with the threat of a monkey.

"Do you know the spell to keep them away?" Muri asked in a whisper.

Bull growled. "You said the magic wasn't real."

"The *merking* magic's not real," Muri said. "But the fairy magic is. Strombidae used a spell to keep the monkeys away."

"Do you know it? Don't lie to me."

Muri huffed at him. "Don't you think I'd tell you if I knew a spell against monkeys? We'll have to hope they stay away." She resisted smiling at Bull's rattled expression.

She resumed climbing the trail. None of the royal wives had ever mentioned problems with monkeys at the hot spring. Hopefully they didn't come near—spell or not.

The terrain grew rougher with the path climbing more steeply. They crossed a stream and followed the trail alongside it as it tumbled down. The gurgle of the water grew, fuller and louder, until the trees parted. Muri gaped at the sight: Water thundered down off a cliff, crashing in white foam in a pool. A creek trickled out from the end of the pool and headed past them, flowing into the stream down the mountain.

Muri pulled herself together. Bull was staring at the crashing water, too. She feigned nonchalance.

"It's amazing, isn't it?" she said. "Strombidae told me the human word is 'waterspill.'"

Bull grunted. Muri continued forward.

Finally she spotted thin vines hanging near the trail. She stopped, reaching out to tug on them. They were strong. "We need these," she said. "Can you cut them, your majesty? I don't have my knife."

"Why do we need those?" he asked, glaring at her.

"We'll need them when we get there," she said, staring at the ground as she wrapped the end of a vine around her wrist. She lowered her voice to a bare whisper. "For . . . for tying things. You'll see."

Bull's lips pursed tight, slipping to the side in a smirk. He pulled his knife slowly from its sheath and handed it to Muri, blade first.

Gingerly, she took the blade in her fingers. Once she had the knife in hand, she sawed through the vines, cutting pieces as long as she could. Bull hovered at her shoulder. He didn't trust her with the knife, but he was too arrogant to do the work himself.

She gathered the vines into coils and looped them over her arms. The weight made the climb harder, and the path became even steeper. Where was the wretched hot spring? Muri was panting now, too. But merwomen were used to working all day, she reminded herself. The mermen were naturally strong, but they never fought for long. Maybe the climb would give her an advantage over Bull, even if it tired her, too.

The trail seemed to be climbing to the top of the mountain. If it did, she could push Bull into the volcano's crater and be done with him. But could she? Would she kill him to protect herself? She didn't know.

At last Muri glimpsed a structure through the green canopy. Her relief swelled when the trail leveled off and arrived at a clear pool surrounded by rocks and steaming in the shade. All around were leafy banana trees and others—mango and papaya, maybe. Maybe a long-ago merperson had planted them here for the merpeople to enjoy.

A path led around the hot pool to a rough wooden bridge across a dip in the ground. Beyond, it ended at the steps of a large circular hut. The hut was open to the air, with thick cane poles supporting the thatched roof and a railing bound into place with woven ropes. Passionflower vines twined up the poles, loaded with frilly purple flowers and green fruits.

Muri headed for the bridge. Bull grunted behind her. He stood beside the pool as if planning to go in. She indicated the hut with her vine-laden arms. "This is where he liked to . . . do things," she said and continued forward, hoping Bull would follow.

She ascended the steps into the hut and dropped the vines along one side. A light breeze blew in. The floor was made of wide canes cut in pieces and pressed flat. She inhaled deeply to catch her breath after the climb.

Bull entered and stalked to the center of the space, taking it in with an air of ownership. This was his, he must be thinking—the place where he'd bring his own wives and enjoy having something none of his miserable subjects had. Maybe he'd change the rule and sire merchildren to continue the endless cycle of oppression. Muri moved away from the railing to give herself space. She waited for Bull to notice her again.

His head turned and his eyes gleamed.

"Did you want . . . ?" she stammered.

"What did Strombidae like to do?"

"He liked me to fight him," Muri said. "He said he liked it when I was rough with him."

Bull stalked toward her. He wasn't moving fast enough to help her toss him to the ground. He came up close. Muri refused to turn toward him.

Bull leaned in like he meant to kiss her. She stepped away. Bull growled and grabbed her, pulling her back toward him. She dropped her weight and he started to fall forward. He let go and caught himself, and she scurried out of reach.

Bull circled her as he'd done with Jack on the wharf that night, but here, he couldn't gain an advantage with trickery. She had to make him angry so he'd rush her. Muri slowly smiled at him, goading him. He stalked forward and leapt to grab her, and she stepped away. She slapped his butt as he passed. He stumbled and caught himself.

When he turned, his eyes were narrow and his teeth bared.

Get angry, Muri told herself. She looked at Bull and the anger flowed in. He'd threatened her friends, and he'd made her leave Jack. If she'd broken Jack's heart, Bull was to blame. Her blood churned, and her body tingled down to her fingertips.

Bull rushed at her. Muri bent her knees and focused. She met him as he came, grabbing his arm to pull and twisting her hips. Bull sailed through the air and crashed onto the floor of the hut. Muri dropped on top of him. He thrashed, frantic, but didn't throw her off. She closed her eyes and counted her heartbeats, waiting, and finally his movement ceased.

It was too easy.

Muri stayed pressing on him a moment longer. She forced her eyes open and studied his unconscious form. He'd wake quickly. She was supposed to use this moment to run away. But if she disappeared into the jungle, Bull could stake out the beaches, knowing she'd have to come to swim. He might take revenge on her friends like Caly or on the villagers. She had to try to secure him.

She stood on shaky legs and staggered to retrieve the vines. She dropped them by the railing nearest to Bull and with a mighty heave, tugged his body to the edge of the floor. The knot Jack had tied around her arm—that one would work. She'd tie it around Bull's wrist and also to the railing.

Her hands trembled as she lifted his wrist. He muttered something, already waking. She wrapped the vine around his arm. What was the pattern? Around the arm, make an X, and slip the end through . . . . It didn't come out right.

"That's my girl."

Muri whirled around. It couldn't be.

But it was. Jack was standing at the entrance to the hut.

Chapter 18

Muri launched herself across the hut and into Jack's arms. She hugged him around the neck, her feet off the floor. He squeezed her back even as he stepped into the hut and across it toward Bull. He pushed her away and set her down.

"Hand me the vines," Jack said, kneeling.

With a few twists, Jack had a vine knotted around one of Bull's wrists and the railing. He took a second vine and secured the other wrist, with Bull's arms stretched wide so he couldn't reach the knots with his teeth.

Muri handed him another vine. Jack was here! Hope filled her. Securing Bull properly had been a lot to hope for. Never had she imagined Jack arriving to do it. How had he found the island?

Jack tied more loops around Bull's arms and neck. The more knots, the better, as far as Muri was concerned. And the knots weren't like the ones Jack had shown her. She touched a finger to one as Bull's head swayed back and forth.

"It gets tighter the more you pull on it," Jack said. He took the last vine and bound Bull's ankles together. Bull lifted his head slightly and blinked. Jack tugged Bull's legs to the side, bending them at the knees, until Bull was trussed tight against the railing. Jack secured the final vine.

Muri backed away as Bull stirred again. One of his arms twitched but the vines held fast.

Jack touched her back lightly.

She turned to him. If any of the mermen discovered him on the island, they'd never let him return to Woodglen. He'd put himself in danger to come here. Now that Bull was secured, everything else came back to her. She had left Jack on land without saying goodbye. And in spite of it, he had followed her here. Why? To convince her to return? Or only to have her explain herself? And how had he found her?

"Oh Jack," Muri whispered, "I'm sorry. I—"

"Shh," Jack interrupted gently. "Let's go outside."

Muri followed Jack down the steps, her gaze soaking up every bit of him she could see—from the curls on his head to the tanned back of his neck to the muscles of his back half-hidden by his loose shirt. And she was naked! Merpeople didn't notice it, but truthfully, it felt a little strange with Jack here. She'd become used to the human habit of wearing clothes. Jack stopped on the bridge, out of sight of Bull. Muri crossed her arms over her breasts as he turned. Jack's gaze darted over her and away, and back to her face.

"I forgot you'd be naked," he said. "I have to remember you don't mind."

"I'd like to put something on, but I don't have anything."

He undid the top button on his shirt and pulled it over his head. Muri's knees wobbled at the sight of his chest and the memories of how she'd lain against him. And ten seas, was it hot in the jungle today! He was smiling as he handed the shirt to her. Muri pulled it on, inhaling the scent of his skin tinged with woodsmoke and the salt of the ocean as the fabric covered her. It slid down onto her shoulders and hung past her bottom.

Muri started to smile back, and now she was the one trying not to stare at *his* bare chest. "It was strange at first," she said, "when I got back. But everyone down there would stare if I wore a dress."

For a moment, they regarded each other. The loud chorus of jungle creatures went quiet under the thudding of her pulse in her ears. Then Muri was in Jack's arms again, held to his chest as he kissed her hair.

"How did you get here?" she murmured at last.

"I knew you'd gone as soon as I woke—"

"I didn't want to! But they never would have stopped, Jack. They would have killed the fish-catchers if I hadn't returned to Glorypool."

"Shh, I know." He rubbed her back until she settled into his arms again. "But I had to make sure you were okay. You said the spring star hung over the island so I headed toward it. And after the sun rose, I used my compass to stay on the right path."

"What's a compass?"

He reached into his pocket and came out with a round metal object. It had a clasp that unhooked so it flipped open into two halves joined by a hinge. Inside, a pointed piece of metal wobbled on a pin.

"It's a spinning magnet," Jack said, turning the compass in his hand. The arrow didn't rotate with it. "It points in the same direction no matter which way you turn it. Sailors use them for navigation when there's clouds or fog, or even when the sky is clear."

"Are they magic?"

"No. Something about the land makes the magnet pull always to the north. Some kind of force we can't see."

Muri remembered the pull she'd felt when she'd crossed the ocean. Maybe she'd sensed the force that made the humans' compass work.

"And once I reached the island," Jack continued, closing the compass, "I had help finding the beach."

"Help?"

Jack let go of her and turned to look back toward the hot spring. Someone was coming up through the trees.

"I offered to bring him back here if he'd help me find you." Jack lowered his voice. "I wasn't totally honest with him. I suggested some of his wives might be glad to see him, but I have no idea. He seemed to believe it."

Strombidae emerged from the jungle, panting with the exertion of the climb.

"He showed me the beach the merfolk use, and when we saw your knife on the sand, he told me to follow the path here."

Strombidae was doubled over by the hot spring with his arms braced against his knees.

"Muri," Jack said, his voice low. "I had to see you were all right. I don't think you're safe here. What happens next with that merman? Won't the others come searching for him?"

"I thought only about fighting Bull off," she said. "I don't have the rest figured out."

"Please come back with me," he whispered. "I'm like a compass; whichever way I turn, I see you in front of me. Everything for me leads to you."

Her eyes filled with tears, and out here the ocean didn't wash them away. "Jack, I want to. More than anything. But we can't, not unless we can stop the mermen from threatening Woodglen."

Strombidae straightened and staggered toward them, and Muri wiped away her tears.

"Muricidae," he said in his hissing voice, stopping beside the bridge.

"Your hi— sir."

"Bullidae is the new king?"

"Yes. But he's also tied up in the hut."

Strombidae's face lit up. "Is he now?" He thumped onto the bridge and hurried past them. Muri took Jack's hand and followed.

Bull lay as they'd left him but now his eyes were open. If he'd struggled to free himself, his attempts hadn't budged the vines. Bull glared at them through slitted eyes as they entered the hut. When he spotted Strombidae, a growl escaped his throat. He could barely twist his neck, but his eyes followed as Muri moved in front of him. His lips were pressed tight, but sharp exhales and the flare of his nostrils betrayed his anger.

Muri took a deep breath and forced herself to meet his gaze. Many seasons of watching the tails of mermen—looking down instead of into their faces—made the habit hard to fight. And looking in Bull's eyes would make him more angry. But who cared if she made him angry? He deserved it.

"Let me go, Muricidae," Bull growled. "I'm your king and I command it."

"I won't, not until you make some promises."

"I won't promise you anything."

"Then I'll dry you out." Muri lifted her chin and gazed down her nose at Bull. His body jerked against the ropes. She had unnerved him.

"I'm the king," he said deliberately, "and my followers will rescue me. They'll search for me if I don't return tonight."

"Not if I stop them."

"You?" Bull sneered. "With your little fighting tricks and your human dog and this waste"—he tilted his chin at Strombidae—"against Turr and Angar and all my mermen?"

Muri shrugged. "It won't come to that," she said. "I'll simply tell them you've decided to select your first wife and no one is to bother you while you make up your mind. Except the mermaids you'll need, of course. I'll bring them to you. The ones who support me."

"Who?" Bull's muscles strained against the vines. "Who would betray me?"

Muri crossed her arms and pressed her lips shut, hoping her lie would hold.

Bull turned his glare to Strombidae. "You! You'd let her do this? Debase the dignity of the merking? Ignore my authority?"

"Me?" Strombidae said slowly. "The waste?"

"What's in it for you?" Bull said.

"Seeing you grovel is fairly satisfying," Strombidae said. "But I have plans. I'm not the merking any longer, but I may still have a wife or two. You know they can choose to stay with me."

Bull laughed. "You think any of them will choose you? When you can't even swim?"

Muri stepped forward. "Lotti will. She loves him."

Bull didn't respond.

"Will you promise not to return to Sylvania?" Muri asked Bull.

"Never. My followers will see through your lies. They'll find me."

"Very well," Muri said. She turned to Jack. "I'll have to go below."

They left Strombidae grinning over Bull in the hut and retreated back to the bridge.

Muri pressed her hands together, thinking. "I'll go down and say he wants mates, and I'll bring back the mermaids I think I can trust. And I'll make it seem like he plans to stay at the island enjoying himself while his followers watch over Glorypool."

Jack swallowed. "How long will it take for him to . . . dry out?"

"About a quarter-moon," Muri said quietly.

"It's what you want to do?"

Muri peered up at Jack. "I don't know! I said it to scare him. But it's not a thing we do as punishment. No one has ever done it on purpose that I know of. I just wanted to make him promise."

"Even if he promised to leave Woodglen alone, I don't know if I'd trust him. Are merfolk bound by promises and oaths the way fairies are?"

"Not with magic. There's a strong sense of honor. But I'd need him to promise in front of the others because I don't think he cares about what you or I think of him, or Strombidae."

"I know it's probably wrong, but I'd love to see him dried out."

"You wouldn't think I'm awful for doing it?"

"After what he's done?" Jack shook his head.

Muri sighed. "He might change his mind. Not having water gets uncomfortable. Maybe once I have the other mermaids here, we can form a better plan. I hoped . . ."

Jack waited, but she stopped. She couldn't tell him she hoped for a revolution like his people had had, where the entire system was destroyed and rebuilt. She didn't know if anyone in Glorypool would follow her the way the humans had followed Rose.

Instead she slipped her arms around him and hugged tightly.

"It won't take long," she said.

"Be safe."

She had to pull herself from his arms.

Muri hurried down the trail and back toward the beach. The return journey went a lot faster. She exited the jungle onto the windy sand. *Alina's Dream* floated in the water, the anchor line holding it in place in the shallows. The sail was lowered but strewn about the cockpit as if it had been left in a hurry.

She'd forgotten to return Jack's shirt. She pulled it off and tucked it beside a rock under the trees before tying on her knife belt. She paused to collect herself.

She didn't have much of a plan. But planning the entire future was impossible. Right now, she had to stop Bull from threatening the villagers in Woodglen. And she had to get Jack home safely, whether she went with him or not.

But what else might she do? If Bull dried out, he wouldn't be merking. Could she stop Bull's henchmen from taking his place? What would they do if they found out she had intentionally dried him out? Merman loyalties shifted constantly toward whoever held the most power, but she couldn't see them shifting to her. The only support she might hope for would be from the other merwomen. Could she rally the merwomen to oppose the ways of the merkingdom and make change?

Could she go home with Jack?

Please come back with me, he'd said. Hope lifted in her breast every time she remembered. He'd forgiven her for leaving him. He still wanted her.

There had to be a way.

Muri stepped into the waves and dove under the water as her tail formed.

Glorypool was straight ahead, down the southern slope of the island. Muri hadn't swum far when she spotted merpeople in a field of seaweed. A harvesting group must have headed out to work after the fight. She slowed her body as her pulse sped up. The guard turned to her, clutching his stick.

"Where's Bull?" he growled.

Muri remembered at the last moment to look down—to play the deferential mermaid.

"His highness is r-resting on the island," she stuttered, staring at the merman's tail fins. "He requested I bring him another mate. Mates. Several." She didn't have to pretend to stumble over her words.

She risked a glance up. The merman was grinning. Behind him, the mermaids had stopped working to watch her. Caly was there.

Muri lifted her chin. "Calyptraeidae," she called out, and Caly shuddered at her name. "Please come."

Caly lowered her face and passed her basket to her neighbor. She sheathed her knife and swam forward.

Muri turned back to the guard, again lowering her gaze. "I'll let you get back to work."

She continued down the incline with Caly silent by her side. When they'd crossed through a dense patch of kombu, Muri reached for Caly's arm and pulled her to a halt. She peeked back through the strands of seaweed and scanned the water around them to make sure they were alone.

"Caly, I need your help."

"Me?"

"Bull did not send for you."

All the stiffness seeped out of Caly's shoulders. "Oh, Muri, thank the seas. I'd hate to lie with him. Was it awful?"

"Caly, will you keep a secret? You don't have to help me if you don't want to. But I need you to keep a secret."

"Muri, tell me. Of course I won't tell."

Muri again scanned their surroundings. "I fought back, Caly. I knocked Bull to the ground and he's tied up in the jungle."

Caly's eyes widened like a catalufa's.

"I told him I'd dry him out if he didn't agree to some things, but he says he won't. So I have to hide him. All I could think was to tell the mermen he's occupied with trysting."

Caly reached for Muri's hand and squeezed.

"Muri," she said. "You fought back. How? He's so strong."

Muri couldn't help her smile. "I met someone on land," she said. "He showed me tricks."

Caly gasped. "Not a fairy!"

Muri shook her head, breaking into a wide grin. "Not tricks like that."

"A human then?" Caly said. "I heard rumors. It's true?"

"It's not like they've said. The humans are kind. And the fairies, too. It's different on land. The women and men are equal, and everyone works, and the women get a choice in everything. And then I met Jack, and he was wonderful and wanted to talk about things and ask me things, and we spent all this time together."

"Jack," Caly said, rolling the name out her lips. "What did he look like?"

"He's as tall as Bull and just as strong in spite of being a land dweller. And he has dark brown eyes and hair only on the top of his head. The human men all have short hair, and some of the women, too. And he's a sailor and a fish-catcher. The humans catch fish using nets cast from sailboats. And Caly . . . he's here."

"*Here?*"

"On the island. He followed me to ask me to go back with him."

"Oh, Muri!" Caly said, her eyes shining.

"Strombidae is here, too."

"But you said he's dried out."

"He is, but he came in Jack's boat. He thinks some of his wives might stay with him even if he has to live on the island."

Caly snorted. "Lotti will." She scrutinized Muri. "Do you want to go back with Jack?"

"Oh so much. I loved it there. It felt like I was home after being lost my whole life. And I can't imagine trysting with anyone else now that I've met Jack. But I thought of all of you and I felt bad leaving you in Glorypool when I was on land. Maybe you could all come—you and Apl and the other mermaids our age."

Caly's smile faded and her brow wrinkled. "I don't know, Muri. I know it's not always good here, but Glorypool is home to me. I wish all the time it could be better though. Maybe it's different for you—why did you leave Woodglen if you liked it on land?"

"Bull threatened the land dwellers. He wouldn't let them catch any fish, and he threatened to tip their boats and drown them unless I came back."

Caly's eyes were wide again. "He wouldn't!"

"He fought with Jack and pulled him into the water, and he held him under like he'd drown him until I went in to get him."

"Oh, Muri, that's terrible! He shouldn't have!"

"That's why I left Woodglen—I had to keep the people there safe."

"So you want Bull to promise to leave the land dwellers alone?"

"Yes."

After a pause, Caly said, "You said the men work, too?"

"Yes, everyone together. And they all get along. It was amazing. The fish-catchers are ruled by a woman! But they don't say 'ruled.' She's like a manager who keeps track of things, but they have a whole system where everyone makes decisions about everything."

"Don't they have a king?" Caly asked, squinting in confusion. "Wasn't Strombidae's bride supposed to be a princess?"

"The people overthrew the king! I wish I could tell you the whole story but there's not time."

"But the human king didn't have magic, Muri. If anyone tries to fight back here, the merking will strike them dead, or worse."

"Oh Caly, the merking's magic isn't real! I heard it straight from Strombidae. It's a hoax. The merpeople got spells from the fairies ages ago, and the merking pretended the magic was his to help him control his subjects—so no one contradicted him. But the spells are almost gone and he has no special power beyond that."

Caly stared. "If there's no merking magic, we don't have to follow a merking any longer."

Muri was speechless for a few beats. "I didn't know if anyone would support a rebellion."

Caly's face was serious. "The reasoning in Glorypool is the merwomen gather food while the mermen offer protection. But from what? I've never seen a shark or even a ray. And if another settlement of merpeople live in the Cold Sea, they've never bothered us."

"I thought the same thing! I saw nothing dangerous while swimming all the way to Woodglen by myself."

"It's like they've made it all up to get out of helping with the work. And why do the mermen make the decisions? And they're pushy about trysting, and there's no punishment if they strike us or grab us.

"The mermaids talk, Muri. You've been kept isolated by Strombidae's court for over a full season so you haven't heard. The past season without the merking here, the mermen have been worse than ever. The mermaids have been grumbling, and even some of the mermen complain—the ones not part of Bull's gang. I think many would support a change."

Was Caly right?

Hope swirled around Muri's breast. "Jack could teach everyone to defend themselves. And the merwomen could refuse to gather food for the mermen if they don't listen to the changes proposed. We could refuse to tryst with them. If we all do it together, they'd have to listen."

Muri and Caly continued down the slope, plotting which mermaids to approach. They might have to be told they were going to mate with Bull, unfortunately, but once they were back on the beach, Muri would explain everything. She could teach them to fight as they waited for Bull to dry out. Hopefully Jack wouldn't mind a whole lot more of being thrown to the ground. And this time, he'd be thrown to the ground by naked merwomen—Muri smothered a smile. He'd be embarrassed, but she was certain he'd want to help.

An hour later, after visiting the stone huts and a few more seaweed patches, Muri had a dozen mermaids with her, all nervously swishing their tails. Everyone they passed watched them. Soon the whole settlement would think Bull was trysting with a dozen mermaids at the hot spring. No one would grow suspicious of him not appearing for a quarter-moon if he had so many mermaids with him.

Muri was eager to put the mermaids' fears to rest. She led them through the arena, where the mermen who weren't guarding something lounged among the rocks during the day. She wanted everyone to see them and believe Bull was staying above willingly. They entered on one side and headed straight across the sand to the opposite entrance.

Turr appeared in the opening.

Dread leapt up in Muri's chest. Turr watched her with his usual arrogant confidence. He was waiting for her. And he had something in his hand, something long and flat.

Something human-made.

She shuddered. As they neared, Turr broke into a smile and held up the object. Muri couldn't read human letters, but she knew what it said.

Alina's Dream.

She let out a wail and rushed Turr, but he swam aside.

"Where is he?" Muri cried.

"He's with Bull," Turr said. "But then, you knew that."

"What have you done with him? Tell me!"

"Don't give me orders, girl," Turr said. But he turned and motioned for her to follow. She glanced back as she swam after him. Caly and the others crowded in the doorway to the arena. Their faces were confused, but they followed her out.

Jack couldn't be hurt. He couldn't be drowned. Bull wouldn't do that. He'd use Jack to get what he wanted from her. There would be a chance to rescue him.

And Muri realized where they were going.

Jack was imprisoned in Strombidae's air chamber.

Chapter 19

೧**ಲ

Muri sped toward the chamber. Bull hovered in front of the wall of glass with more wreckage of *Alina's Dream* at his tail. When he noticed her, he swam aside to reveal the inside of the horrible glass prison. Jack knelt on the ground, hunched over and coughing. Water trickled down his naked back, dripping from his wet hair.

Muri raced to the glass and pressed her palms against it. She didn't dare pound on it since she didn't know how strong it was. But Jack's head turned as if he sensed her there. His eyes were wide and wild with fear.

He staggered to his feet and came toward her, shouting, but the glass trapped his voice and reduced it to a muffled yell. Bull yanked her elbow and dragged her away from the glass. He pulled her backward as she reached toward Jack. Muri struggled against him.

"Let him go!" she cried, twisting, but Bull held her fast.

"He's not dead yet," Bull said, "but he will be if you step out of line."

Muri froze in Bull's arms. If she fought again, he'd become angry and he might hurt Jack. "What do you want me to do?"

"Strombidae and I reached an agreement," Bull said, "after you left the hot spring. He let me go while the human wasn't watching."

"What did you promise him?"

"You."

"Fine. I'll go lie with him. Now let Jack go."

"You won't just lie with him," Bull said, lowering his voice. "You'll live with him. You'll be the perfect wife for him once I dry you out, too."

Muri's stomach lurched. She couldn't. She couldn't lose her tail and live as Strombidae's wife. Such a future was too horrid to imagine.

But she'd offered to dry herself out for Jack. If drying out was the only way to save him . . .

"You'll let Jack go if I do it?"

Bull smirked. "We'll see."

"Why would I agree to anything if you're going to kill him anyway?"

"Agree? I don't care if you agree."

A ring of merpeople had formed around them. Bull's henchmen hovered with arms crossed over their chests and smug grins spread on their faces. But Caly and the mermaids Muri had gathered flitted behind the mermen, looking from her to Jack, and their faces betrayed confusion and fear. And other mermen and merwomen had come to see what the fuss was. They left a wide radius around Bull, stared at Jack, and murmured among themselves.

Bull grabbed Muri's wrist. "Time to go above. I'm guessing we'll have to tie you to stop you from going in the water. But you know all about tying people up, don't you?"

Muri couldn't help it. She jerked her arm against Bull's thumb, the way Jack had shown her, and freed herself. She swam back from Bull.

He reached for her again and she backed away.

Arms came around her from behind—Turr. She couldn't drop her weight, not in the water. She bent forward and bit his arm as hard as she could. He bellowed a curse and his arms loosened, and she broke free. Bull rushed her, his tail swishing and his arms pinned to his sides. She couldn't grab his arm the way she had practiced on land. She reached for his head, getting two fistfuls of his hair and yanking him forward and past her. As he flew past, she caught the end of his tail. She bit into the thin tail fin as hard as she could.

Bull roared in pain, but he couldn't reach her and he couldn't jerk his tail free without damaging it. Muri held on, digging in her fingernails as Bull tried to maneuver his upper half backward to reach her. For a moment, the scene swirled in chaos with Bull's screams and the crowd crying out around her. Then hands pulled her back, causing Bull to cry out again. They pried her mouth open. Too many of them had her—she couldn't fight three mermen at once. She spit out the taste of Bull's skin as they pulled her off him.

Bull hung in the water panting, murder in his eyes. His hair had tangled in his frenzy.

Not Jack, Muri thought. Please not Jack.

Bull swam forward and grabbed her wrist again. With the mermen holding her from behind, struggling was futile.

Bull's gaze darted around at the ring of merpeople, all watching for his next move. Their chins were up. The usual deference to the merking was wavering. She turned to Jack, who still pressed his palms against the glass. He ran to the door and struggled to open it, even though it would've meant drowning. Thankfully it held fast. The merpeople nearest the door backed away, watching him.

Bull growled and rose up in the water, pulling her—and the mermen holding her—with him. "Strombidae has returned to the island using the boat of this human," he bellowed. "I've destroyed the boat to stop the human from returning to land. We don't want him telling the other humans how to find our island. Strombidae has shared with me the secrets of the merking's magic. Muricidae will be the first to see me wield it."

Bull turned to Turr and said in a low voice, "Help me get her to the grove."

Two mermen yanked her forward and the crowd parted. Muri twisted, trying to see Jack, but merpeople filled the water between them.

"He's lying!" Muri shouted. "The merking's magic is a hoax! The humans are kind! Everything's a—"

A hand clamped over her mouth.

No one spoke as the mermen hauled her away. But the crowd watched her pass.

She had to save Jack. But how? Even if she got free and got him out of that chamber and up to the island again, his boat was gone. How would she ever get him back to his village safely?

They'd moved beyond the crowd. Turr held her on one side, and Bull took her other arm and sent the rest of his mermen back.

"Aren't we taking her to the island?" Turr asked once they'd gone.

"There's no time," Bull said. "I had to shut her up before she riled everyone. I need to deal with that mess." He gestured back toward the crowd. "I'll lock her in the grove and deal with her later." His free hand came up and pinched Muri's arm hard.

"Just show them your magic, your highness," Turr said. "That'll shut them up."

Muri narrowed her eyes at Bull but didn't interfere. Turr would never believe anything she said, and winning him over would be pointless anyway. He wouldn't help her even if he believed the truth about the merking. He'd keep tagging along behind Bull and doing his bidding. At least she had told the other royal wives and Caly the truth before she was stopped, that the merking's magical objects were just—

Muri started. Fairy spells. The merking's magic was stolen fairy spells. And one of them was the shell she and Lotti had used. She'd left the other half with Hyacinth. Maybe she could reach Hyacinth to ask for help.

She had to get into the vault with the spells.

Muri glanced sideways at Bull. He had no idea what he was doing, but he was desperate to retain his power. Strombidae had told him about the magic, eh? And she'd be the first to see him wield it? Bull knew the vault contained only old fairy spells. But did he know how to use any of them?

"Your highness," she said, looking down. "I need to discuss the merking's magic with you."

Turr regarded her, but Bull ignored her.

She couldn't offend him. She couldn't imply he didn't know what he was doing, not in front of Turr, or he'd never listen even if he floundered because of it.

"I spent time with fairies on land," Muri said. "They showed me their magic, and some of it could be used by anyone. It could enhance your power."

Bull's nostrils sucked in with a sharp inhale. Now he was interested.

"Perhaps we could trade," she added.

Bull jerked to a stop. Turr stopped behind her. The grove lay a little further ahead, no longer guarded now that no one was imprisoned inside. Since Bull had become the merking, Strombidae's former wives had returned to their huts.

"Move back, Turridae," Bull said. "I've got her."

Turr exhaled, hesitating to let go of her arm. Finally he dropped it and swam quickly back.

Muri lowered her voice. "Strombidae may have told you how to enter the vault, but did he tell you how to use any of the spells?"

"I can figure it out once I'm inside."

"Can you? Are you sure? Because that crowd at the air chamber didn't seem like they'd tolerate a misstep. You wouldn't want to appear weak."

His hand tightened on her arm. She'd upset him. Good.

"I could help you. I could show you how to use the spells, if you let Jack go."

Bull's lips mashed tight like a fist. She had him.

"You'll show me first," he said.

"Take me to the vault."

The royal vault was tucked behind the arena and the grove. It shared the tall rock walls but wasn't open on top like the grove. Instead, it was a cave with a solid door mounted to block the entrance.

Only the merking was allowed past the chains—human-made chains—hanging around its borders. The lie was that anyone else venturing inside the chains would be struck dead by the magic unless they had the merking's permission. Bull and Turr flinched slightly as they swam in. It was strange to remember how fearful she used to be of this spot. It had always seemed mystical and dangerous. But the vault entrance was nothing special, just old chains covered with barnacles and slime.

Inside the chains was a wall of rock with the vault door in the center. The door was also made of human metal, rusted and decrepit. They stopped in front of it. Bull let go of Muri's arm and swam down to the ground to shove aside the boulder leaning against the base of the door. His eyes darted up to Turr as he hovered above it.

"You're never to touch this," he said. "It could kill anyone other than the merking."

Muri kept her face passive. Mocking Bull would only ruin her plan. And her plan was working so far, but once they were in the vault, what would she find? She hadn't seen many fairy spells on land. If she couldn't show Bull anything useful, he'd be angry. She'd have to watch for a chance to get the shell, no matter what else happened.

Bull rolled the boulder aside and the door swung out. Turr peered into the dark interior, his lips parted.

"Wait out here," Bull said, and Turr started forward and jerked to a stop. He stared at Bull—a memory popped into Muri's head of Captain staring at Jack when he'd wanted his bone. Muri could imagine Turr whining the same way at being left outside the vault.

Bull rested a hand on Turr's shoulder. "Make sure no one enters."

"No one would dare, your highness. They'd be fools to enter into the magic's domain without your permission."

"I'll feel better knowing you're out here," Bull said. "And Muri might try more of her tricks. Whatever happens, don't let her out of here without me."

Turr lifted his chin.

Bull swam into the vault. Muri followed him down a tunnel. The rocks closed in overhead, and the light from the doorway dwindled until even her underwater vision wasn't enough to see clearly. But something ahead glowed a strange color, a blue-lavender like the horizon at dawn. As they reached the end of the tunnel, the glow brightened. It coated the walls and ceiling. Bull twisted to keep his wide shoulders away from it. Maybe he thought it was enchanted. Behind his back, Muri put out her hand and touched it, and the sparkling color came off on her fingers. It was some kind of luminescent substance.

The tunnel opened into a single room. The glowing light of the walls revealed objects strewn about, but nothing looked magical about any of it—a rusted human tea kettle, and mugs like the ones she'd had her ale in at the pub, but with the handles broken off. Why had Strombidae kept any of this? Maybe he hadn't known what was what, either—maybe he'd suspected the tea kettle had fairy powers he didn't understand and he'd hoped to figure out how to use it. Supposedly each merking passed knowledge about the magic down to his successor, but with all the bitterness of the fights for the throne, Strombidae might have assumed he'd not been told everything.

Muri spotted a round metal object and reached for it. She popped open the clasp. Four human letters were spaced evenly around the edges and a needle was pinned in the center. She turned the object. The needle wobbled but kept pointing off to one side—to the north. Muri broke into a smile.

"It's a compass," she said breathlessly, as if it were the greatest treasure in the world.

Bull leaned in.

Muri turned the compass, pointing to the needle. In the water, it started to turn with the body of the compass but then righted itself.

"It always points toward the Warm Sea," she said. "To the north. The fairies enchanted it to do so. You can use it to navigate the oceans without checking the sun and stars."

Bull grabbed it from her.

"Careful, your highness. It has a delicate balance." Bull gawked at the compass in his palm as he twisted his body back and forth.

Okay, what else? Muri moved away from the pile of junk in the center of the room. Objects leaned against the walls, including a stick with ribbons hanging off the top. She'd seen that before—Strombidae had used it once when she'd been present in the arena. It truly was enchanted by the fairies, or it had been. She picked it up at the bottom the way Strombidae had and waved it through the water. A thin stream of rainbow light trailed out of the ribbons.

"What's that do?" Bull asked, pulling it from her. He jiggled it back and forth, and bits of rainbow color sputtered out.

"It makes rainbows," Muri said.

"Rainbows?" Bull's brows lifted. "What use is that?"

"I believe it's for entertainment. The merwomen like it."

The side of Bull's mouth cracked open with a huff. He dropped the stick to the ground.

Around the edges of the room, the glow disappeared from the walls in a few places. Leaning closer, Muri made out shelves in the rock with more trinkets on them. Maybe these had been placed above the rubble because they had spells on them. She glanced over a bell-shaped stone object. A glass jar with a strange lid and dried herbs inside. A curled shell.

She forced herself to swim past the shell as if it didn't matter. It was shaped like the shark-eye shell she'd left in Woodglen but much bigger, too big to hide in her palm. Bull would think it an ordinary shell.

She needed something—something she could hold over Bull to make him let Jack go. Something with real power he could use to his advantage, but power she could control.

A razor clam shell! She picked it up carefully. Underneath it, bands of metal crossed it—it was a fairy blade like the one Hyacinth had used to cut flower stems. Muri's lips broke into a smile. Strombidae must not have known what it was because she had never seen him use it.

"You'll like this one, your highness," she said, slipping the metal over two fingers. She gently touched the blade, and her fingertip stopped a hair's width off it. The blade was protected. Hyacinth had said fairy words to remove the protection.

Muri pictured Hyacinth as hard as she could and murmured the sounds she had heard, not knowing what they meant but hoping they would work. The band around her fingers warmed slightly—or had she imagined it?

Muri turned to Bull and held up her hand. "It's a fairy blade. It's enchanted to cut. It can cut through anything. Here, watch." She leaned down to grab one of the broken pottery mugs as her pulse pounded. Would the blade work? She held the mug up and put the edge of the shell to the remaining stump of the handle. The shell sliced right through.

Bull's face lit up.

Muri bent away to place the mug down and murmured the spell again.

Bull seized her wrist, careful to avoid the edge of the razor clam shell.

"I've protected it," she said. "The blade won't cut you now. There's a spell you say to use it." She slipped the metal off her fingers and held the shell out to him.

Bull pulled the blade onto his finger. He turned to Muri.

"Say the spell," he said.

"Let Jack go."

Bull grabbed her neck with both hands, and the clam shell

pressed into one side but didn't cut her. "You viperfish, I've had enough of you. Tell me or I'll kill him right now."

"If you harm him, I'll never tell. I'll never tell you a thing more about any of this." Muri lifted her hand, gesturing at the walls. "All these spells, and you won't know how to use any of them. And Strombidae won't tell you because he doesn't even know. The merpeople will learn the truth about the 'merking's magic.' I don't care what you do to me. Dry me out, starve me, I'll never tell if you harm Jack."

They glared at each other.

A faint call came from the entrance. "Bull!"

Bull narrowed his eyes and exhaled. He swam to the tunnel and disappeared down it. Muri started for the shell but hesitated. She didn't have a satchel or a pocket to hide it in. She swam partway down the tunnel until the light of the ocean returned.

Bull blocked the exit. Beyond him, Turr hovered with Angar.

"But your highness," Angar was saying, "some of the people are saying we should return the human to the island. We're—"

Bull exhaled. "So stop them. You're a royal guard."

"We tried, but—"

"Never mind," Bull said. "I'll go back with you."

Turr pulled himself up and nodded toward the tunnel. "What about . . . ?"

Angar scowled at her over Bull's shoulder. He'd had it in for Muri ever since she'd stood up to him, back before Strombidae had left. "Lock her in the vault," he said. "That'll teach her. Remember when Strom shut Aplysiidae in for a night?"

Angar laughed low and Turr joined in. "Good idea, Angar. It's perfect, your highness. She deserves the merking's punishment."

Bull hesitated, and Muri could imagine what he was thinking. Leave her in the vault with all the fairy spells? He couldn't post a guard at the door without drawing suspicion about his magical power, and his hold on the people was already tenuous.

Bull turned and she pretended to cower back. "You'll spend the rest of the night here," he said, "and when I return, you'd better be prepared to talk."

He turned away. "Shut her in," he said. Angar grinned at her as he swung the door shut, leaving her in darkness. The boulder grated on the metal door as they slid it into place.

Muri waited to let them swim away. She felt her way to the door and pushed. It strained, but the bottom held fast with the boulder wedged against it.

She held the walls and made her way back down the tunnel until the glowing luminescence lit the way. She went straight to the shell.

It was three times bigger than the one she'd carried to Woodglen, but it had the same spiraling shape. She cupped her hands around it and lifted it carefully from its perch, bringing it to her lips.

"Hyacinth?" she whispered. She felt nothing. "Hyacinth? Gray?" She projected her voice. The shell warmed with a slight vibration and went still. Had she imagined it? In the wan blue light, nothing felt real. She moved her fingertips across the surface of the shell. It was dull and cold.

Hyacinth wouldn't hear her. She was in her flower shop, not under the water. The shells worked only in the water.

Muri rested her cheek against the smooth shell. "I have to save Jack," she murmured, tears leaking from her eyes. "I have to save him, and I need a boat to get him back to Sylvania or he'll be trapped in Glorypool forever and his life will always be in danger. I don't know what to do."

Muri cradled the shell in her palms and rested her forehead on it. She repeated the words, calling to Hyacinth, until her voice wore out. She hadn't slept well in days. She hugged the shell as she curled her tail in. She had to rest. When she rescued Jack, she'd need all her strength to get him to the surface fast enough.

Chapter 20

꼉✸ಛ

"Muri?"

Muri curled into a tighter ball, not wanting to leave the peaceful emptiness of sleep.

"Muri?"

But reality worked its way in. She was back in Glorypool. Bullidae was the merking.

And Jack was trapped below the water.

Muri sat up, allowing the nightmare to return. The vault around her glowed with the eerie blue-purple light. The shell was on the floor beside her.

"Muri?"

Muri shot up. A merwoman's voice floated down the tunnel from the entrance. A young voice . . .

"Caly!"

Muri swam into the tunnel. The door to the vault was open and her friend hovered in the water outside.

"Oh, Muri," Caly said as she neared. "Thank the seas you're all right. We didn't know what he'd done with you."

"Has he hurt Jack?"

"No, Jack's fine. But we need to get him to the surface."

"You'll help me?"

Caly took her hand. "We've been talking it over all night. Bull's behavior is wrong. And anyone can see Jack is more than a mindless beast. All of us want to help. And I think you'd find support among the older merwomen as well. After Bull took you away, his mermen shooed everyone back to their huts, but people were grumbling."

"How did you find me?"

"His men were laughing about how he'd left you here. Why did Bull change his mind?"

"I tricked him into putting me in the vault. I wanted to try to reach the fairies using one of the spells. But I don't think it worked."

"I was scared to open the door. The merking's magic truly isn't real."

"No. The vault is mostly a room full of junk. Thank you for coming."

"Let's go before anyone sees," Caly said.

Together, they shut the vault door and pushed the rock back into place.

"Stay back and I'll watch for guards," Caly said. "Most everyone's sleeping. Bull's mermen were drinking phyta all night. We spied on them until they passed out. We should be able to get to Euli's hut without being seen."

Muri followed Caly through the water. They stayed low, down among the rocks and seaweed, as they wound between the arena wall and the royal hut.

Caly looked back as they neared the air chamber. "Stay behind the seaweed, Muri. Bull has guards around the chamber." Muri forced herself to stay hidden, resisting the pull to peek out. They needed a plan to get Jack out or they'd end up drowning him.

"Don't worry," Caly whispered. "We'll get him to the surface."

"I can't let him die, Caly. I can't let him stay in that cage. It's monstrous."

"I see that now," Caly said. "And so do the others. He tried to break the walls as Bull carried you off, and he hasn't stopped watching for you since. And the way he looked at you . . . Everyone could see how he cared about you. Merpeople were whispering and a few even called for his release before the guards ushered them away."

They came to the thick cluster of kombu separating the royal hut from the smaller stone huts. Once they were among the thick brown strands, Caly peeked out and motioned Muri forward. They slipped out, moving between the silent huts to the one shared by Euli and several other mermaids. Caly pushed aside the woven drapery and hurried Muri in the door.

A ring of mermaids rose to meet her.

"Blessed seas!"

"Come, Muri, can you eat?"

Euli, Perse, Apl—all the mermaids she'd gathered yesterday and more besides. They pulled her into the hut.

"We don't have much time," Caly said, and everyone quieted and turned. "We've all agreed to help Muri rescue her human. And we've agreed we want Glorypool to change. We want the mermen to work, and the merwomen to have more say in things. Muri saw how things are on land. We want to hear more about it."

Caly turned to her. "We saw you fight back, Muri. You broke free of Bull's hold and Turr's, and when Bull charged you, you didn't let him get you. We're planning to lure the guards away from the air chamber, but we want to be ready to fight if we need to. Tell us how you do it."

Muri gazed around at the faces, all eager and wide-eyed.

"I can show you the moves Jack taught me," she said. "Jack is the human," she added.

"He taught you?" someone asked. "Why?"

"He wanted me to be able to defend myself if anyone tried to harm me."

The mermaids stirred, expressing surprise. Muri wished they could all experience the kindness she had from Jack.

Muri bit her lip, thinking. "We don't have much time. I can show you moves that might be useful under the water, but there's more we could do on land."

"Show us," Caly said, "so we can help you get Jack to the island. We can learn more up there."

Muri moved forward and motioned Caly toward her. Using Caly as an opponent, she showed the others how she'd broken out of Bull's hand grasp by using the weak spot at his thumb, and how she'd used Bull's momentum to fling him away from her instead of meeting him head on. She told them the tricks she'd learned, like using her teeth and attacking the sensitive spots on her opponent.

And she told them to harness their anger.

"They want us to think we have no power," Muri said. "But we do. The mermen might be bigger than us, and they show off their bulging arms when they wrestle, but we work every day. They've used fear to hold us back—the threats of the merking's magic and of danger lurking outside the settlement—but those were lies. And we're as strong as they are. We don't need a king to boss us around."

"Treasonous viper."

The drapery at the door pushed aside and Angar towered in the doorway.

Muri drew herself up as Angar swam into the hut. Behind him, the mermaids nearest the door moved to block his exit. Muri smiled.

Angar's scowl deepened. "The merking will reward me for catching you."

Muri smiled wider. "I guess you better try to catch me then."

Angar growled and moved forward, and Muri moved aside. Around her, the circle of mermaids watched. Angar tried again, faster, and Muri caught his arms and flung him past her.

"See how I used his momentum?" she asked the others. The mermaids who'd caught Angar turned him around and held him up. He yanked his arms from their grip, baring his teeth as he fumed.

Caly swam into the center of the hut. "Let me try." She turned to Angar, narrowing her eyes. "Come on, Angar. You wanted me once and Muri stopped you. Now's your chance. Come and get me."

This time Angar bellowed as he started forward. Caly caught his arms and pulled them so hard he thudded to the ground, even with the water buoying him.

"Good!" Muri said. She dropped onto the back of Angar's neck with her hands. "Push me down," she added, and two of the mermaids obliged. Angar flailed beneath her, but with all the mermaids holding him down, he couldn't get up. "You can stop his breathing by pushing here, and once he's unconscious, you escape. It's easier to do when you don't have water all around, and if he's on his back."

"Here," Caly said, "let's flip him over and you can show us."

Muri floated away and Angar flicked his tail and tugged on his arms, but mermaids had grabbed ahold of him. They lifted him and flopped him onto his back. He snapped his teeth as Muri descended. She took a fistful of his hair and held his head so he couldn't bite her tail.

"When you have legs on land, you use them to press here." Angar struggled harder, but the mermaids held him fast. As Muri came off him, he inhaled and opened his mouth.

Caly appeared beside his head with a clump of kombu. She pushed it into his gaping mouth. Angar tried to shout, but the seaweed muffled his cries.

"Are there any loose vines?" Muri asked.

"Out by the nets," someone said. She swam out and returned with an armload.

They flipped Angar again, and the mermaids pulled his arms behind his back as Muri looped a vine around his wrists and tied a square knot, working the loop smaller and smaller before pulling the knot tight. Next she tied a clove hitch around both his wrists, but she couldn't tell how strongly it resisted his wiggling, so she tied a few more random knots around him to be safe. None of her knots were as tight as the ones Jack had used, but hopefully they were enough to hold him.

Since he didn't have ankles, Muri tied a vine around the narrow part of his tail and looped it around his neck and pulled it taut. His tail folded behind him, curved like a seahorse. He writhed as they moved him behind a row of baskets. Caly covered him with woven mats to hide him. His smothered curses were barely audible.

Caly turned to Muri. "Now let's go rescue your human before the settlement wakes."

Chapter 21

֍

THE GROUP OF MERMAIDS SWAM from Euli's hut to the kombu forest shielding the royal hut and the air chamber. When they were hidden among the strands, Caly peeked out and turned to the group.

"It's only Mitridae," she said. "Maybe Angar was the second guard. This makes it easier. So . . ." She began pointing at the mermaids as she spoke. "Euli and Perse will lure Mit away. That should be easy—he's such a sap. If you can, subdue him the way we did Angar. Apl and Riss will work on the chamber." She addressed Muri. "We think we figured out how it works. The little compartment is an antechamber that fills with air or water, depending on if you're going in or out. Muri, you want to be the one who brings him up, right?"

Muri nodded.

"You'll go in and bring Jack into the antechamber, and we'll fill it with enough water to offset the pressure of the ocean. When you tell us, we'll open the door, and you'll have to pull him out quick and go straight up. We'll cover you in case anyone comes after you."

How fast could she swim to the surface? Thirty heartbeats? Fifty? And how long could Jack hold his breath?

It didn't matter. Trying this was the only choice.

"Everyone ready?"

Muri started forward, and Caly pulled her back. "We need to clear the guard off first."

Euli and Perse pushed through the strands of kombu, and their tails slipped out of sight. A moment later, their voices drifted through the water. The words were unclear, but the tone was sultry. Mitridae called out for Angar. The mermaids' voices resumed. They grew louder, coming toward the kombu.

"Wait for Angar," Mit whined. "I can't leave my post without him here."

"We'll go in the kombu," Euli replied. "You can keep watch the whole time."

"If Angar comes," Perse added, "he'll want to join us, and he's the worst kisser."

"We both wanted to spend time with you."

The kombu rustled, and the mermaids pulled Mit in. His eyes widened and he jerked back, but he'd realized too late he'd been tricked. Euli and Perse held his arms fast as he twisted and flapped his tail, and Caly pried his fingers off his stick until he dropped it. As they tied and gagged him, Muri pushed past and through the kombu.

Jack stood in the chamber, waiting with his hands flat against the glass wall and watching in her direction. When he saw her, he leaned forward. He followed as she rounded the glass to the door. Caly came beside her and the others hovered near.

Apl and Riss slid aside the door into the antechamber and Muri swam in. They shut the door behind her. Jack was beyond the next door, with only a thin sheet of glass between them. He pressed his palms against it, and Muri placed hers opposite.

"Can you hear me, Muri?" Caly asked, her shout faint through the glass, and Muri nodded. "You're sealed in. Open the door to the chamber."

Muri found the latch with a hook that locked the door shut. She lifted the hook. Before she could slide the door open, Jack had done it. The water from the antechamber spilled onto the dry ground, and Muri fell into Jack's arms.

She had no time to revel in being with him, not while they were down here.

"I'm taking you back to the island," Muri said. "I'll swim faster without your clothes."

Jack shifted her in his arms to unbutton his trousers and push them down. He'd already lost his shoes. He shrugged the damp clothing to the ground and stepped out of it.

"Lock yourself back in," Caly shouted.

Jack carried Muri back into the antechamber and reached one arm back to slide the door closed behind them. Muri fumbled to hook the lock. Water swirled around Jack's feet as the mermaids refilled the antechamber.

Muri stared into Jack's eyes. "I'm going to get you to the surface," she said.

"I trust you."

The water reached their knees and then their waists. As the water rose higher, Muri pushed herself from Jack's arms, able to swim again. She placed his arms on her shoulders and hugged around his bare chest.

"Don't try to help," she said. "Just keep still and hold on and hold your breath." She turned her body sideways so Jack was at her hip, leaving her tail free to move back and forth without hitting his legs. She tightened her hold on him.

"No matter what happens," he said, "I'm glad I saw you again."

She kept her face forward. She was not going to fail.

"Get ready," she said. The water was up to their necks. Jack took a deep breath, and Muri looked at Caly.

"Now," she said.

The door slid open and Muri shot out.

She swam as hard as she could straight for the surface, counting in her head. Five heartbeats passed. Ten beats. She held Jack tightly against her to reduce the drag of the water. Twenty beats.

No light came from above. She didn't dare look at Jack. He hadn't moved a smidge.

Thirty beats. Her tail thrashed through the water. Her breathing strained, her muscles ached, but she refused to slow down. In her peripheral vision, someone appeared behind Jack. Jack lurched upward against her arms, and her load lightened as she accelerated. Apl was beside him, helping to carry him. Together, they propelled him upward into the darkness.

Forty beats. Faster. Faster! Do it for Jack. Her tail ached but she pumped it back and forth. Fifty beats. Shouts sounded around her but she focused on swimming. The rest of the mermaids came in a circle around her. Someone reached a hand in to push her upward, and the others were pulling up on the helpers, creating a ring of motion all working together to reach the surface. A faint light shone down. Muri sprinted, no longer counting. The mermaids on the edges disappeared, one by one as they shot above the surface.

Muri broke into the air, hauling Jack up with her as she launched them into the sky. He sucked in a breath as they fell back toward the surface, crashing into the sea. His arms around her shoulders pushed her under the water as he floundered. Muri sank and let him go, but only for a moment. She flitted behind him, surfaced, and held him up from behind.

"You're okay," she whispered. "You're okay."

Jack's struggling ceased. His panting was harsh, and his pulse pounded against her cheek where she rested it on his neck, but he sank down into the water against her. His chest expanded and contracted under her arms, and for a moment, she forgot everything as she held him tight, burying her face in his wet hair.

"Come on, Muri," Caly said. "They'll be after us."

Muri gazed around. The mermaids bobbed in the water nearby, staring at her and Jack in her arms. Their expressions ranged from wide-eyed wonder to smiles to lip-biting smirks. The waving trees on the island were a short distance off. The sun was climbing the sky in the east.

Muri squeezed Jack one more time. "We've got to swim," she said. "Are you all right?"

He barely nodded. She folded one arm across his chest to keep his head above the surface and set off.

Within minutes, the mermaids were crawling onto the beach. As the sand scraped Muri's tail, Jack twisted out from her arm and fell onto his knees in the water. He staggered up and onto the beach.

Muri pulled herself onto the warm sand and watched his back as he stood alone. His shoulders heaved with each breath he took. He covered his face with his hands. His broad back was smooth and tan, but below his waist, his skin turned pale like a moonfish, from his bottom all the way down his long legs to his calves, where the tan resumed. Humans and their weird clothing habits! As their tails faded, the mermaids were tan-tinted-green from their faces to their toes.

Muri's scales tingled and her tail became legs, but she stayed on the sand waiting, and the other mermaids did the same. Jack rubbed his face and ran his hands over his hair. He slowly turned.

She stood to face him. He stared at the sand. He was blushing.

Muri stepped forward and took his hand. She cleared her throat.

"This is Jack," she said, locking her fingers through his.

One by one the others stood and gathered round, and Muri introduced them. Not a single one of them glanced down at his pale naked body, and his shoulders slowly relaxed.

"Thank you for rescuing me," he said at last, and that low voice she loved rolled down Muri's body and settled between her legs, but they had no time for that now.

"How did Bull get free?" Muri asked him.

"I don't know. I turned my back for a moment, and when I returned, Bull jumped me and knocked me out. I woke as he dragged me into the water. I never saw Murkel again."

"Strombidae betrayed you," Muri said, scanning the trees. "Bull promised to bring me to him and he let Bull go. They were going to dry me out and leave me on the island as a wife for Strombidae."

A few mermaids gasped.

"Bull's gone too far," Caly said, addressing them all. "He's following no code of merman honor."

"We'll tell everyone what he threatened."

"We have to defeat him."

"Will you really teach us to fight?" Caly asked Jack, and the mermaids pressed in closer.

Jack blushed again but he nodded.

They moved up the beach and when Jack was ready, he began his lesson. Soon he was showing the mermaids the moves he'd taught Muri, and they practiced on each other and on him. Muri searched the trees again, but nothing moved in the shadows. Strombidae had better stay away. If she ever saw him again, she would tie him in the jungle and leave him to the monkeys. She would never forgive him for betraying Jack.

She turned back to watch Jack. If he was uncomfortable wrestling with a crowd of naked merwomen, he was certainly hiding it. She winced as Apl slammed him onto the sand.

"Good," he gasped.

They practiced until they grew tired. Then they sat in the shade to wait. The settlement should be awake by now. They'd find the guards missing and Jack gone from the air chamber, and they'd soon notice that mermaids were missing, too. If anyone searched the vault, they'd find Muri gone. They'd come to the beach. The mermaids had nowhere else to go unless they swam into the open ocean.

"I wonder what Bull's up to," Muri said.

"Maybe he's trying to find Mit and Angar," Caly said, and everyone laughed.

"They were the ones guarding you this morning," Muri told Jack. "We've tied them up in Euli's hut."

"Who was the one who grabbed you last night?" he asked. "Before you fought Bull."

"That's Turr."

"Bull sent him to destroy my boat," Jack said quietly.

Muri touched his arm. "We'll find a way to get you home." He regarded her, and his eyes were sad. He was probably wondering if she'd go with him.

Jack broke their gaze first. "You all carry knives," he said to the mermaids, indicating the pile of gear on the ground. They'd removed their belts before practicing together. "What do you think of fighting with those?"

"We just use them for harvesting," Caly said.

"It seems foolish to fight with a knife," Apl added, "when the opponent could take it from you."

"I would agree," Jack said.

"I have a question," Perse said. "Do we need to fight? Can't we just tie them up when they flop out of the water?"

"You could," a voice said from the jungle, and Muri shot to her feet. Everyone around her stood, too, staring into the shadows.

Bull stepped forward amid the undergrowth. Behind him among the thick leaves and trunks of palm trees lurked Turr and two other mermen—but not Mit or Angar. Bull carried a knife upright in his hand, in addition to the useless fairy blade on his finger.

The mermaids clustered around Muri, and they backed away onto the beach. Jack scooped up the pile of knife belts as Bull and his mermen advanced out of the trees.

"You could tie us up," Bull said again, "if we came out of the water."

Even sorely outnumbered, Bull's arrogance wafted off him. Why had he brought only three mermen? Angar and Mit might still be tied up, but Bull had at least a dozen more mermen who'd been with him in the bay at Woodglen or acting as guards the past few days. Maybe he didn't want all his minions to see that he had opposition. Maybe he hoped to quell their rebellion quietly. Muri smirked. His mistake.

He and his lackeys grinned, and his knife hand tightened. He might cut their throats without a second thought.

"Let me fight Bull," Jack said quietly, "until I can get those knives out of his hands."

"The fairy blade is dull," Muri said. "He doesn't know the words of the spell."

"It should be even quicker then."

"I thought you didn't like fighting with knives?"

"That doesn't mean I've never fought against one. Don't worry. I'm betting Bull's not skilled with his legs."

Skilled with his legs? Before she could ask, the mermen started forward. The mermaids split to avoid Bull, leaving only Jack in his path. Bull's eyes narrowed as he stalked forward. And Muri couldn't stop watching, even as Caly and Perse darted forward beside her to tackle one of the other mermen. As Bull lunged, Jack sidestepped from him. Jack's whole body swiveled and tilted, and one leg came up and he kicked the knife from Bull's hand. It flew across the beach and embedded in the sand.

"He's all yours, ladies," Jack called. The three mermaids waiting for a fight moved in to surround Bull. Beyond them, the other mermaids had the three mermen down on the sand in various states of skirmishing. Muri couldn't see a place to help so she watched with pride, standing beside Jack after he retrieved Bull's knife. After a brief struggle, Bull and all three others were pinned to the sand.

Bull strained against the mermaids holding him one last time before wilting. "We've reached a stalemate," he panted from the ground.

"A stalemate?" Muri snorted. "All of your mermen are down. Are you ready to bargain, or do you want us to go below and take out the rest of your henchmen?"

Bull's lips curled in and he exhaled forcefully. He didn't speak.

Well then. They'd have to get vines and secure the mermen on the beach. Muri prepared to direct the others.

Someone splashed out of the waves and lurched onto the sand. As everyone turned to see who it was, more merpeople appeared in the waves. They were not Bull's followers but all different merwomen and mermen. Someone must have rallied them to come to the island.

What would they think of the situation? Would they support Bull? She'd drag Jack into the jungle to hide if they went for him. Muri stood taller and waited.

Soon the merpeople lined the shore—the entire population of Glorypool, minus Angar and Mit. A few of the mermen, the ones who followed Bull, cried out when they saw him. As their legs formed, they started toward where Bull was held, but other merpeople stopped them.

Muri waited as one by one the residents of Glorypool stood up on the beach. Bull fumed silently. Everyone would know he'd lost a fight. As the merpeople stood, they gathered closer. Lotti stood at the back, scanning the tree line—no doubt hoping to find Strombidae.

Hipp walked forward first. "What's going on here?"

Muri gestured at Jack and the friends who'd helped free him. "We were spending time on the beach when Bull and three mermen attacked us with a knife. We fought back and subdued them."

Bull struggled and the mermaids let him go. He scrambled to his feet. "Muricidae disobeyed my rule. She freed my prisoner."

Muri crossed her arms over her chest and raised an eyebrow. "You have no right to take a human prisoner. And you nearly drowned him bringing him down to Glorypool. You'd make enemies of the humans and endanger us all."

"He attacked me first!" Bull said. "He ambushed me and tied me up at the hot spring."

The crowd murmured. This must not have been the story Bull had given when he'd returned from the hot spring with Jack.

"That's not true," Muri said, turning to the crowd. "I'm the one who fought the merking and defeated him. But I was only defending myself. He took me to the island against my will."

Bull began to move, to argue, and several merpeople stepped forward to block him.

"Let her finish," Hipp said.

"We've been lied to," she continued. "We've been told the merking possesses magic we need to fear, but it's not true. Ages ago, the fairies gave the merpeople spells to help them survive, and only a few remain. The merking uses them to pretend he has magic. Bull locked me in the vault last night, and Caly came this morning and opened it to let me out, and neither of us were struck dead.

"And we've been told the fairies and humans are our enemies, but I went to a village on land. Fairies helped me, and the humans were nice to me. They're not beasts like we've been told—they're kind and intelligent."

"But the fairies abandoned the merpeople," someone called out.

"They didn't mean to," Muri said. "Forty seasons ago, the fairies were forced into isolation by a terrible queen. She didn't let them leave their home. That's why they stopped meeting with the merpeople and sharing their spells."

Muri stepped back to stand among the mermaids who'd fought with her. "We're tired of the way things are in Glorypool. We fight to choose a king and we end up with someone like Bull, who endangers us all by causing trouble for the humans. We could have a different process. We could choose someone with new ideas or someone who helps others. And we've been told the mermen need to protect the settlement instead of working to harvest food, but when has the settlement ever been threatened?"

"What about Janthinidae?" someone asked.

Muri's heart stuttered. Janthinidae *had* disappeared—but no one had ever found her remains. Muri lifted her chin. "No one knows what happened to Janthinidae."

A murmur went through the crowd. They parted at the back and Lotti stepped forward.

"I know," Lotti said, and everyone turned to her. "Janthinidae always spoke out of turn. She caused trouble. When Strombidae became king, he . . . asked her to leave. She went back to Merianalis."

The merpeople stirred at Lotti's revelation. Muri sorted through the words—Strombidae wouldn't have asked Janthinidae to leave. He'd have ordered it. Janthinidae might have been glad to return to the place she had loved. But could she have made the long journey alone? Hopefully she had made it safely home.

Muri drew herself up taller. "Has anyone here ever seen a deadly shark or any other threat to the settlement?"

No one spoke.

"The merwomen do all the work in Glorypool. I propose a change. I propose that everyone works and everyone helps run the settlement. No one is bullied or ordered around."

In the crowd, many of the merwomen whispered. Lotti's head was down. Would enough merpeople be in favor of such a change?

Hipp stepped forward. He regarded Muri, frowning. He lowered his gaze and turned to the crowd. "I support this."

Eyes widened and merpeople gasped. Whispers filled the air. Bull gave a low growl.

Hipp looked up and waved his hands in the direction of the crowd. "Look at our settlement," he said. "We live in the same huts our ancestors lived in. We eat from the same few patches of seaweed, and we never have enough. We've not been graced with merchildren for twenty seasons. What do we live for? The merwomen work and rarely have a moment to enjoy themselves. But I suspect the mermen who are idle are not much happier."

He lowered his hands, pausing. "I too visited the land settlement." Voices rose in disbelief, but Hipp continued. "When Strombidae didn't return, I was curious. I swam to their shore and watched the land dwellers. And I saw they were not like we've always believed. They're smarter than animals and they form bonds of friendship.

"I also saw how they work together and what it has done for them. They have comfortable dwellings and plenty of food, and they have families that bring them joy. If we worked together, perhaps we could have that here. We could plant new fields of seaweed and harvest more. We could encourage the fish to thrive and fill our nets. We could harvest more fruits from the island and find ways to store them to give us a steady supply. And we could have enough food to support merchildren."

Muri's hope swelled. Hipp's words were moving the crowd, she could tell. Everyone thrummed with excited voices, talking to those around them. Only Bull and his guards glowered.

Bull lifted his hand and pointed toward her. Muri followed his gesture as everyone turned to look . . . at Jack. Jack straightened as his eyes darted over the crowd.

"What about him?" Bull asked. "We can't have a human living on our island. And now he knows where it is. If he goes home, we risk more of them coming. They'll come with their ships and their machinery and cut our trees, and seduce the mermaids the way he's seduced Muricidae. And they'll bring their fairy friends to help them with magic."

"Sounds good to me," Euli quipped, but some in the crowd muttered.

Bull pressed on. "Muricidae and Hipponicidae say they want a better society, but how do we know we can trust them? Muricidae's obviously been swayed by the human and her so-called fairy friends. And Hipp admits he went to land against all of Glorypool's rules! We have those rules for a reason. The humans have poisoned him, too. Or maybe even a fairy poisoned his mind with their evil magic. They could both be poisoned in the head by the fairies and spreading that poison to all of you."

"It's not true," Muri said, but the crowd was rumbling louder. She was going to lose them to Bull's idiotic fearmongering.

"Something's coming!"

The cry from the crowd repeated, and merpeople pointed out to sea. Something was moving across the water along the island.

It was large, but what was it? It glinted in the sunlight like metal. It moved across the water like a sailboat, but it didn't have the usual triangular sail. Instead, large square sails swelled over it like on a large traveling ship, filled with wind over the metal hull. It was as if a pirate battle ship had mated with the metal of the human tools.

The craft shifted direction, although the sails stayed eerily filled with wind. It headed directly toward the beach. Overhead, a swarm of gulls circled the ship, crying loudly. Now seen head on, metal tubes protruded from both sides of the ship. One of the tubes flashed with light, and a moment later a boom rolled across the water as smoke belched out of it.

Everyone gasped. "Cannons!" Everyone knew the humans possessed such weapons, but no one had ever seen one in action.

The boat was in the waves, speeding toward the beach, moments away from landing. Gunshots banged from it, and another cannon fired. The merpeople had backed away, up to the top of the beach near the trees.

A figure stepped up onto the prow of the ship. It was Hyacinth.

Chapter 22

It was Hyacinth, but not the Hyacinth Muri had last seen in the Fairweather Florist. This Hyacinth wore tight britches and a tunic emblazoned with a bluebird, while a cape billowed out behind her in the ocean breeze. And her hair was pulled up and held in place by—Muri squinted to make sure she was seeing it right—a pair of small birds. Living, flapping birds who let out sharp little screeches from the top of her head. In her hand, Hyacinth brandished a wooden staff topped with a cluster of hyacinth flowers.

The boat slowed as it skimmed toward the sand, although what caused it to slow was a mystery because the sails still appeared full of wind. As it hit the sand and jerked to a stop at the waterline, the flock of seagulls circling above let out a loud cry all together and swooped behind Hyacinth and straight at her. The merpeople cried out, but Hyacinth only held up her arms. The seagulls caught her arms and lifted her, and everyone stumbled into the trees as the birds carried her to the sand.

Hyacinth stepped onto the beach and lowered her arms. She coolly regarded the crowd as the birds flapped off to settle on the water. The sails on the ship now hung limply. The two birds in Hyacinth's hair nestled down, watching the merpeople with intense, beady eyes.

"I am the fairy Hyacinth," she said, holding the staff before her, and her voice boomed out clearly. Her words reverberated over the beach. The merpeople glanced all around, but the length of the beach was empty. Hyacinth continued, "I have been called by the merwoman Muricidae."

All the heads swiveled toward Muri.

"Why did you call, young mermaid? Tell us, so we may aid you."

Muri swallowed. "The merpeople want peace," she said. Her voice was faint compared to Hyacinth's.

"The merpeople want peace, you say?" Hyacinth said, echoing the words loudly.

Muri took a steadying breath. She spoke as loudly as she could. "The merpeople want peace and to keep our island safe. Several days ago, a group of mermen led by Bullidae went to the human village and threatened the fish-catchers. This was wrong of them and brought danger to us all. The humans might retaliate. But most of us don't want to cause trouble to the land dwellers or to have them trouble us. Do you agree?" She addressed the question to the merpeople. As she waited, many nodded or lifted a hand.

"We were discussing our settlement and how to make it better," Muri continued. "I want a just society where leaders are chosen by all instead of by a fight. I want the things Hipp talked about—enough food to be comfortable and to support merchildren. Is this what the merpeople want?"

Across the crowd, heads nodded and hands raised.

Hyacinth lifted her arms. "The fairies will leave the merpeople in peace, as will the humans, provided you do the same."

"We can't trust them," Bull said with an angry shout that carried across the crowd. "We should kill them before they take our secrets back. Before they all know where our island sits."

"It's too late, merman," Hyacinth said, and her amplified voice overpowered Bull's. "The birds know the way here, and they will tell the other fairies how to get here if you harm me."

Bull scoffed. "You can't make them do that."

"Can't I?"

Suddenly the gulls floating on the water lifted their wings. All together they took off, and once in the air they swooped into a circle over Hyacinth's head. A dozen broke off and dove at Bull. The merpeople scrambled out of the way, leaving Bull alone on the sand. The birds swerved away at the last moment, and when the air cleared, Bull's head was dripping with seagull droppings.

Muri smothered her laugh.

As the seagulls landed on the beach around Hyacinth, she lifted her staff again. "All the creatures of the earth bow to me! I speak with the birds of the air and the creatures of the sea! If you harass the humans, I will know and I will find the ones who do it and give you to my strongest followers. Not the birds or the fish, but creatures of the land."

A keening wail started in the jungle. The merpeople shuddered at the sound, turning to the trees and staggering back from them. They surveyed the trees with wide eyes and hands lifted in dismay.

Hyacinth's lips curled into the cruelest smile Muri had ever seen. Muri's heart skipped a beat, and she reached for Jack's hand, but he had it clamped over his mouth. His eyes were crinkled and his shoulders quaked. He was laughing.

"I call the monkeys," Hyacinth said.

The wailing intensified, and the entire crowd stumbled away from the trees and down the beach. Several merpeople ran for the water, diving in and swimming out a safe distance. The remaining merpeople huddled together at the water's edge, their eyes wide with terror.

A monkey appeared in the trees. It swung on a branch high over the sand. More monkeys leapt out of the shadows, filling the treetops and crying in their eerie voices. The tops of the palms and the coconut trees became thick with the hairy brown bodies and gangly arms and legs, the clawed feet gripping the bark and grimacing faces peering down. When the canopy was completely filled with monkeys, their call silenced, and they perched in the trees with their tails uncurled.

"They will not harm you," Hyacinth said, "if you keep your

word. If you keep peace with the land dwellers and among yourselves. If you abide by the rule of peace and love."

"You lie to us," Bull said, but the crowd ignored him.

"You'll have to trust me," Hyacinth replied. Her gaze scanned slowly over the crowd. "I will send the monkeys away. But remember. If you cannot keep the peace, I will call them back. Whoever causes harm will never be safe on the island. You will not be able to pick fruit without a monkey finding you. You will never lie together on a moonlit night without a monkey leaping onto your body and nipping at your . . . fingers. The monkeys will follow you."

Hyacinth lifted a hand. Silently, the monkeys disappeared into the forest.

A collective sigh went up from those who remained on the beach.

Hyacinth said, "From now on, it will be as you've discussed. Your leader will be chosen by the group."

"We've always had a king," someone said. "How will it work?"

Muri exhaled quietly. "We can still have a king," she said. "We'll choose one all together instead of fighting to see who wins. We've always let whoever wins the fight be king. And what has that gotten us? Have we been ruled with grace and intelligence? No, we've been lied to and isolated, and the king is constantly challenged and replaced. It gets us nowhere."

"So how do we pick the king?"

"The humans have a system." Muri hesitated. Jack had never explained to her how it was done.

Jack stepped forward. "It's called an 'election.' Anyone who's interested in being . . . king puts in their name, and everyone in the village gets to pick which candidate they like best. And whoever gets the most votes is the king."

"And," Jack added, "anyone can be king. Even a merwoman."

"I vote for Muricidae!" came a cry from the back of the crowd.

"Me too!"

A moment later, the entire crowd was chanting her name.

Muri's gaze met Jack's. He gave a small smile, but his eyes were sad.

Chapter 23

☙ ✳ ❧

Muri had no idea what to do about the crowd. They buzzed with excited voices, and her name repeated in the air as voices rose and fell.

Hyacinth stepped up to her and spoke in a low voice. "Can you send them back into the water?" She tipped her head toward the strange metal ship, and Muri abruptly realized where the strange ship had come from. She had to clear the merpeople away before they realized the invincible ship Hyacinth had arrived on was an illusion.

"Everyone!" Muri called, and Hyacinth repeated her call with her magic-enhanced voice to get the crowd's attention. "Let's meet in the arena this evening to make plans. You can return to the water now." Giving an order—even a mild one—felt awkward. And to have people follow the order was even stranger. Muri never wanted to be a king, but it seemed like she'd have to be. For now.

The merpeople began wading into the water and diving under. Hyacinth moved across the beach, herding them a bit as they hastened away from her. Bull tried to go quietly, but Hyacinth caught him and snatched the fairy blade from his finger.

Someone had retrieved Jack's clothing from the air chamber, and it now hid most of his untanned bits. He had his wet trousers draped over his arm. Muri tilted her head, watching him across the beach. When she considered human clothing, she did find one thing nice about it . . . the way it hid parts of a person—parts that could be revealed later when just the two of them were alone together. But when would that be?

The merpeople had cleared from the beach except for one. Lotti stood at the edge of the jungle, peering into the shadows. Muri went to her.

"Lotti, go to the hot spring."

"Do you think he'd want to see me?" She wrung her hands.

"Go find out."

Muri seethed inside when she thought of Strombidae handing Jack over to Bull, but she hated to see Lotti suffer. And it wasn't like they needed Lotti in Glorypool. The next time they needed to vote on something, she'd probably vote to reinstate Strombidae.

Lotti didn't move. "I know I was hard on you. I always had your best interests in mind."

"I know."

Still Lotti hesitated. "You spoke of what happened ten seasons ago."

Muri glanced quickly around. Jack and Hyacinth were waiting across the sand by the water.

"When Strombidae became merking," Lotti continued, "he wanted to do better for the merpeople. He got an idea to bring more fish to Glorypool. He went to the human shore with several mermen, and they came home with nets filled with fish to release in the waters here. But later I found out they'd caused an accident—they'd tipped a human boat and sank it, and the humans along with it. It was an accident. They didn't mean to harm anyone."

"But they could have saved the people!" Muri's whisper was frantic. "They could have brought them to shore—it wouldn't have taken a moment!"

Lotti stood unmoving and refused to meet Muri's gaze.

Muri lowered her voice. "Those were Jack's parents Strombidae murdered." She let out a long exhale, getting herself under control. "You'd better find your husband at the hot spring and make sure I never see him again."

Lotti turned away. She crossed the sand and disappeared onto the trail into the trees.

Muri turned back to the water.

"Thank the stars!" a voice called out, and the huge metal ship vanished. In its place was a small wooden sailboat with Gray slumped against the tiller. His hair was plain and black, and his shirt was the same white all the villagers wore. He pushed himself upright and let go of his hold on the boat as he slowly stood. He was shaking. He crawled toward the front of the boat, hanging onto the sail, which had been lowered down the mast and pooled in a heap. As Muri rushed across the sand, Jack hurried into the water to help Gray climb over the side of the boat and onto the beach.

Gray sank onto the sand and lay back, closing his eyes. "Hyacinth," he said in a weak voice, "you were marvelous."

"You were pretty good yourself," Hyacinth said. She shook her head, and the birds holding her hair up lifted off and flew into the trees.

"Pretty good?" Gray opened one eye with his lips parted in disbelief. "Creating an entire battleship with booming cannons while I was steering an actual sailboat?"

"All right, your illusion was amazing."

"Not to mention," Gray continued on, "I held it steady for ten hours while Muri overthrew the patriarchy." He gave a frail grin and slowly winked at Muri before his eyes closed again.

"Will he be all right?" Muri asked.

"Sometimes he needs to rest after using so much magic," Hyacinth said. "He can sleep it off on the ride home." She rounded on Jack. "What were you thinking, coming here by yourself?"

Jack faced the sand and ran a hand across his hair, but he didn't sound sorry when he said, "I had to go after Muri."

He glanced up at her, and she leapt across the sand and into his arms.

"Still," Hyacinth said more gently as Jack rubbed Muri's back, "they could've done more than destroy your boat. They could've drowned you."

Muri nuzzled harder into Jack's chest, and he didn't say anything.

"They tried to drown you!" Hyacinth said, and she leaned on her wooden staff. "Was it that Bull fellow again? Thank the stars you're safe."

"Muri saved me," Jack murmured, and he kissed the top of her head.

Muri turned in his arms and leaned back against his chest, and he rested his chin on her head. "Bull dragged him down to Glorypool and put him in the air chamber and locked me in a vault down there. But the mermaids let me out and helped me get Jack to the surface."

Hyacinth had gone pale and clutched her staff.

"But his boat was gone," Muri said. "That's why I tried to contact you. But I didn't think it worked. You heard me?"

"Not exactly. Something woke me, and I felt so distressed that I got up and paced around the room. And it got stronger when I went near your shell. And when I touched it, I felt sure something was wrong. I woke Gray and we searched for Jack, and when we saw that he was gone—and his boat, in the middle of the night—we guessed he must've come here following you."

"But how did you find the way?" Muri said.

"The birds guided us. At first we headed east, and once we got closer, we found some seagulls who knew exactly where to go."

"Minions," Gray muttered where he lay with his eyes closed.

"How did you do that with your voice?" Muri asked. "It was echoing across the beach."

Hyacinth lifted her staff with the hyacinth blossoms tied to the top.

"I told you she can do anything with hyacinth pollen," Gray said, stifling a yawn. "Luckily we have about ten horse-weights of it in the storage room. In case we encounter any more despotic merkings."

For a moment, the three of them stood in silence beside Gray. Jack's arms tightened around Muri.

"What will you do?" Hyacinth asked at last. "We should leave soon to make it as far as we can before the sun sets."

Panic seized Muri. She didn't want them to leave. But they *should* go right away, before anything else went wrong. Even if the merpeople wanted peace, Bull might discover that Hyacinth's battleship was merely a wooden sailboat and destroy this one, too. Then they'd all be trapped on the island instead of only Jack. The sooner they were home safely, the better.

She wanted to go with them. But if she left, the tentative beginning of a new society for the merpeople might fall apart.

Jack leaned down. "I'll wait for you," he whispered in her ear.

"I'll come back," Muri said, turning her face up to his. "As soon as I can. I'll tell them to elect a new king. I don't want to do it. I want to be with all of you." She twisted her body around to hug Jack tightly.

"Do what you need to do here," he said, "and come back to us."

When Jack let her go, Muri knelt beside Gray. His eyes slid halfway open. She took his hand.

"Thank you," she said.

"You can make it up to me when you get back," he said, blinking once slowly. "Maybe teach me to swim."

"You can't swim?!"

Gray's eyes fell closed. "Neither can Hy," he said. "But she has enough dolphin friends to rescue her if she falls in."

Muri gazed at his face, overcome with emotion. Jack had come for her knowing he'd be in danger. And Hyacinth and Gray had sailed a tiny boat across the Cold Sea to come when she needed help, when they couldn't even swim. They truly were her friends.

She let go of Gray and stood. As Gray sat up, Jack reached out a hand to pull him to his feet.

"What if this fails?" Muri said to Hyacinth. "It's not like you can actually attack with monkeys if someone does something wrong."

"Oh, you don't think—" Hyacinth began, but Gray interrupted.

"She means you can't do it from Woodglen," he said. "No one's questioning your utter dominion over all the creatures of the world."

Hyacinth softened. She bit her lip. "It's true, the threat of monkeys might not last long if they don't attack anyone."

"Actually, you'd be surprised—" Muri began.

"But you won't need to threaten when the merfolk see things improving. You mentioned having enough food. What do you need to do to make that happen? Make a plan and appoint dedicated people to carry it out. It won't matter what Bull says if the people are well fed and happy."

"I just don't know if I'm—"

"Muri," Hyacinth said, "look at everything you've done! You can do this, too. Just ignore those self-doubts and pretend to be confident, and you'll succeed."

Muri nodded.

"We'll see you again soon," Hyacinth said, reaching to touch Muri's arm.

And suddenly Muri understood all the hugging the land dwellers were always doing. An empty ache rang in her chest and she stepped forward to fill it with Hyacinth.

"Jack," Hyacinth said when Muri let her go, "do you have your compass? Only the birds have flown off and I hate to ask them to come back and guide us home."

Jack dug into the trousers over his arm and pulled out his compass. He flicked it open. The magnetic needle inside pointed to

Muri standing above him on the beach. He smiled, turning his hand. The needle stayed on her.

"It seems to work in spite of its journey to the bottom of the sea." He gazed up into her eyes as he closed the round case. After a few heartbeats, he turned away.

Jack waded out and held the boat steady as he helped Hyacinth and Gray scramble in. Gray curled up on the floor near the bow, and Hyacinth settled toward the back. Jack stashed his trousers, then came back to the beach.

Muri met him at the edge of the waves. He took her hands in his and used her arms to pull her into him as he leaned down to kiss her. And kiss her again. He dropped one last kiss on her nose and rested his forehead against hers.

"Come home soon."

Muri didn't trust herself to speak. She nodded.

Jack kissed her forehead and let her go. He stepped neatly onto the bow of the boat, pushing it off the sand and out into the water as he did. He balanced as it swayed, kneeling to reach the rope that raised the sail up the mast. As the sail slid up and the boat caught the wind, it turned away from the beach. Jack hopped down over Gray and reached for the tiller.

Hyacinth peeked under the sail, waving goodbye. Muri waved back, no longer trying to stop the hot tears falling from her eyes. Jack turned back once, dipped his chin toward her, and shifted his attention to the boat. It carved a line across the water, with the wind carrying them away from Muri far too fast.

Muri watched as they sailed off until the boat was tiny, then a mere dot on the horizon, and even after it was gone. She pretended she could still see it until she blinked and lost the spot she'd been watching and could no longer pretend.

She wiped the tears trickling from her eyes. She'd see him again. She just had to deal with the situation here first. She stepped toward the water but stopped. She turned instead, walking to the trees beside the end of the trail. Jack's shirt was there, rolled in a bundle beside the rock. She took it out and buried her face in it, breathing it in and remembering his skin and lying in his arms in the cottage. The place she wanted to call home.

Chapter 24

෨✳︎ɞ

When Muri entered the water, she met Caly waiting for her halfway down the slope by the seaweed patch. Caly swam up alongside her and they descended together.

"Is Jack gone?" Caly asked.

"Yes."

"Will he be safe with that . . . magic person?"

In spite of her breaking heart, Muri chuckled. "Oh Caly, that was my friend Hyacinth. She's the nicest fairy you'll ever meet. She just said all that stuff to make the merpeople listen."

"But she called the monkeys!"

"She can communicate with animals. A lot of fairies can. Probably she asked them to come to the beach and make noise—she wouldn't really have them attack."

Caly frowned. "Did you really use magic to call her?"

Muri explained about the pair of shells. "The one I used is in the vault. I left it there when you let me out and we went to save Jack." Muri's smile vanished as she again remembered he'd gone.

Caly pulled her to a stop. They were outside the settlement.

"You should go after him," Caly said.

"But I can't let things fall apart here."

"I don't want them to either, but the merpeople don't deserve your loyalty. You should be happy—away from here and with the human you love."

Muri squeezed Caly's hand. "Maybe once we have a new system in place I can go after him."

The settlement was silent when they swam in past the royal hut. Muri was tempted to find a large rock and smash through the glass wall of the chamber that had imprisoned Jack, to prevent it from ever being used on another human. She held back, sensing it would be better to have the entire community agree to such a thing. Hopefully they *would* agree.

Murmuring voices drifted through the water from the direction of the arena. She and Caly swam to the entrance. The residents of Glorypool had already gathered. They hovered over the sand and lingered around the walls. Muri scanned the faces. Bull, Turr, and a few other mermen clustered near the opposite entry, speaking, their faces angry. The other merpeople left a wide gap around them. Good. Forming a new society would be easier if Bull didn't have many supporters. Angar and Mit were still absent. Perhaps they were too embarrassed to show their faces. Or perhaps they were still tied up in Euli's hut—she'd have to check. But that could wait.

Niggling doubts crept into Muri's chest, but she ignored them and swam into the center of the arena. It was time to pretend to be confident. The voices died down and everyone turned to her. How many times had she seen a new king in this very spot? New kings always involved fist-pumping and bellowing and parading about, and lots of "I will do this" and "I will do that." She bit her lip. How should she begin?

"Thank you," she said, "for coming together like this. On the beach, we heard some ideas. I think we'd all like to have enough to eat each day and comfortable huts to live in. And Hipp mentioned having merchildren. I'd like to hear what everyone thinks about these proposals and any others."

Several merpeople stirred as if they'd swim into the center of the arena.

"We'll take turns," Muri added. "Um, wave your tail if you'd like to speak."

One by one, the merpeople took turns speaking. They unanimously supported Hipp's suggestions about food and merchildren. They also brought up the use of guard patrols (no one could remember anyone ever seeing a predator around the settlement) and what to do with the remnants of the "merking magic" and the places on the island that had been restricted for most of the merpeople. When Apl spoke about wanting the mermen to respect her decision not to tryst with them, many in the crowd dropped their gaze and no one replied. Apl kept her chin up. Muri hoped that no one arguing against her was a positive sign.

Still, all it would take was Bull whispering in people's ears and seeding doubt, and the whole place could fall apart. Muri needed to show them the benefits of working together for the community good.

When she made a final call for speakers and no one else waved their tail, Muri again took the center of the arena.

"We've shared a lot of excellent ideas," she said. "And we should pursue them all. Solving our food shortage seems like a logical place to start."

The crowd murmured in agreement.

"The land dwellers use groups of people called 'committees' to work on projects that benefit everyone. We'll form a committee to plant new seaweed fields. They can scout new locations and test out transplanting different varieties. Once we have more information about what works best, we'll make a plan to plant more and assign people to tend the new fields.

"And we'll have a second committee to consider how to better manage our fish supply and how to bring more fish to the area. So . . ." Muri swallowed. "Who'd like to volunteer?"

To her relief, several merpeople waved their tails. Soon they had the two committees formed, plus a third that was eager to work on restoring the settlement's huts. The crowd began to talk in a buzzing hum that resonated through the water.

Muri watched the merpeople all around her. The nervous tightness lodged in her chest drew her attention again. The meeting had gone well. Why was she still nervous?

Maybe it wasn't nerves. The feeling was . . . it was just a sad, lonely feeling. The people around her didn't feel like her family, and the undersea settlement didn't feel like her home.

"You didn't make any suggestions." Hipp swam down to her.

"Everyone else had so many ideas."

"Isn't there anything *you* want to do?"

"Yes," Muri said. "I'd like to destroy that horrible air chamber so no one can ever use it again."

"Where is your human?" Hipp asked, cocking his head to one side.

"He returned home. He went on the fairies' . . . battleship."

Hipp considered her, his demeanor calm. Everyone in Glorypool must know about her and Jack. What did they think?

All her life, finding love had never been her goal. She'd had a few lackluster encounters with mermen and watched warily as the odious ones like Angar skulked around looking for mates. She'd never considered falling in love with a merman. And later, she'd spent all her time with Lotti and Strombidae's other wives. She'd thought love was pathetic obedience, the way Lotti behaved around Strombidae.

But now that she knew what love felt like, she wanted it in her life, and she didn't care a smidge what anyone thought of her.

Hipp blinked. "I'll help you destroy the chamber," he said, bringing her thoughts back to the scene around her. As she scanned the crowd, she noticed the couples—many merpeople had come forward to echo Hipp's desire to have merchildren, and some of them hovered near a partner, their tails brushing. And Apl, after she'd spoken about not being pressured to tryst, had settled beside another of the former wives, and they sat close together.

Muri turned to Hipp. "I didn't like to do it without asking the others. Since we're making group decisions."

"Would you like me to ask them?"

"Thank you."

Hipp swam up and called out to the crowd for their attention. "Muri would like us to destroy Strombidae's air chamber," he said. "Does anyone disagree?"

Muri froze in anticipation. No one spoke. A few nodded, and the tension she'd felt at his words dissipated. She didn't know where Strombidae had found someone to make such a thing, but she hoped there was never another one.

"Thank you," Muri said, rising beside Hipp. Unexpectedly, tears welled in her eyes—the invisible tears of a mermaid in the water. The tightness in her chest was stronger than ever. Destroying the glass prison would not be enough to ease her sadness. She'd made a mistake and she wouldn't feel better until she followed the path she needed to be on.

The merpeople waited, watching her float in the center of the arena. Couples held hands and rubbed shoulders. Maybe some of the merpeople *had* found love with each other, beyond trysting on the island. Maybe they would understand her plight.

"I don't want to begin as king by lying to you," she said, and as she spoke, her pulse began to hammer and her hands to shake. "I want Glorypool to succeed and thrive as a new community run by everyone. And I think it can. But . . . I don't want to live here anymore."

She fought to stay calm as everyone stirred around her.

"When I went to land to find Strombidae," she continued, "I fell in love with a human. Jack. Many of you saw him trapped in that chamber yesterday, and on the beach today. He loves me, too. That's the only reason he came all the way here—not to threaten you but to make sure I was okay. Bull made me leave the land village to return here, and I didn't say goodbye to Jack, and he wanted to know I was okay. I sent Jack home, but I want to be with him." Her voice cracked as she finished. "I miss him so much."

Her vision blurred with the tears washing from her eyes. How were the merpeople reacting? Caly, Apl, and her other friends swam up beside her.

"I learned so much from the land dwellers in just a few days," Muri said. "I can learn more about how they do things and share it with all of you. I know my friends there would want to help. The fairies will want to help, too, now that they know how to find you. I could be a—an ambassador of the merpeople on land. And you can elect a new king—or maybe multiple kings to share the responsibility." She scanned the crowd and made a wish that the merpeople would make a smart decision. "What do you all think?"

The murmur of voices began, and it rose to a hum, and Muri sensed excitement and hope. She found Caly beside her and lifted her eyebrows.

"What do you think?" she asked Caly. "Should I nominate you?"

Caly gasped quietly, but a smile crept across her face.

"You work hard and you're fair and honest," Muri said. "I think you'd be a wonderful king."

Muri called for a new election, and she nominated Caly, and Caly nominated Hipp, and most everyone cheered for them before anyone else could come forward.

And then Caly ordered Muri to rest until the next morning so she'd be alert when she made the journey home.

Chapter 25

☙ ✴ ❧

Muri's friends were awake in the morning to see her off, along with most of the residents of Glorypool. They gathered around the broken pieces of the glass air chamber to wish her well.

This time she had no satchel, just herself. And this time the trip took forever. Once she was on the way, she wanted only to be there already. She had to force herself to travel at a steady pace, not sprinting across the Cold Sea to reach Jack.

Her body sensed the direction to go—each time she rose to the surface to check the sun, she was already going the right way. Maybe her heart was pulling her toward Jack. But probably she felt the pull of the land, the mysterious force that made the compasses spin. By noon, clouds had covered the sun and she stopped surfacing to check it, trusting that her course was steady.

And finally the water temperature changed. She'd entered the bay at Woodglen.

She poked her head above the waves and happiness filled her as she spotted the points of the castle under the heavy gray clouds and the hill of the village that descended down to the water. Only a few sailboats were out in the bay, and they were heading back toward the village as the wind gusted chaotically. Thunder rumbled in the clouds, and raindrops flecked her wet cheeks. She faced Jack's cottage, then dove back under, letting herself sprint the final distance.

When she resurfaced, she saw Jack. He was sitting on the rocks over the water, staring past her toward the sea. The rain was steady now, splattering on the waves, and his hair was plastered against his forehead. His shirt clung to his shoulders and stuck to his chest.

She slipped toward him, gliding through the water. As she placed her hand on the rock at his feet, he noticed her and startled.

He was on his knees and reaching for her faster than a minnow darting after its shoal. As he hugged her, she pushed back against him to stop him from toppling off the slick rock into the water. He let her go and cradled her face in his hands. They were damp and chill. How long had he been sitting here?

"Did something happen?" he asked.

Muri shook her head. "I told them I wanted to be with you. We elected new kings."

"I can't believe you're here. I worried you'd never come. That Bull would take over and trap you somehow." He was stroking her face, wiping away the raindrops as they landed.

"No," she said. "Bull stayed quiet." She stopped Jack's hand with her own as thunder boomed around them. "Let me get out of the water."

Jack backed off the barest bit as Muri pushed herself up onto the wet rock in the downpour. The moment she was seated, she and Jack were tangled together again. As he held her to his chest, the heat deep inside him radiated out, and she willed it to spread to his fingertips and warm him from the inside as the rain drenched him from above.

She pulled away and flipped her tail up onto the rock beside them. The raindrops spattered against her. "It's never going to dry," she said, indicating her tail. She'd never dealt with needing legs in the rain. The humans had towels for drying themselves after bathing. "Maybe—"

Jack shifted to crouch on his feet, slid his hands beneath her, and lifted her in his arms.

Muri clung to him as he climbed over and up the slippery rocks with her. He went carefully, and a moment later, the green of the clifftop spread before her and the wind over the fields stung her wet cheeks. The tall grasses tossed as another roll of thunder shuddered.

Jack held her tight and strode up the bare path to the cottage. Rain slid down the window glass and stained the patio stones. The hyacinth flowers were bent to the soil, as if they were bowing as Jack carried her past.

She held on as he balanced her on his arm and unlatched the cottage door. The scent of a wood fire and human bread and warm comfort rushed over her, and a moment later, they were out of the rain and it was warm.

Jack lowered her onto a seat beside the door. "Wait here," he said, kicking off his shoes and shutting out the noise of the wind and sea. He opened a cupboard and pulled out blankets. A scuffle in the back of the room caught her attention and she smiled as Captain lumbered to his feet before the hearth and stretched his legs. The old dog ambled over to greet her as Jack took his place before the hearth, spreading the blankets and placing two logs onto the embers glowing in the fireplace. After a few pats from Muri, Captain flopped down on the rug inside the door.

Jack returned to lift her and carry her to the fireside. He sank onto the blankets and pulled her onto his lap.

Flames crackled as the fire caught the new logs, and Muri shivered as a wave of heat wafted over her back and left cold in its place. The heat returned. Jack's skin was faintly steaming against her. She brushed his hair off his forehead, running her fingers through to dry it as he watched her. Before he could lean in, she tugged on the collar of his soaked shirt. She slipped her fingers down to undo the top buttons, and he let go of her body and pulled it over his head.

Muri caught his cold hands and held them to her breast as the last of the outdoor chill vanished from his fingertips. She wanted to stop time, sitting against him and staring into his eyes, deep with the flickering of firelight. But not forever. Just long enough to realize that this—Jack, the cottage—truly could be her home.

Her hands were tiny over his as she moved them up to her neck, scuffing his calluses over her soft skin. The fire was hot on her back now, and Jack's chest was warm and dry when she pressed herself against him, leaning up to kiss his neck. His fingers slid into her hair, tangling in the damp strands. Her lips tugged on his skin and a moan trembled through him as her teeth found him and gently bit.

His rough fingers skated down her back and held firm as she nipped at him, and the sound of his uneven breaths stirred a fire inside her. She shifted her hips, rubbing against the erection pressing into her, and he whispered a curse. She bit him again, and the heat inside her spread up her chest and down her tail. The last of the rain's damp sizzled and evaporated, and her tail vanished into legs.

Muri was on Jack in an instant, pushing him back and moving her leg over to staddle him. She kissed over his stubbled chin to his lips, all the while fumbling with the buttons on his trousers.

He pulled away to help, pushing the damp material down and off his legs. She wished she could dry his damp thighs and bottom with her hot skin, but she was too impatient, and the sight of his erection erased all thought from her mind. She climbed back onto him and sank down on it as he cursed again.

Her own body wanted to be touched, but for now, having him filling her and seeing the waves of ecstasy crossing his face was enough. She found his hands on her sides and brought them to her hips, and as she pulled herself off him and back on, he gripped her and began to help.

"Is this—?"

"Shh," she said. "Just keep going." She let him take control, balancing herself with her hands on his shoulders as he thrust into her, pulling her body against his and pushing it away. All reason fled his face as he thrust faster, until he cried out and shuddered and went still.

His body sagged under her touch, and he leaned his face on her shoulder. All of him was hot now.

Muri wiggled her hips, nestling onto him before he lost his erection. He hugged her back.

"What was that called?" she whispered.

He shook his head against her shoulder.

"The two-headed octopus," she decided, and he convulsed with a laugh.

Jack lifted his head and watched her face. He was waiting on her to decide what came next.

She rubbed his arm and found his hand, pulling it around to her front and bringing it between them, where their bodies were coupled together. He traced the backs of his fingers over her belly and down into the curls of hair until they danced over her exposed skin. His touch was gentle and light as he watched for her response.

Muri rose on her knees, giving him better access. With her body less open and exposed, he pressed harder, rubbing his knuckles into her. He leaned back, taking her with him. He left her propped on her arms on the blankets as he slid under her.

His knuckles ground harder between her thighs as he took one nipple in his mouth, sucking from beneath her. She rocked her hips into his hand. His other hand had grasped her hip again and held her steady. He bit her breast gently before releasing it and continuing down her body. He gripped both her hips and replaced his knuckles with his tongue.

She sprawled over him as he swirled delicious patterns on her, his hot breath teasing and his tongue roving, back and forth. He pulled back and his wet lips found her. His tongue forged a path for them to close and suck on her. Her knees started to shake, and he smoothed her legs down until her body rested on him somehow, his warm exhales assuring her he could breathe.

He sucked her in front, and his hands cupped her bottom. He pulled an arm in, wedging it under her thigh before settling her again. Then a callused thumb scratched between her legs. He rubbed across her straight to her center. He slipped his thumb into her wetness with no effort, but pulled it out to knead her from the outside.

"More," she gasped, struggling to press down on his thumb.

He pushed it inside her again, circling, and her body strained against it. He withdrew it, and for a desperate moment Muri wanted to object. Then his fingers were in her, the rod of them stirring and pressing until he found a place that made her body jerk in response. His tongue worked her between his lips as he massaged her with his fingers on the inside. The tumult of pleasure at last overwhelmed her. She thrashed in his hold and cried out over and over before trembling after the release.

He helped her crawl backward over his body to collapse in his arms. His hair had dried, and the firelight reflected in his gaze. As she settled against him, his body relaxed onto the blankets. Raindrops thrummed on the roof and spattered the windows, but here inside they were dry and safe.

"I'm so glad you're here," he whispered, his voice huskier than usual.

"Me too."

"I never thought I'd find someone like you."

She hugged his chest, burrowing her hands to get her arms around him properly. "I didn't either. I didn't know what it was like to fall in love." She pulled back to see his face. "I love you, Jack. And I won't leave you again. I'll be your family."

"And I'll be yours," he choked out before pulling her back into his arms and whispering that he loved her, too.

Three Moons Later

೮⟡ఔ

MURI STOOD AND STRETCHED HER back. The long rows of marigold plants crisscrossed from one bed to the next across the castle gardens. And above them fluttered hundreds of butterflies, just as Gray had promised. He hadn't mentioned that butterflies came in all sizes and colors, or that their wings were iridescent and went motionless when they landed on a flower, preening slowly opened and closed until the butterfly floated up into the air and on to its next location.

Since their arrival, the butterflies had gathered at the flower shop each morning as the sunlight filled the village square. Sometimes, if Muri passed by early enough, a cloud of them would take off and join her to cross the clifftop to the gardens. The morning wind on the bay would buffet them, but they'd fight back and swoop over the tall garden wall and down onto the flowers to begin their day as she began hers.

Muri bent to retrieve her trowel and carried it to the toolshed. She couldn't see any symmetry to the marigold seedlings she'd just planted, not like the orderly grid of chrysanthemums she'd done a few days ago. But Hyacinth had insisted Muri plant each marigold in the exact location where Hyacinth had left it lying on the dirt. She'd also said something about warding against beetles and maximizing soil fertility so Muri hadn't dared vary the pattern, lest a plague of beetles descend on Woodglen as a result. She'd been on the garden crew for only one moon, but she knew better than to stray from Hyacinth's directions.

For a while after her return from Glorypool, Muri had spent her days out on the water with Jack. She'd wanted to spend every moment with him. Plus, she couldn't stop worrying that Bull would return to the bay and drag Jack under the water.

But as one moon and another had passed, she'd become restless. She wanted to contribute to her new community, and she was pretty sure Jack didn't catch more fish when he had her onboard. If anything, he caught less fish because they spent half the day with the sail down, lying in its shade atop the nets and making love. One time, they'd even capsized the boat and lost all the fish he *had* caught.

And she could no longer use her fear of Bull as an excuse. She talked to Caly every quarter-moon using the enchanted pair of shells, and she knew Bull was behaving. Well, more or less. He and his small group of mermen had interrupted the next community meeting to challenge Hipp to a fight for dominance, resulting in shocked silence in the arena. But Hipp had refused to fight and Caly had swum into the middle of the mermen and loudly reminded everyone that they didn't fight anymore, and the crowd had sighed in relief and gone back to discussing their committee tasks, leaving Bull alone in the center of the space.

The merpeople had planted trial seaweed fields around Glorypool, testing several varieties in different locations around the base of the island. They had agreed that if the first harvest succeeded, they'd plant more and the ban on having merchildren would lift. In the moons since her departure, they'd created new committees for several projects, and their enthusiasm seemed to grow with each accomplishment.

What's more, after the failed attempt to seize power, Hipp had asked Bull to lead a group on the island locating and repairing the old huts used for pregnancies. He told Bull they needed someone brave to do it, given the threat of monkeys. Being in charge of a project that scared all the others seemed to agree with Bull, and he stopped grumbling about Hipp's mind being poisoned by fairies and went about his work without fuss. One evening, he reported finding Strombidae and Lotti living in a cave on the far side of the volcano.

With the threat of Bull diminished, Muri left Jack on the water and joined the gardening crew at the castle. Most of the castle workers were older volunteers. With Muri helping, they could get a lot more done. She was used to the physical labor, plus she could do any heavy lifting. She liked bringing the gardens to life, but the more she learned about life in the village, the more she wanted to try everything—planting land vegetables and sewing new clothes and even making cheese. And she was learning to read with lessons at the village printshop. She would try it all, one thing at a time.

On slow days at the gardens, she woke before dawn and went fishing with Jack. Or, if he sneaked out and left her sleeping, she followed him later in the day, swimming across the bay in a few moments to reach the fleet. From beneath the waves, Muri could easily recognize the underside of *Alina's Blessing*, with its new boards and shiny coat of varnish.

She might pack her satchel with a picnic of waterproof foods to share with Jack at lunchtime—cheese and plums and those sticks made from cut-up carrot roots that the human children loved, and a tin of the spread made from ground-up nuts to dip them in. Sometimes, she swam into Jack's net and let him pull her to the surface just to see the look of surprise on his face when he found a naked mermaid instead of fish.

Caly kept a list of the problems the merpeople encountered and ideas they had, and Muri went over the problems with Hyacinth. Hyacinth was excellent at problem solving. Together they amassed a pile of tools they could bring to the merpeople and simple spells that could help them. Initially, Muri intended to bring the items to Glorypool, but dread seized her each time she imagined returning.

So instead, Caly offered to come to Woodglen to get the items. She called it a "research trip." And once she'd decided to come, Euli and Perse and Apl and several others wanted to come as well.

Finally, Caly cut off new participants so that she wouldn't arrive in Woodglen with a crowd of merpeople, terrifying the villagers with an apparent invasion. Muri arranged to meet the mermaids on the stretch of sand where she'd first arrived so she could get them all clothed before the humans saw them.

Seeing her sisters again was wonderful. Once they were fully clothed and able to walk, Muri took them by her and Jack's cottage. Jack had stayed off the water that day to help Muri host the mermaids on a tour of the village.

First they explored the shops at the wharf. No one had any coins, but they tried on hats at the milliner's and the candymaker gave them samples. Muri took them for lunch at the grange home. Margery and the ladies had prepared a feast called a buffet, where giant platters of food filled the table and each person could take whatever they wanted. They had a dozen kinds of cheese, and slices of bread that had been toasted until they were crisp, and fresh snap peas from the garden, and all the pickles and jams the grange home had stockpiled the previous autumn, which Margery said they needed to clear off the shelves anyway now that summer was come again.

Muri hadn't been sure if the mermaids should visit Hyacinth. Caly knew the truth about Hyacinth—that she wasn't a terrifying, monkey-wielding killer. And Muri hated for the others to think badly of Hyacinth, especially when Hyacinth had procured most of the tools and spells the mermaids were taking home. But with everything progressing smoothly in Glorypool, Muri felt hesitant to spread the truth too widely. It might be too soon. She didn't want to change anything when it was all going as well as it was. In the end, Hyacinth arranged for her human friend Ladi to watch the shop that day, in case the mermaids wanted to see the flower shop.

Finally, as the sun set, Jack took them all for pints of ale at The White Pony. Of course, by now, most of the mermaids had tried phyta, but Caly said the merpeople had decided not to make so much of it in the future since it seemed to make the mermen sloppy and unproductive. But human ale was potent. And the mermaids wanted to celebrate. Drunk on ale, they staggered back to Jack's cottage to sleep the rest of the night before swimming home. They planned to come back in a few moons' time.

Today, Muri waved goodbye to the butterflies and exited the castle gardens. She crossed the clifftop, scanning the bay for any late fishing boats, but only the blue waves and the circling gulls were out. As she entered the square, she glanced at the Fairweather Florist. A few butterflies lingered on the window frames, flexing their wings in the afternoon sunshine, and the noisy bluebird sang from atop the shop's sign. Gray called the creatures Hyacinth's "fan club."

Muri missed Gray. He'd gone off on some adventure shortly after her return to the village, and now Hyacinth said he might stay longer in a village up north. Hyacinth said he'd met someone—someone he was in love with! Muri was glad about that even if she missed him. At least he was on the coast. The village of Cliffside was several days journey by road, but Muri could swim there in an hour, and she would someday soon. She still owed Gray a swimming lesson.

She turned to the village park in the center of the square—no longer haunted by Strombidae Murkel, the deposed merking, and now filled with roses and lilies and other summertime flowers. And sitting on a bench, watching for her, was Jack. He grinned the moment she spotted him.

"Why are you smiling like that?" Muri asked as she neared.

He reached for her, pulling her between his knees. She bent down to kiss him.

"I have a present for you," he said, still grinning. A small, square package rested on the bench beside him.

Muri turned to sit, but Jack stood. "Let's go home first."

And still he was grinning.

She took his hand, eyeing the package as he tucked it under his arm. It could be a block of cheese, but it was rather wide and flat.

Together they walked out of the square and down one of the lanes. They came out on a path across the fields toward home.

Captain lay in the late sun on the stones beside the door. He opened an eye at their approach, thumped his tail once, and went back to sleep.

Inside, Jack handed Muri the package. She undid the twine carefully and tucked it onto a shelf for later use. She opened the folded paper. Inside was a book, like Hyacinth's book of flowers but smaller and more compact. It had naked people on the cover.

Muri's lips parted as she stared. The cover showed a beautiful naked woman surrounded by a border of tall stalks dotted with delicate pointed blossoms. The vines and leaves of the plants twined suggestively around the woman's legs and arms—as did the hands of the naked man behind her, gripping her arms. Her head was tilted back and his lips were on her neck. Just the sight of the picture made Muri start to tingle. Curling letters crossed the top and bottom of the cover. Q-U-E . . .

"What does it say?" she whispered, trailing her fingers across the letters.

"*Queen Delphinium's Book of Love-Making*," Jack said.

Muri tentatively opened the book to a page in the center.

"Ten seas!" she exclaimed. The picture showed the naked man standing and holding the woman sideways at his hips. Their bodies were locked together, and her legs wrapped around him as she stretched her arms languidly over her head.

"What is this?" Muri said, her fingers hovering over the page.

"That one's called 'The Vine and the Tree,'" Jack replied.

"But what is this book? Who's Queen Delphinium?"

"Apparently," Jack said, "she was an ancient fairy queen who did a lot of, uh, 'research' on lovemaking."

"Wherever did you get it?"

"The villager printer. He's just started printing it."

"What's this one?" Muri asked, turning the page. The queen was face down on the grass with a man atop her. He pressed himself against her bottom and held himself up on his arms over her back, with his legs stretched alongside hers.

Jack actually blushed. "The eggplant sandwich."

"Eggplant?" Muri asked.

"It's a late summer vegetable. It's shaped like, uh, like a fat purple banana."

Muri snorted.

She continued flipping as Jack read her the titles: The Lazy Sweet Pea. The Transplanted Hellebore. The Grapevine Wreath. Each pose appeared to involve a different man.

Muri stopped at a page. "It's the two-headed octopus!" From the look on her face, Queen Delphinium liked it just as much as Muri did.

"She calls it 'The Water Lily,'" Jack said.

Muri had seen water lilies in one of the pools at the castle gardens. She would never look at them the same. In fact, after studying Queen Delphinium's book, she suspected she'd see naked people in the shapes of every tree and plant in the village.

"Ten seas," Muri said again, flipping gingerly through the pages. "It'll take us a half-moon to try all of these."

"Maybe a whole moon," Jack said, "if we need to try some of them twice."

"I guess we'd better get started," she said, and met his grin with her own.

A Note from the Author

🕮 ✱ ☙

DEAR READER,
Thank you so much for reading *The Ocean Girl*. The story originated because a friend who read *The Forest Bride* said she felt sorry for Prince Murkel. I didn't, but I kept thinking about her comment. It made me wonder, just what was his deal? I imagined the merpeople wondering why he never came home and what their awful society must be like to have produced him. I didn't intend to write a second book with someone overthrowing another terrible king, but there it was. Hopefully Sylvania is now free of patriarchal monarchies and we can return to road trip comedies and office romances. But with fairies.

I love writing cozy fantasy romances, and I'm hoping the subgenre will grow as more like-minded readers find such books and enjoy reading them. If you liked the story, please consider leaving a review online to help other readers with similar interests find the book. I would really appreciate it.

I'm planning to have the next book in the Sylvania series, *The Woodland Stranger*, out in 2024. As you may have guessed, it is Gray's story! Although it is told from his love interest's point of view, someone who is mentioned briefly in *The Forest Bride*.

You can subscribe to my email list at https://janebuehler.com for an email when the new book is available. I send only a few emails each year, with slightly more when a new book is coming. When you subscribe, I'll send a link to bonus material. I also give away advance review copies via my email list.

You can connect with me online on Twitter as @ephemerily or on my various author pages, listed on my website. And you can email me at jane@janebuehler.com.

Sincerely, *Emily Jane* ♡

Acknowledgments

✿

I AM LUCKY TO HAVE A whole bunch of supportive friends and family members in my life. I generally don't list them by name in the acknowledgments because once started, I would need to keep going and I'm sure I would leave someone out. I'm grateful for all of them!

But also, writing has been kind of a solo activity for me so far. I haven't had a crew of writing buddies or draft-swapping partners to thank, and since I self-publish, I don't have agents or an editorial team or anyone like that. I do have a fabulous copyeditor, Kelly Urgan, and cover designer, Cory Marie Podielski, whom I'm very thankful for. Thank you also to my friend Angie McMann, who's always willing to beta read and also to help me fight my imposter syndrome. And thank you to Adrienne Moore, also a fabulous beta reader and friend.

And thanks to all the other romance readers and writers for your support. I appreciate every single person who sends a note or tags me online or shares my book or even just gives it a chance without me ever knowing. I might write romance novels even if no one else ever read them, but having other people who like them means the world to me.

About the Author

෴✻౷

Emily Jane Buehler published two nonfiction books—one on the science and craft of baking bread, the other a memoir of a bicycle trip from New Jersey to Oregon—before venturing into fiction. She writes "cozy fantasy romance": lighthearted stories that focus on a protagonist finding their courage and happiness, as opposed to plots with a lot of fighting and darkness.

Emily lives in Hillsborough, North Carolina, with a bossy cat named Coco. She can often be found walking or bicycling through town. Her favorite things include letters sent through the mail, Made-in-the-USA knee socks, and very dark fair-trade chocolate. She is passionate about living waste free.

Emily writes romance using her middle name, Jane. Email her at jane@janebuehler.com. Find her on Twitter as @ephemerily. Subscribe to her email list at https://janebuehler.com for occasional email updates and news about new books.

CPSIA information can be obtained
at www.ICGtesting.com
Printed in the USA
BVHW040201230323
661002BV00004B/93